FREEDOM

Letting Go of Anxiety and Fear of the Unknown

JIM BRITT

A Dandelion Books Publication
www.dandelionbooks.net
Tempe, Arizona

Copyright, 2003 by Dandelion Books, LLC

All worldwide rights exclusively reserved. No part of this book may be reproduced or translated into any language or utilized in any form or by any means, electronic or mechanical, including photocopying, recording or by any information storage and retrieval system, without permission in writing from the publisher.

A Dandelion Books Publication
Dandelion Books, LLC
Tempe, Arizona

Library of Congress Cataloging-in-Publication Data

Britt, Jim
Freedom: letting go of anxiety and fear of the unknown

Library of Congress Catalog Card Number 2002113859
ISBN 1-893302-74-1

Cover design by Maverick Design, Nevada City, CA;

Book design by
Amnet Systems Private Limited
WWW.amnet-systems.com

Disclaimer and Reader Agreement

Part I of this book is a fiction work. Any resemblance of fictional characters in this book to living or deceased individuals is purely coincidental. Neither the author nor the publisher, Dandelion Books, LLC shall be liable for any damages or costs related to any coincidental resemblances of the fictional characters in this book to living or deceased individuals.

Under no circumstances will the publisher, Dandelion Books, LLC, or author be liable to any person or business entity for any direct, indirect, special, incidental, consequential, or other damages based on any use of this book or any other source to which it refers, including, without limitation, any lost profits, business interruption, or loss of programs or information.

Reader Agreement for Accessing This Book

By reading this book, you, the reader, consent to bear sole responsibility for your own decisions to use or read any of this book's material. Dandelion Books, LLC and the author shall not be liable for any damages or costs of any type arising out of any action taken by you or others based upon reliance on any materials in this book.

Dandelion Books, LLC
www.dandelionbooks.net

Dedicated To
Freedom and The American Spirit

Acknowledgements

To my family for their continued support.

To JoAnn Arnold for her relentless research, creative skills and editing, without whom this work would not have been possible.

To those who know, or seek to know, freedom.

Contents

Part I

Part II

Eight Steps to Personal Freedom

Author's Preview

In a few short minutes of one day, the lives of the American people were dramatically changed forever by the most violent and tragic terrorist attack in the history of humankind. It was as if we were awakened from a deep sleep. We have had to rethink our circumstances and retrain our thoughts to function in a different world than the one we once knew.

Our wake-up call came at 8:45 AM on September 11, 2001. However, with the tragedy and some passing of time, we began to realize that something wonderful had happened. We are now more aware, more alert, more united, more loving and more charitable than before. We are less tolerant of crime and vicious acts, and quicker to act against them. We are no longer complacent, but have brought to the surface our strong feelings of patriotism. In fact, we have all but redefined patriotism. The flag we proudly fly and salute, represents what we proudly stand for. Our bravery is far beyond our fear.

The question comes to mind. Were the Trade Center and the Pentagon the real targets or were the terrorists after the minds of the people by planting fear in them, knowing if they can control our minds through fear, they can control our country?

Everywhere I turn, people from all walks of life are experiencing fear, anxiety, anger, grief and what seems to them to be insurmountable challenges in the way they should live their lives. And I know from talking with hundreds of individuals, most are still searching for relief.

Though the story in this book is fictional, much of the story-line is based on events that took place during the two weeks following the attack on America.

The truth in this story is stranger than fiction. Its reality is inconceivable and its tragedy is almost unbearable to forgive. Yet forgiveness is part of the healing process.

Jeremy Carter, a fireman from Missouri, in New York for the day, decided to take a tour of the Trade Center, only to watch, in shock, the attack on its twin towers from a block away. The story takes Jeremy from the pits of the rubble into the lives of the people and into the depths of his own soul. He learns who he is and what it takes to overcome the fear, anger, grief and anxiety this kind of evil brings.

Jeremy, the main character in this book represents a composite of conversations with many individuals. Any resemblance to yourself, and to people you know is highly probable, as well as intentional. By identifying with him and his experience you will be provided ample opportunities to heal. You will rejoice as he leads you on a journey of understanding of present events and of what lies ahead, as he rebuilds the dynamics of his life and yours.

At this time, for all of us, it is essential to unravel old patterns of belief and to teach our minds new ways to function from this day forward. As you read the story, you will be gripped by the truth Jeremy discovers. You will also discover intense interaction as a mental switch is thrown and understanding falls into place.

The work contained on these pages offers practical tools that can be used to manage your life, your emotions and feelings. You will find it to be no less than self-healing for processing the feelings of fear, anxiety and grief brought on by the attack on America and our freedom. It also provides tools for living life to the fullest from this day forward.

The first two decades of my adult life, I lived without these principles. But about 20 years ago, as a result of searching for answers to heal my own life, I discovered these methods of inner healing that I'll be sharing with you. This work is not a by-product of someone else's teachings or based on any curriculum. It is based on my own experiences. I have used these principles in my own life and I have also shared them with over 1,000,000 people in my workshops and in my other books, *Rings of Truth and Unleashing Your Authentic Power.* Discovering these principles was a great gift that brought forth immediate results and long-term rewards. The tools work! The rewards for using them are extraordinary!

The goal of the Author's Application section in the back of the book is to offer additional, applicable tools designed to create a framework from which to view life differently. Above all, I wish to express the simplicity of the journey you are about to take. Though it may initially appear complex, it is not. All I ask is that you approach it with an open mind. Healing can only happen with your full participation. Put your old beliefs aside for a time and just look for and feel the truth behind the words you are about to read.

I would be the last one to tell you or to lead you to believe that these tools will solve all your problems, or that you won't need to know anything else after reading this book. The journey of life and the problems we experience along the way are ongoing. I only know that through using these principles in my own life, I have been able to alleviate about 90% of the hardships I used to experience, the results of which have opened the door to many gifts. Peace of mind, patience, tolerance, contentment, love and joy are all now dominant in my life; and stress, anxiety, anger and fear of the unknown are "almost" a thing of the past.

I felt compelled at this time to share my work with all the people of America and the world who would listen. If you are prepared to be accountable for your feelings, thoughts, beliefs, behaviors and your freedom, it will work for you as it has for so many others.

Enjoy the journey! And be prepared. Your life is about to change!

PART ONE

Chapter One

A Wake-up Call 8:45 AM, 9-11-01

Why us? What did we do to deserve this? Who could have done such a thing? Why should we have to live in fear? Who committed this terrible crime? Why was our government so unaware of what was about to happen? Why do I feel the way I do? Why can't things go back to the way they were?

These questions and similar ones have been in the minds and hearts of people since the September eleventh terrorist attack on America. We are a generation that has lived in abundance. We have never witnessed the tragedy of war in our own land. It has always been somewhere else, far away from us. We have always felt safe and secure living in our country.

It reminds me of a man I met by the name of Bob. Bob was a good man who lived a good life, a peaceful life. As a result of the abundant society we live in, he was able to raise a family and live a life free of conflict. He always managed to make "inside" match "outside"; therefore he was always satisfied. Bob didn't recognize that with all the abundance he enjoyed he had become complacent, taking what he had for granted.

Bob felt he was living a well-balanced life. He went on vacation to the same places, year after year. He woke up at the same time every morning and went to bed at the same time every night. Bob was a very organized man. He believed there was a place for everything and everything should always be in its place.

The one thing Bob did not like was "change." He felt safe in the sameness of things. You see, Bob was simply into survival. As long as he was able, in his own mind, to make "inside" match "outside," he was happy.

On September 11, 2001, Bob's life was turned upside down and "inside" no longer matched "outside." That day he became a friend to "change."

Emotions swell inside me as I think of all that happened that day I met Bob and what happened in the days that followed, for I was there. I have an unyielding feeling that I was supposed to be there to see, with my own eyes, all that occurred so the change in my life would be felt even deeper, and the impact on my life would be more dramatic.

I wasn't even supposed to conduct the training meeting in New Jersey that week. I was filling in for another man who had become ill at the last minute. Was it, then, a coincidence that my one free day was September eleventh and that I would choose to visit the famous Twin Towers before I went back home to the Midwest? No one will ever convince me that it was.

I was just minutes away from walking through the doors of the Trade Center. It was around 8:30 AM, and the sun was perfect for taking a few good pictures before I started my tour of the magnificent structure in front of me that seemed to touch the sky. I watched hundreds of people disappear through its doors as I snapped pictures with my camera. I tried to imagine how many thousands were employed there. I laughed to myself as I decided there were more employed at the Trade Center than actually lived in my hometown.

I had just put my camera away and started walking toward the doors of the South Tower when I heard the sounds of a large plane flying low. Too low, I thought to myself. I looked up just in time to witness the explosion as the plane hit the first tower. I stood there in stunned disbelief for several minutes. Was it real or was I dreaming? Then, before my brain could fully register the scene before me, I watched as another Boeing 767 struck the second tower and another explosion filled the air with its flames and debris. The world was suddenly moving in slow motion and my brain was shouting for me to run but my legs wouldn't respond. I could only watch as several stories of the towers became engulfed in smoke and flames, the debris falling everywhere. I could hear people shouting and screaming, but I stood silent. I was swept into a nightmare from which I couldn't awake.

All the training I had received in the past eighteen years hadn't prepared me for what I had just witnessed. My body and my mind were numbed with shock. It wasn't until I remembered all the people I had seen enter the building just a few minutes before that my brain started calculating numbers and I suddenly became alert to the disaster in front of me. Debris was falling all around me and I found myself automatically directing people away from the danger, if possible. Though I doubted they needed directions, I needed to feel useful.

Flames and smoke were shooting out of the buildings and I wondered how long the structures would be able to withstand that kind of heat. The burning fuel and the explosions themselves would cause temperatures to exceed that which the steel cores could bear without buckling.

I kept turning to watch the doors of the building, hoping all the people I had seen enter, now were able to come back through them to escape. And hundreds did come through those doors. But some of them made it through only to be killed or injured by the debris that continued to fall from the sky like rain. Except it wasn't rain. It was fragments of metal, luggage... even body parts. I was sickened at the sight. But it was the shoes, the empty shoes, that kept falling, that woke my mind to the horror of the hundreds of bodies literally being vaporized. People's lives were disappearing as if they never had existed. Only their shoes were proof they had lived.

A tremble was felt as the Trade Center suddenly began to quiver and a loud booming sound shattered windows and shook the ground beneath me. Instinctively I knew one of the towers had given way.

"The tower's coming down," screamed a police officer standing near the door of the building. "Get out, get out... run!" He was pushing people ahead with all the strength he had. He grabbed a woman who had been struck by falling debris and was bleeding. He literally threw her over his shoulder and began to run. Without hesitation I ran with the rest.

Dust, smoke and ash began to overtake us and I glanced back just in time to see a woman stumble and fall as she tried to escape the horror behind her. As she fell, her head hit the concrete and blood began its immediate flow. I quickly made my way to her side just as another man stopped to lift her from the ground. Together we picked her up and carried her to safety, the clouds of dust and gray matter moving past us as if they, too, were anxious to escape the devastation they left behind. I could taste their flavor in my mouth and as I inhaled, I choked on its odor.

When we reached a spot we knew to be a safe distance away, I had a chance to look into the face of the man I had assisted. Although the ash and dust had settled on his hair and his face, giving him a ghostly appearance, his eyes remained clear and filled with calm. "You stay with her until the ambulance comes," he spoke softly. "I'll go and see if there's anyone else who needs help." He then took off his jacket and laid it on the ground. Together we gently lowered the woman onto the jacket. I sat next to her, and leaning against the building behind us, I placed her head on my shoulder. I fumbled in my pockets until I found a clean hand-kerchief to wipe the blood from her face. Then I carefully placed it on the wound until the ambulance could get there, knowing by the sound of the sirens it was not far away.

As I sat, mindful of the scene around me, an unnatural quiet and unexplainable calm came over me. There were people holding up people, people consoling people. Tears and confusion were evident, but I sensed a strength among those who were around me. I saw compassion, kindness, unity, and most of all, charity... the kind of charity that only comes through love. What I was witnessing was love in its most tender form. These people had not known each other until today, yet in those few short minutes they came to know each other in a way that would never be forgotten.

I had watched horror movies with people screaming hysterically as they ran over other people, pushing them out of the way so they could escape. The real life version was nothing like that. What I saw were people grabbing people, dragging them to safety. The strong assisting the weak, guiding them to safety, the young protecting the elderly, the uninjured holding the injured in their arms until first aid could be applied. It was incredible. It was like nothing I had ever seen before. I was suddenly swept into a moment where time no longer existed. Only love was present.

While smoke and dust filled the world around us, and while we watched the gaping hole in the remaining tower through the growing cloud before us, while flames leaped through the air, casting an eerie glow, for just one precious moment, we were untouched by the pain. Time was silent while love penetrated the fear and calmed our souls. Though no one could speak of it, I could see in their eyes that they, too had felt what I had felt; and that brought comfort to us all.

I wondered how many of those thousands of people were safe. How many innocent people were killed in the planes? How many were in the tower that had collapsed? Why was this happening? Who was responsible for this?

There were no answers. Once again I felt the numbness return to my body as tears began to make their way through the dust on my face. I cried for people without names and faces.

I became conscious of the woman I was holding, and I looked down to see tears streaming down her cheeks as well.

"I was late for work," she said through her tears. "I should have been on the eightieth floor and I was late for work for the first time in fifteen years. I only hope there were others who were late today." She laid her head against my shoulder once more. There was nothing else I could do for her until first aid arrived. I watched her face for a few minutes as she closed her eyes. Deciding the wound on her forehead had stopped bleeding, I took the handkerchief and began brushing away as much dust as I could from her face.

As I worked I noticed she had rather a lovely face, perhaps a little on the pale side. I laughed at myself, thinking she might say the same about me. Everyone around me looked a little on the pale side. Her hair was auburn, as far as I could tell. She was slim built, around five and a half feet tall. Her age, I would guess was approximately thirty-five. During this evaluation I somehow managed to come to the conclusion that she might have a concussion. I decided it would be best to keep her awake.

"My name is Jeremy Carter," I said. "What's yours?"

Her eyes opened and she looked at me for a minute before responding weakly, "Shana. Shana Stewart... I think." I watched as a quick smile touched her face. Then it was gone.

"Well, Shana Stewart," I said, smiling back, "the cut on your forehead has stopped bleeding. That's good. However, I think you have a slight concussion so I need you to stay awake and talk to me. Can you do that?"

She nodded in the affirmative, opening her eyes.

"You work on the eightieth floor in the Trade Center?"

She nodded again. "At least I hope I still do," she said drowsily as her eyelids closed once again.

I decided to change the subject. "I'm a firemen from Missouri. Actually I'm the fire chief. I've been a fireman for eighteen years and I like being a fireman. In fact I like being the fire chief."

"What is a fire chief from Missouri doing in New York City on a day like today?" she asked, trying to stay awake.

"Well, actually, I was teaching a class in a training seminar in New Jersey and had this one day to myself. I decided to see the sights of New York City, first stop the Twin Towers of the Trade Center. I've never seen the city from the top floor and that was on my 'must see' list."

Before she could respond, an EMT tapped me on the shoulder and asked if he could take the lady from my arms and get her to a hospital. I helped put Shana into the ambulance, then waved goodbye as the door closed in front of me. I hoped to see her again.

As the ambulance pulled away, I looked at my watch. I had to brush away a layer of dust and ash before I could see the time. It was 10:22 AM. In the past one and a half hours, the twin towers had been hit and the south tower had collapsed. How much more could the north tower stand before it, too, became a mountain of rubble?

Without thinking I turned and began making my way back toward the scene from which I had not long before escaped. In my mind I kept replaying the scene of hundreds of people walking through the doors of the Trade Center just seconds before it was hit. I didn't know what I could do. I only know

I had to try to help those people whose faces I had seen through the lens of my camera.

Through the foul, thick air, the north tower could still be seen, its top floors hidden in the smoke. Flames were shooting everywhere through the dense clouds. A parade of ghostly figures holding pieces of torn fabric over their mouths and noses, ran past me as I made my way toward the burning building. As I walked, I removed my jacket and literally tore my shirt off and ripped it into several pieces, handing them to anyone who didn't have a covering over their face.

"Thank you," the voice of a young man shouted as he took a piece of material I handed to him. "It's terrible back there." His voice was shaking and he was crying, openly and unashamed.

"Is everyone out of the buildings?" I stopped long enough to ask him.

"I don't know. You can't see your hands in front of your face. There is nothing you can do to help, the other tower is going to go any minute." As he turned to go he hesitated. "I understand there are hundreds of people caught in the debris of the first tower along with a crew of firemen who had gone in on a rescue attempt. Don't go back, mister, there really isn't anything you can do." He touched my shoulder, then quickly moved toward safety.

I still had one piece of shirt in my hand. I put my jacket back on and placed the cloth over my mouth and nose, then continued on. I checked my watch once again. Five minutes had passed since I'd left Shana with the EMT. My lungs felt like they were on fire and my eyes watered and blurred as the smoke thickened around me. Although I tried to keep my mouth closed, my tongue felt caked with ash.

Then it happened. The ground began to quiver once again and I knew I wasn't going to get there in time. There were still so many people running, trying to get away and I couldn't help them any more than they could help themselves.

I heard the horrible sound of steel folding under the weight of the concrete. Floor after floor collapsed and all I could do was watch. I remember thinking I was too close and needed to get back. But before I could move, everything went dark. The sun was no longer visible. I was choking. I couldn't open my eyes because of the thickness of the smoke, ash and dust that was swept out from under pieces of building as they landed. I lost all sense of direction, and a feeling of panic swept over me like a heavy blanket as I tried to get my bearings. I found myself back in my nightmare. I could hear people screaming and moaning but I couldn't tell which direction the sounds were coming from.

Then, without warning, I felt a tremendous pain in the back of my head and the world was suddenly silent. Yet, in the silence I heard a voice, soft and soothing. I couldn't connect a face to the voice, but it seemed familiar to me. I had heard it before; I just couldn't remember where. I could see a small white book on a table, its title written in gold script. I wanted to take the book and hold it so I could read its title but I couldn't reach it. "The truth is found on the pages of the book," the voice was saying. "Search for it until you find it. There you will find the truth of what surrounds you as well."

I tried to comprehend what the voice was saying, but it didn't make sense to me. My head began to ache and I felt confused because I couldn't understand.

I opened my eyes to the throbbing pain in my head and found myself lying on a blanket next to another man who had been injured. I heard a moan escape my throat.

"Just lie still for awhile and rest," I heard a different voice say. "You have a pretty good size bump on your head, a few scratches and probably a lot of bruises, but you'll be all right."

I looked up to see an EMT working on the man beside me. The injured man was wearing firemen's clothing. Instead of a helmet, however, he was wearing a thick bandage around his head. As the EMT attended to his wounds, the man turned his face toward me. His eyes were puffy and irritated from the ash and his face was swollen.

"A lot of my buddies died back there," he said, almost to himself. "I'll never forget what happened. Dear God, I wish I could, but I can't get it out of my mind."

I didn't know what to say to him so I just listened as he talked, forgetting all about the throbbing in my head.

"The call came just as the shift was changing," he continued. "Most of the firefighters coming off their shift climbed right back onto the ladder trucks when they heard what had happened. We came from Brooklyn so we were one of the first to respond, meaning we were the first to go in on the rescue. Then the others came. They didn't know the tower would collapse, but it did. I can't tell you how many firefighters were in that building at the time, trying to find survivors, but it had to be in the hundreds. Our whole ladder squad had gone into the building just before it collapsed, and I don't know if they're dead or alive."

He closed his eyes and took a quick breath. I could see the tears glistening beneath his lashes. He swallowed several times before he spoke again.

"Every time I close my eyes I see the horror of what happened. How do I explain to you what I see in my mind? If I could explain it, maybe I could get it out of my head. Tell me," he begged, "tell me, how do I explain it when there is no explanation evil enough to describe the scene?"

I had no answer. There was no answer.

"How am I supposed to feel?" he continued. "What am I supposed to feel? I can't handle the pain that is in my heart without feeling hate. I'm not supposed to feel hate toward another human being. I don't even know who caused this, but yet I hate them. How can I not feel hate? The pain is too great, how can I bear it without feeling hate?" He broke down and let the emotion overtake him. His sobs were heart wrenching. I raised myself to a sitting position, reached over, put my arms around his shoulders and let my heart break with his. All I knew how to do was hold him and cry with him until there were no more tears. Once the burden was lifted from him, his eyes closed and he slept.

I lay back down on my blanket and thought about the firemen and police officers who lost their lives trying to save others. I watched the people. I listened to what they had to say. I watched as tears turned to prayers and the proud discovered humility. I watched as confusion turned to fear and sadness.

In my career, I've had a lot of experience with tragedy and the sense of loss it brings, but no amount of experience could have prepared me for what I had just witnessed, or the incredible emotional pain that I'd shared with another human being. I wasn't prepared for the deep feeling of love and friendship I felt for a man whom I had only met a few moments ago. I needed to know his name so I could find him again.

"Can you tell me this man's name?" I asked the EMT.

"I believe it's Lenny... Lenny Roberts."

"Lenny Roberts," I whispered, "I will talk with you again, my friend."

I looked at my watch. The time was 2:00 PM. The sky was still black with ash. Breathing was still difficult and my eyes burned in spite of the cleaning solution the EMT had washed them out with. My head was feeling better, however, and I needed to find out if they would let a firefighter from Missouri be part of a volunteer crew to help in whatever way I could.

"I think I can be on my way," I said to the EMT, standing up to prove I was able.

"Let me check you over first before you leave." He walked over, looked first into one eye, then in the other. He then checked the goose egg on the back of my head.

"I think you'll be all right now." He put four capsules into my hand. "For your headache, when it returns. Take two at a time."

"Could you tell me who I talk to about volunteering?" I asked. I'm a fireman and have had the kind of experience that would be useful."

"They'll be glad to have you, then." He pointed me in the direction I needed to go, and told me whom I should ask for.

After getting the approval I needed, I took my badge from my wallet, pinned it on my jacket and began making my way back to the disaster site. Emergency workers were attempting to clear the streets, but making slow progress. One of the workers was sitting on a curb drinking from a bottle of water. He had removed his hat and was leaning against a light pole with his eyes closed.

"Is there anything I can do here?" I asked, looking at the destruction in front of me.

"Yep," he replied. "I'll get you started in a minute. Want to sit for a minute, and I'll tell you what we're doing."

I sat down. "Where do you get water?" I asked. My head had begun pounding again and I was glad for the capsules in my pocket.

He reached over, pulled a bottle out of his bag and handed it to me. I washed down two of the capsules. "Thanks. I got a bump on the head this morning."

"We'll put you on paper clean-up for awhile, until the headache's gone. As you can see, there's plenty of it around. All kinds of paper from all kinds of companies. Just think of it as giant confetti," he grimaced. "Your badge says you're from Missouri. How did you happen to be at the wrong place at the wrong time?"

"Good question," I sighed, shaking my head. "Do they know what happened yet?"

"Not for sure, but in case you hadn't heard, the Pentagon got hit too. Don't know what the death toll is there yet. A plane hit it just before 9:45 this morning, leaving a massive hole in the side of the building. Crazy terrorists. They think the U.S. will take this lying down."

He stopped and looked at me, concern showing in his face. "You don't look so good, I think you'd better wait until tomorrow to do any real work. The Salvation Army has set up a camp for out-of-town volunteers. They've got cots and blankets. Maybe you should spend some time there."

I thanked him and decided to take his advice. I found out as I talked to workers along the way that I wasn't alone. Many who had escaped death that morning had offered to stay and help. A local volunteer group was providing food. I found a cot in the Salvation Army camp, and while I ate my supper, I watched the sun as it began to set through the heavy haze. I felt so grateful to be alive. I felt grateful to be sitting there eating and watching the sunset.

As I looked out in the dimness, I whispered a prayer for the thousands trapped under the debris. A man sat down beside me, reached out his hand and introduced himself.

"I'm Bob Goldberg,"

I reached out my hand. "Jeremy Carter." He looked every bit as tired and ragged as I felt. He found a place on the cot next to me and we sat silently and watched the sun disappear before Bob spoke again.

"I'm a good man," he said. "I've raised a good family and I've lived a good life, a peaceful life, and I liked my life. I like order and I hate conflict. Most of all, I don't like change." He looked at me and then beyond, at the mountains of debris. Wiping the tears from his eyes, he continued. "Today my life changed. I can never go back to the life I knew and I don't know how to feel about that. Everything I thought was so important for the 'good life' I find has little meaning now."

"Did you work in the Trade Center?" I asked softly.

"I did. And today for the first time in all the years I've been there, I got to know the people who work for the same company I do. It's not that I didn't have the opportunity. I just didn't want to complicate my life with people. So every day I saw their faces but I never cared enough to ask their names. Today, I met the most wonderful people and I know their names..." He paused as a sob caught in his throat. "I know their names... and I feel such an overwhelming love for them. Today I found I've missed out on so much over the years because I've lived a life of total and complete complacency. I just never cared about anything except what I wanted. In fact, I think I liked being complacent."

Bob shook his head, tears in his voice. "Today I hugged more people and felt love for more people than I have ever felt in my life. It took all of this for me to see that not only have I not lived the 'good life.' I haven't even lived '*life.*'" He stopped speaking and took a deep breath. "I just had to tell someone and you looked like the kind of person who would listen."

"I've been told that before," I smiled through my own tears. "I don't think you're alone when it comes to complacency. I think we just received a 'wake up call' today because so many of us have that same problem. I think sometimes our lives have to be stirred up a bit so we can understand the meaning of 'wake up.' But once we catch the meaning, we can see what's really around us."

"I understand that, but I have to tell you," Bob shook his head, "I felt such anger, this morning, toward those who brought this tragedy upon America. I feel even more anger, tonight, toward myself for not doing my part as an American. I feel anger toward myself for what I represent. You see, if I am so self-absorbed, I can't contribute. Then what can I expect? I make my demands. I wanted to be left alone, in my good life, to do my thing, with nothing required of me in return. If I can't give in return, then I, too, am at fault.

"I've learned something today as I watched helplessly while the towers collapsed. I learned it's so easy to place the blame on others and complain to others because my freedom is jeopardized. But it's hard to do a self-evaluation and ask myself, what have I done to protect it? I've complained, I've whined, I've insisted. I've even favored that which is wrong if it meant I would gain from it.

"So, my friend, must I not also share some of the responsibility for this tragedy?" He wiped his eyes with the back of his hand. "Today, I received a gift from each person I met. I didn't expect that. Some gave me insight, some, a simple piece of knowledge. Others hugged me — and from all I felt love. To them I owe my gratitude. America has given me a most precious gift, the gift of freedom. To Her I owe my loyalty. I agree with you that there are many who are complacent, but that doesn't excuse me. It doesn't make it right for me. I also agree with you when you talk of a 'wake up call.' My wake up call hit me like a bolt of lightning, and boy was it painful."

I listened intently to Bob's words and was caught up in his analysis. I knew he spoke the truth, not just for him but for every American who demanded freedom without accepting responsibility. I watched him as he expressed his feelings, watched as the tension seemed to drain from him as he talked. He took another deep breath, then quickly changed the subject.

"Here, I have confessed all my sins to you," he said, a smile crossing his face, "and all I know about you is your name. So tell me about yourself. Have you got a family?"

"My wife, Addie, died a few years ago," I responded. Then I found myself sharing with him the feelings I hadn't shared with anyone else concerning my wife's death. It surprised me, yet it felt good because as I shared them I was able to let them go. I realized what happened to him as he talked was also happening to me. I could feel the tension leave my body. I told him about my sixteen year-old son Kyle and my ten year-old daughter, Kaylee, that when my wife died my parents had insisted we move in with them. "They have a small mansion," I laughed, "and it works great."

We talked for several minutes more before Bob decided he'd better find the cot where he'd laid his coat and blanket. As we stood, we hugged. He was a big man, probably 6'4" compared to my 6'2"frame, and outweighed me by at least a hundred and fifty pounds. Even though I considered myself muscular, I felt the crunch of his bear hug.

I watched him as he walked into the darkness, and I thought about this day and how it had changed Bob's life... how it had changed my life. What is it that had prompted the change? Was it the tragedy itself, or the fear caused by the tragedy? Was it fear that opened Bob's mind to the truth? Did I feel fear this morning?

Most certainly.

Was it the fear that numbed me, or was it the fear that gave me the courage to move?

I lay on the cot with a blanket tightly wrapped around me. I tried to concentrate on the questions in my mind, but a feeling of heavy fatigue swept over me. I must have slept because when I opened my eyes, it was light. At first I couldn't remember where I was, but as I looked around me and saw the debris and devastation in the daylight, the memory of yesterday refocused my mind and suddenly I was wide awake.

The scene was much worse in the daylight and I forgot my questions about fear because fear itself filled me. I didn't want to move. I just wanted to close my eyes and pretend it wasn't there, or hope it would go away... all along knowing it wasn't going anywhere. The words Bob had spoken last night about responsibility began swirling around in my brain as I lifted my head from the blanket. In spite of my fear, I stood, folded the blanket and set it with the others. I turned my face to the debris and knew it was going to be a long day.

Breakfast had been provided by one of the local restaurants. Hunger seemed to replace fear for the time being as I gratefully ate the bagels and drank the juice.

Cell phones were finally working, so I called my mother and my children to let them know I was safe and where I would be for the next several days. My mother started to cry. "I love you, Jeremy. And – I'm so proud of what you're doing."

As I tucked the cell phone in my pocket, I felt a twinge of homesickness for my family and a deep sense of gratitude that they were safe in Missouri.

I wasn't expected back to work for several days and along with hundreds of other people who had volunteered their help, I could give all my time now to what lay ahead of me.

That day as I searched with the others for life beneath the rubble, I saw a little girl standing near the yellow tape, crying. I hurried over and knelt down beside her to ask her if she was lost. She shook her head, no. "But my doll is lost, in there," pointing to the rubble.

I looked into her eyes and recognized a child's fear. Then I took her hand and walked with her, away from the devastating scene. I reached into my pocket, pulled out my money clip and removed two twenty-dollar bills.

"I'll tell you what." I handed the little girl the money. "I'll give you this to buy a new doll if you promise me that you will name her Addie. Will you do that for me?"

She lifted her tear-stained face. "Addie's a nice name," she said softly.

I could see a woman hurrying toward us, concern showing on her face, and I knew this must be the little girl's mother. "Promise me one more thing?" I asked. "Promise me that you will not be afraid and you will teach Addie to not be afraid."

Her eyes softened as she smiled gratefully, clutching the twenty-dollar bills in her hand. "I promise," she whispered.

"Shellie," her mother called as she ran to us, her face pale with worry, "I've been looking all over for you!"

"Shellie was looking for her doll," I greeted her mother, "but she and I have decided that she'll buy a new doll and her name will be Addie."

"Oh, thank you for finding her!" The woman reached out to shake my hand. "Thank you so much! I was taking Shellie to her grandmother's for the day when the planes hit. She never went anywhere without her doll. I didn't realize her attachment until now. Thank you again for everything."

As they walked away I felt I had quieted my own fear by consoling someone else's fear. I didn't quite understand how that could happen.

That evening I found a vacant spot and had just sat down to rest against a wall of broken concrete and bent steel when an elderly gentleman, his face etched in fear, walked by me as he cautiously stepped around the bits of debris that cluttered the sidewalk. I stood, and taking his arm, walked with him until we reached a place where there was less debris.

As we walked we talked. I reassured him that he was safe. I felt my own fear subside as he shook my hand and thanked me.

After making sure the gentleman was safely on his way, I returned to my spot, sat down once again and leaned my head against my pillow of steel. Just as I closed my eyes, someone spoke.

"Hello there." It was the familiar soothing voice of the man I had helped the day before. I opened my eyes and looked up into those same clear, calm eyes. "I thought it was you." He sat beside me. "Were you able to get our friend into an ambulance?"

I smiled at him. "I was actually able to keep her talking until they put her inside." I could see his fatigue. His dark hair, slightly longer than my own, was wet with perspiration. "How have you been?" I asked him.

He proceeded to tell me about a man he had helped free from the rubble, and how, tirelessly so many volunteers had labored until they could no longer lift their arms. As I listened I was aware of something about him that I hadn't noticed before.

His voice was calming and although his face looked tired, his eyes remained untouched by fatigue. They were intense; deep-set, almost black in color. He was neither old nor young.

Ageless would be the word to describe him. His height was equal to my own. But it was not his physical features that were so striking; rather, it was the feeling of peace I could sense as he sat near me. There was something else, also; something I didn't know how to describe, yet was familiar. What was it?

"You look tired," he observed as he drank from a bottle of water.

"I was just thinking the same thing about you," I laughed.

He chuckled softly as he leaned back on the pillow of concrete. As we sat there, the feeling of peace seemed to enfold me. I felt like I wanted to tell him about my fear.

"This morning," I began, "I woke up full of fear. Then during the day I comforted a little child as I knelt down beside her, looked into her frightened eyes and said, 'Don't be afraid.' Her eyes softened as she smiled at me, and my fear was quieted. This evening I eased the fear of an elderly man and my fear was lifted."

I sat quietly for a minute, not saying any more. Then I turned to him. "Can you tell me why?" I asked, knowing he could answer my question.

His eyes seemed to penetrate my thoughts and I could almost feel his answer before he spoke. "Courage dwells in each of us. Courage is simply strength of heart. When we experience fear, we sometimes have to dig deeply to allow the courage to shine through," he said simply. "In helping to free others of their fear, you accepted responsibility for your own fear, and let it go. And through letting go of your fear, courage surfaced. You have learned a beautiful lesson, my friend. For without fear there is no need for courage. It simply becomes a natural act."

Author's Notes

I think almost every person at some time in their life has had an experience that caused them to be distracted, directed or moved just long enough for danger to pass them by. I wonder how many people, employed at the Trade Center and the Pentagon, were held up in traffic or ran into an unusual situation on the morning of September 11 that kept them from getting to work on time.

Sometimes when we have something to learn, we find ourselves in situations that allow us that opportunity. I wonder how many people whose routines would not have normally taken them there that day, found themselves a witness and participant of this tragedy.

I wonder why there were only a total of 266 passengers on the four flights that held over 1000. I wonder why those passengers who called their loved ones were able to maintain calm in the face of such grave danger. I wonder why the towers were able to stand as long as they did before collapsing, allowing so many to escape?

I wonder how many of us recognize divine intervention. I, myself, believe in miracles.

I wonder how many of us had a wake-up call because of the complacency in our lives. I wonder how many of us responded to that wake-up call with a renewed dedication to the country that allowed us the freedom to be complacent.

In all this wondering, one thing is apparent. In a time of crisis, as human beings, in the midst of all the questions, we tend to remember what we are here for. Our hearts become tender. Our eyes open to the needs of others and we are not afraid to step out and do what is necessary in order to maintain our way of life. Our true character is that we know how to *be* in a time of tragedy. We know how to respond, because it is within us to know. We know how to be courageous, like those aboard flight 93 who chose to give their lives so that others might live — because courage lives inside each of us. It is a power within, a gift that has been bestowed upon us by those who came before us and brought with them the desire to be free. To them we owe our dedication. To America, who has given us the precious gift of freedom, we owe our lives. And to those who experienced a loss in this tragedy, we owe our compassion.

Chapter Two

Courage in the Face of Fear

The gentle man seated beside me proceeded to explain more about courage, and fear. "How do we recognize courage if we don't first experience fear? I had never thought about that before. I had always considered the feeling of fear to be a sign of weakness, but instead, I find it is the first step toward reclaiming our natural state of courage. If we don't experience fear, we have no thought of courage.

"But when fear is present and we experience courage for a certain period of time, it becomes an antidote to our fear. Fear brings us to that point of choice. Courage already lives inside, but when fear is present, we must make a conscious choice to honor that courage rather than the fear. When courage surfaces, fear dissipates."

I wanted to hear every word he spoke, but as I listened, my eyelids grew heavy. I fought to keep them open but the fatigue was so great within my body, my muscles quivered like Jell-O and my head ached. My lungs burned and my throat was dry. Even the fresh water I drank from the plastic bottle couldn't quench my thirst or wash away the taste of the ever-present ash, dust and smoke that burned in my lungs as it polluted the air. I was so weary, my pillow of steel felt soft and comfortable against my head. Finally, I slept.

In my sleep, I could still hear the soothing voice, and I began to dream. I remembered I was going to ask his name before I fell asleep, but I was so tired. I will just think of him as my friend, I told myself. In my dream, however, it seemed as if I already knew his name and didn't need to ask. I felt my body relax as the warm and restful dream overtook me.

"Walk with me and we will talk of things that will help you understand," he was saying as I found myself beside him in the dream. I could see in the distance a door, slightly ajar. By the door was a small table and on the table, a book. As we walked toward the door, words of a scripture came into my mind. *"Knock and it shall be opened; seek and ye shall find; ask and it shall be given unto you."* I wondered if the book on the table was the Bible, but as I got closer I could see that it was too small. It was about an inch thick and was bound in a white cover. The book seemed familiar to me as if I had seen it somewhere before but I couldn't remember where. The words on the front of the book were written in gold, and though I could see them, I couldn't make out the title. Then we stepped through the door, and the book was gone.

My thoughts returned to the question that seemed to have brought me into this dream. I had asked to understand fear because fear had filled my day as it had filled the day of those with whom I had worked, clearing away the rubble. We were afraid of what had happened, afraid of what might yet come. We were afraid of what we might find under the debris, afraid of what we might not find; yet we tirelessly searched, pushing away fear with this act of courage.

"Understanding your fear," my friend said as the door opened before us, "is like opening a door and finding what's on the other side. You have experienced fear many times in your life, Jeremy, and you will experience fear many more times in the years to come. Fear is part of being alive. It is a result of what is taking place in your life or in the world around you. It is not there to torment or protect you. It is not there to alter your life, but to move you forward in your journey, to move past it so that you can be elevated to a higher level of awareness."

As he spoke, I thought of Addie. When we found out she had cancer, I was so afraid of losing her I could hardly breathe. Every day as I watched her become weaker and every night as I held her in my arms, fear was my companion. I would plead with God to make the fear go away so I could be strong, but fear remained. I thought I could never be that afraid again, but I was wrong. On the day she died, the fear of going on alone was even greater and more painful, and I wanted to lie down beside her and die too. But I couldn't. I had two children who needed me more than I had needed Addie, and I had to find the courage to let go of the fear so that I could be the kind of father Addie wanted me to be.

Had I been elevated, then, into a higher level of awareness? I would like to think so. I had learned to walk around that fear and leave it in its place... behind me. Now, as I began to understand fear, I began to understand that God had heard my plea and had, in His way, held me as I had held Addie, until I could evolve enough to find the courage I needed to go on without her.

Because of my own experience, I was able to identify with the fear in the little child and the elderly man. Because I understood, I could help take away their fear, and in its place, help them find courage. What I thought was a simple act of kindness was a simple act of courage; and I, in turn was healed. That is what I began to comprehend as I walked through the door to the other side.

I understand better now the scripture that had gone through my mind. The word *knock* could mean simply to be willing. I didn't have to literally knock on the door, for the door was already open. I just had "to be willing" to walk through. Perhaps *to seek* means to observe, then *to listen*, so the answers to the questions we are asking can be answered.

I don't know when the dream ended and my thoughts took over, or if they were both the same, but when I awoke my nameless friend was gone. In his place was a blanket that had been tucked around me. The sun was rising amidst the ash and smoke, and Bob was standing over me singing a wake-up song of his own. In his hands were two Styrofoam cups of coffee each balancing a bagel and a donut. Under one arm he held two bananas, under the other, the morning paper.

He looked like a clown who had forgotten to put on the rest of his makeup. His hair, white with ash, stood on end. His face was pasted with white dust and his clothes looked as if he had slept in them, which I'm sure he had. His size just added to the humor of his appearance. The chuckle that escaped his lips told me he found the picture before him to be every bit as amusing.

"Thought you might be hungry." He handed me one of the cups with a donut and bagel on top and one of the bananas. He sat down beside me, set his cup on the ground next to him, then opened the paper so we could read the headlines.

The date on the top of the paper was Thursday, September 13, 2001. Two days had passed since this nightmare had begun. The headlines gave this information:

Four hijacked United Airlines 767's set out the morning of September 11, 2001, before 8:45 AM. (two from Boston, two from New York) on a mission of evil. One plane crashed into the area of the 92nd floor of the north tower at 8:45 AM. The second plane struck the area of the 80th floor at 9:03 AM. A passenger on the third 767 called her husband and calmly described the attackers and the weapons they were using, shortly before the plane struck the Pentagon, at 9:38 AM, opening a hole that spanned five floors and killing at least one hundred and fifty.

The fourth plane, United Airlines Flight 93, crashed into a vacant field about 80 miles southeast of Pittsburgh, Pa., at 10:10 AM. Destination was unclear at the time of the crash. One man on that flight, called his family to tell them he loved them and in calm assurance, once again, explained the situation and that he and other passengers were going to jump the hijackers. These people saved lives of many others by giving theirs in this heroic deed.

At 10:05 AM, the south tower of the World Trade Center collapsed, burying many rescuers.

At 10:28 AM, the North tower of the World Trade Center collapsed.

The picture on the front page was the picture still frozen in my mind of the explosion of the first tower. It brought back the shock of what I had seen just forty-eight hours before. I turned my head away for a second to let the shock wear off before I could look at the paper again. Giving me the time I needed, I went about the chore of putting the bagel between my teeth, removing the lid from the cup of coffee, placing it on a piece of concrete, and carefully setting the donut on the lid. I was trying to keep everything from touching the dirty concrete, and suddenly I considered how humorous that was, since my own hands were certainly far from clean. I was so tired last night I hadn't even bothered to wash them.

"They don't know yet how many people were in the towers when they collapsed, but it is in the thousands." Bob's voice broke as he finished speaking and tears spilled out of his eyes, rolling freely down his cheeks. He tried to put down the paper, but the shock of what he was reading held him spellbound.

"What will we find under that rubble?" he almost whispered. "Will anyone be alive? Will we reach them in time? Where was God when this was happening?"

The answer to his questions came quickly to me, but it took a few seconds to control my own emotions before I could reply. "He was there, waiting to receive those who would not survive," I answered as tears filled my own eyes, "just as He was there waiting for Addie the day she died in my arms. I think he was creating obstacles for many who, because they were late for work, lived." I thought of my friend Shana Stewart who lived because for the first time in fifteen years she was late for work. I think He was very busy that morning.

We sat there silently for a few moments and finished our breakfast, each trying to understand the purpose of this ugly tragedy, crying for those who died and crying for those who would be personally affected by the deaths.

"Let's clean up here and see where we're needed today," I finally said, gathering up the cups and banana peels. "I think we have another full day ahead of us."

"Maybe today we'll be lucky and find someone alive under all that…" In exasperation Bob used a sweeping gesture of his hand to finish his sentence. Rubble couldn't begin to describe it. Debris hardly touched the surface of what it was.

As the hundreds of men and women worked tirelessly through the third day, the mushrooming effect this disaster was having on both humanity and on the economy of the United States and the rest of the world, became evident. I needed to focus on how the tragedy had touched human lives and leave the economy to those who understood that aspect far better than I did.

Fearing more terrorist attacks, the airlines had shut down. People had begun flooding the supermarkets to buy enough groceries to last for several weeks, in case the trucking industry would be immobilized. People had begun living in fear of a second attack. Fear literally swept the nation.

I think that was what was supposed to happen. I think that was part of the plan. To control the minds of the people through fear is perhaps the greatest of all control. And as long as there was fear in the Nation, one man would be in control. But I think one man did not understand the American people. In all of his research, he did not research the hearts of the American people.

Minds can be controlled for only so long if the heart refuses to give in, and our hearts desire... no, they *demand* to be free at all cost. Nowhere in the world are there people with the strength of Americans when they are tested or challenged. And though the fear was evident, courage had begun to take its place in our hearts.

Reports came in almost by the minute, telling of the heroic deeds of the people giving of their time, their means and their money. Monday, they may have been divided into race, religion, color or creed, but Tuesday there was no dividing line. They stood as one, united... millions of people united together to stand up for freedom and to give freely to those in need. Funds were set up for the families of the firefighters and policemen who lost their lives that first day, and money was pouring in.

On Monday, our heroes were athletes. By Tuesday evening, our heroes were the firefighters and policemen who lost their lives in the rescue attempt. Our heroes were those who were held captive in the planes and died. Our heroes were those who stopped the plane from reaching its destination by taking a stand, knowing it meant their lives. On Tuesday patriotism was reborn and it felt good in spite of the tragedy. America had received a wake-up call and she had responded with "God Bless America."

While taking a short break mid-morning, several of us sat and watched the huge cranes as they dug beneath the wreckage and lifted their cradles full of steel, metal and concrete.

"I wonder how many days it will take to remove all this?" one man asked.

"Things will never be the same, will they?" another responded.

"Will they ever find all the bodies?" a third man mused aloud. "So many questions and no one has an answer. So many changes."

To help lighten the mood, one fireman talked of how things had changed in one day at home. "On Monday, my wife complained that we didn't have enough money," he smiled. "On Tuesday, she gave half of it away."

"My daughter called just a few minutes ago and said she was in line to give blood," an Irish volunteer, his accent giving him away, said with pride. "And from where she was standing at the time, it was a three-hour wait. She was excited to be there, waiting for her turn to give her blood. Last Monday," he chuckled, "she complained because she had to stand in the supermarket line for five minutes."

The two stories broke the somber mood and the men began to relax and visit with each other. They talked of home, family and pride for their country. Not once did they mention fear. They had no time to think of fear. Their courage ran deep. They told of experiences of survivors, and of falling airplane and body parts.

One man related the story of how a tire from one of the planes fell through the sky and landed within a few feet of a man who felt lucky to be alive. They talked of the sadness they felt as they found hundreds of shoes lying everywhere; the only explanation given was that the bodies had either vaporized or the shoes were blown off the feet of the victims. They talked with pride of the way the New Yorkers had handled themselves as they made their way to safety after escaping the towers.

They talked of the calm that was ever present in the exodus. How unusually calm the people felt in spite of their fear. They talked of the love and concern that was felt on every street, in every store and on every sidewalk.

As I sat and listened to the stories, I felt like I was viewing a scene from a science fiction movie, the acting so good, it had drawn me into the excitement of the moment. None of this seemed real to me. It couldn't be real — but it was; and I was there with these amazingly courageous people. People of every race and almost every religion. Everyone was the same color, a ghostly white from the ash and dust. No one cared who voted for whom in the last election. Politics had no place in this setting. There was no age difference here. We were all young enough to work and old enough to know how. It didn't matter what we believed about God, or even if we believed in a higher power. Here God represented love, faith, courage and humanity.

About an hour after we had all gone back to our duties, three others and I were working in an area, dislodging bits of concrete when, without warning, I reached down and touched something that felt like clothing. My heart stopped beating. My breath was caught in my throat and I tried to speak but no words would come out. I swallowed and tried again. I heard myself scream, "I found something here! Hurry! I found something here!"

The other men dropped what they were doing immediately and were at my side. We all fell to our knees and gently removed the debris around the still lifeless body of a man. As soon as I could reach, I felt for a pulse. There was none. I began to cry, and I couldn't stop crying. Slowly and gently I began brushing the ash and dirt from around his face. He was an African American about my age. As I freed his body from the filthy rubble, I kept asking him to please wake up, but he just lay there in sleep. I couldn't let anyone help me as I worked diligently. I felt as if I were responsible for him now, and I couldn't let him get hurt anymore.

The others there seemed to understand and they stood back waiting to assist me if I needed it. I wished I could stop crying so I could explain to him how sad I felt that we couldn't get to him in time. When the stretcher arrived I allowed the others to help me lay him on the body bag. I had to walk away then, because I couldn't watch them zip him in. I couldn't believe the intense pain I felt inside was for a man I had never met. The pain seemed familiar to me somehow, and I didn't want to feel it. How was I to live with that pain? Why wouldn't it go away? Why did it keep coming back?

I needed to get away from the destruction for a while to see if I could make some sense of all of this. I needed to get back to New Jersey to pick up my things at the hotel and check into a place nearby if I was going to stay for a time. Now was a good time to take care of that.

Traffic was moving somewhat and I was able to get back to New Jersey. I climbed into the shower once I was inside my hotel room. I just stood under the hot water, letting it cleanse my body while it thawed my mind. I shampooed my hair until there was no shampoo left in the bottle. I shaved, brushed my teeth and put on clean clothes for the first time in two days. My body felt so good, but my heart was sad. It was a sadness that shook my being, and I was afraid once again.

The hunger pangs in my stomach reminded me that I hadn't eaten since breakfast and it was after 3:00 PM. I ordered room service so I wouldn't have to go out. I didn't want to be around people. I didn't want to think, yet thoughts exploded in my mind and my head ached with the emotion. I just wanted to close out the tragedy and all that I had seen. But my mind wouldn't let me.

Room service arrived with my dinner and I ate slowly, concentrating on chewing. I felt better then, but the sadness wouldn't go away. How could I make the sadness go away?

I lay back on the bed, closed my eyes and let sleep come to me. When it finally did, my mind was quiet.

It was after 7:00 PM when I awoke. I called the desk to let them know I would be checking out in the morning, then turned on the TV to listen to what the media was saying about the attack. I was fascinated with the coverage, but as I continued to watch, the sadness surfaced again and I had to shut it off.

I remembered I had purchased a book on the 10th, the day before all this began. I had placed it in my travel bag. I retrieved it and sat back on the bed to see if reading would help.

I began thumbing through the pages and noticed the titles of the chapters. The chapter entitled, "Letting Go," peaked my interest. What did the author mean by the phrase, letting go? As I read the first few pages, I found myself agreeing with everything I read, and I began to see myself in this chapter. He talked about how we hold onto feelings in case we may need them for later use. One statement caught me off guard. *"What about all those past mistakes, pains, hurts, and failures? Well, we never know when we might need one of them to protect us from that ever happening again."*

I thought about Addie and the helplessness I felt while she was dying, and the pain I felt the day she died. I had hung on to that for two years. I had held onto pain and nourished it so it could grow inside of me.

Further down he explained what happens to us when we don't get rid of those destructive feelings. We experience stress, loneliness, anxiety, worry, depression, fear... there was that word, fear again. I thought I understood fear and what it can do. I didn't know that it can steal our happiness, but I did understand that it could affect our peace of mind. I was, only now, realizing what it could do to us physically.

What was the solution? I skipped down to "how to let go." He talked about really knowing yourself. I thought I knew myself pretty well until today. Now I realize I am just beginning to learn who I really am. The book explained that I am who I honor within myself. Fear, or any other painful feeling is a point of choice; I can honor the fear or I can let it go and honor my peace of mind.

The next sentence struck me. *Our lives are about discovering who we really are, uncovering our true self.* I had to admit I had no idea who my true self really was.

I continued to read until I got to the questions he had outlined: *How do we resolve the issue? How do we let go? How do we stop the pain?*

How do I stop the pain?

I realized as I read through the questions, I had hidden my true self after Addie died. The pain I felt that day, the pain I keep nurturing inside, I continually bring back every time I go through an experience, like the one I went through today.

The words on the pages continued to grab at me. *How do we let go of the past without losing control of our lives in the present?*

As I read, I found that learning to let go is just like learning to read, to walk, or to ride a bike — you take one step at a time. So what were the steps?

The first step I needed to take, in order to let go, was to observe my feelings as if I were viewing them from a different angle, from the outside looking in. This helps you to discover that the feeling you are experiencing is not really you, but rather, an experience you are having. The second step was, wanting to let go of those feelings that stopped me from being who I really am. The third step was the willingness to let go. And, finally, the fourth step was making a firm decision to let go. As I read further, I discovered that "letting go" required self-observation, intention, willingness and commitment. Did I have what it took to let go? Everyone has what it takes to let go, I decided. We just have to search it out in our own minds.

So, I began observing myself. First I looked in the mirror to see if I could find the real me in my own eyes. I was surprised how hard I had to look before I could begin to uncover the person I had hidden away. As the minutes passed, I could see something happening. I found something I had a hard time admitting to myself. I had blamed myself for Addie's death. Although there was nothing I could do, I had judged and sentenced myself to pain.

The strange thing was that, in some way, I also blamed myself for the death of the man I had found in the rubble today. Why? Maybe it was because I felt that same sense of hopelessness I had felt two years ago. There was nothing I could have done then and there was nothing I could have done today to change the outcome. I now knew I needed to let go of the feeling of guilt and pain that lived inside of me.

As I read about the process that the author had outlined in the book, I decided to try it for myself. I first observed my pain for a moment. I could feel it churning inside as if it were ready to leave. Then I asked myself if I *liked* feeling that way. I could truthfully say that I didn't. I also thought about Addie. Would she want me to hang onto the pain of her death or would she want me to let it go and be happy? I knew the answer to that question. My next question was, "Do I *want* to let go?" Most assuredly, was my answer. However, a wave of fear swept over me with the thought of letting go.

Can I let go? I don't know. How will I feel if I let go? I almost laughed at myself. Whatever I would feel, it had to be better than what I felt now. My answer was a definite "yes," I want to let it go.

My next question was, am I truly *willing* to let it go, or did I want to continue believing that by hanging on I was somehow keeping the memory of Addie alive or protecting myself from being hurt again? I decided I would trust my intuition. I was willing to let it go.

My final question was, *when* did I want to let go? That only brought forth other questions and fear flashed through my mind. If I let go, will I forget what Addie and I had together? What would fill the space of my pain?

Despite my fear, I knew the right thing to do was to let it go… and there is no better time than now. I felt a huge lump in my throat that seemed to want to surface and be released. I took a deep breath and when I let it out I felt lighter, as if a heavy weight had been lifted from me.

The lump in my throat was gone. I felt free for the first time in two years. I could let Addie go and it felt right. I knew I was letting go of not her *memory*, but only the *pain* I felt from losing her. I felt a sense of peace and happiness come over me. I also felt the warm presence of Addie and I knew she was pleased.

I finished reading the chapter before closing the book. As I placed it on the nightstand I relaxed my body, lay back in bed and began to observe myself without the pain. It felt so good to no longer feel afraid. I knew now, that I could go back to New York and put myself into the work I needed to do.

I switched on the TV, watched the disaster sites and listened to the commentator as he spoke about the tragedy. The picture of the towers collapsing was shown again and I watched and knew I was going to be just fine.

I think it is all right to be afraid. Sometimes I think we need to experience fear so we can become acquainted with courage once again. Courage sometimes lets us cry. It lets us feel our fears and let them go instead of burying them. Having courage doesn't mean you don't feel emotion. Courage is full of emotion... the emotion of love rather than fear.

I know the fear that is being felt in the Nation at this time is a temporary thing. In our strength and our unity, fear will subside and courage will once again prevail as we pledge our patriotism to the country that we love.

Author's Notes

How do we recognize courage if we don't first experience fear? First, we have to realize that fear is man-made. In fact, fear is proof that we create. We can allow fear to elevate us to a higher level of understanding and awareness or drag us down to the depths of depression, loneliness, hopelessness, sadness and pain. Fear can inspire us to move past it if we see it for what it is, which is simply a past experience being re-lived in the present. Or fear can destroy, if we accept its false reality. It is our choice.

Fear awakens courage. Once we recognize fear for what it is, courage can then become a natural inner response to any given situation. Courage can then become the dominant force in the way we approach life.

Eleanor Roosevelt said, *"You gain strength, courage and confidence with every experience by which you really stop to look fear in the face. You are able to say to yourself, 'I lived through this horror, I can take the next thing that comes along.'"*

Were those firefighters and police officers afraid when they ran into the Trade Center? If so, fear was quickly forgotten and courage, which had been their constant companion, was their driving force. Those who survived the attack and helped others to escape, let go of their own fear and courage was instantaneous. The volunteers who helped search the rubble for survivors, then for bodies, did so with courage. Those who helped pull people to safety during the attack on the Pentagon let go of their fear and courageously did what had to be done. The people who stood in lines for hours to give blood had courage. Those who helped bring food and supplies to the site for those who were working endlessly had courage. The children who have sent in more than $1 million for the children of Afghanistan, and those who held their neighbors' hand or sat with another in their grief, all showed courage.

Courage isn't loud and boisterous. It is quiet and reverent. It is not spoken; it is witnessed. We witness it as we watch the servicemen and women prepare to put their lives on the line for our freedom. We witness it in the eyes of their families as they say their goodbyes and watch their loved ones leave. We witness it through the willingness of the postal workers to continue handling the mail. We see it in the health care workers who provide treatment around the clock.

As our freedom is challenged and as our lives are interrupted and changed, we have all experienced the feelings of fear, sadness, anxiety, grief, and even depression. They are natural responses. *It's what we do with those feelings once they surface in us that matters most.* Bin Laden is not our enemy. Fear, left unchecked, is our enemy. Depression is our enemy when it feeds our minds with hopelessness and unyielding sadness. Anger is our enemy. When we use anger to try to control something over which we have no control, we become a part of the problem instead of part of the solution. All we have to do is awaken our courage by letting go of our fears, anxiety, anger and grief, and let that courage be the dominating presence in our thoughts and feelings.

It is important to understand that God does not cause disasters, but sometimes allows disaster to happen for reasons only He understands. Then He is found in the healing of every soul. He gives us support until we can stand again. He is witnessed in miracles that are not always visible to the human eye. He protects the freedom of our hearts, and no one can touch our freedom when it is carried so proudly and openly.

With that kind of courage in the face of fear we become heroes. Quiet, strong heroes, who stand beside those firefighters and policemen who are our heroes; and we share with them the freedom of America. We stand with those who died and we live, with courage, in their defense.

Chapter Three

What Can I Do for My Country?

I was born in 1963, the year President Kennedy was assassinated. My mother told me, years later, that it was a terrible time. "The nation," she said, "was deeply traumatized, and a feeling of great mourning swept the whole country." As she talked to me I noticed a folded newspaper in her hand. I could tell it was an older paper because it had started to yellow slightly. She didn't make an attempt to open the paper. She just held it on her lap.

"I was at work when it happened," she recalled. "Someone, I don't remember who, came running into the office screaming that the President had been shot. My boss quickly turned on his TV and we all crowded around it, in total silence. We watched and listened as the news commentator described, in detail, what had happened. He could hardly contain his emotions as he spoke, the shock showing clearly on his face. I remember there was total silence in the office... the shock was almost too great to bear. As we watched with unbelieving eyes, even the men began to cry. We all cried most of that day."

I could feel the emotion in her voice as she continued. "In the days that followed, the shock began to wear off, and fear took its place. We were afraid of what might happen to the nation. We waited for the truth to come out so we could understand, but the assassin was, himself, murdered. It felt like the final chapter was never written. We never really knew if Lee Harvey Oswald was the true assassin. If he was, was he acting alone or was he just a hit man for some power in another country? Were we a target for war? With these questions came anger... anger that someone dared target our president and our country. But through it all we came together as a nation. We mourned openly with each other. We cried together in honor of this man, and as we wept, we healed."

My mother then unfolded a newspaper so the front page was visible. The paper was dated November 23, 1963. The picture on the front page showed Jacqueline Kennedy leaning over the President after he had been shot. The caption written underneath gave the details: *On November 22, 1963, at 12:30 p.m., President John F. Kennedy was shot to death while riding in a motorcade in Dallas, Texas. An assassin fired several shots striking the president twice in the base of the neck and the head. The president was rushed to Parkland Memorial Hospital, where he was pronounced dead about a half hour later.* I'll always remember when, how and where he died. And I'll always remember how carefully my mother folded the newspaper before placing it back into the drawer of her desk.

On the twenty-fourth of November, as the nation and the world mourned, President Kennedy's body lay in state in the rotunda of the U.S. Capitol. Leaders of ninety-two nations attended the funeral and a million people lined the route as the horse-drawn caisson carried his body to his burial place in Arlington National Cemetery.

I don't know why my thoughts turned to that day. Maybe because it seems relevant to the horror people were going through now. Many thought the nation would never recover then and some wonder if the nation will ever recover today. I remember my mother reciting a statement that Daniel Patrick Moynihan, the assistant Secretary of Labor made at that time. If I can remember, it went something like this: *"Mary McGory said to me that we'll never laugh again," and I said, 'Heavens, Mary, we'll laugh again. It's just that we'll never be young again.'"* And America did recover and America did laugh again.

My generation has never seen the effects of a national tragedy close up. The wars have always been somewhere else, far away from the safety of our homes. I couldn't grasp the emotion of what my mother was trying so hard to make me understand until now. This tragedy has brought maturity to my generation and to our nation. We will no longer be innocent — which may not be so bad. We will however, be older and wiser and we will still be able to laugh again.

It was President Kennedy who stated these words, "Ask not what your country can do for you, ask what you can do for your country." These words have greater meaning today than they did the day before September 11; maybe even a greater meaning now than they did in 1963. We have a greater responsibility to the country that we love now that war is closer to her shores. We have to make a deeper commitment to our children and grandchildren now that we know their country needs to be protected. What can I do for my country, should be the question in all our hearts and minds.

I didn't sleep well that night and was grateful when the morning sun peered through the window. I turned on the TV to listen for any new developments while I shaved and finished dressing. The commentator was reading from some notes in front of him. "This attack by the terrorists," he said, "under the leadership of Osama bin Laden, is considered, by their own words, a Holy War.

I stopped what I was doing and gave my full attention to the man speaking. Two days ago Osama bin Laden was just a suspect. This morning there was confirmation. It wasn't that I hadn't heard of "holy wars," but how could a group of terrorists kill thousands of innocent people and call it holy? How can a religious belief be interpreted to give one man the authority to decide for God, that thousands of innocent people should be murdered in His name? If there is only one God, isn't He the God of all of us?

I began to feel such anger inside, I could hardly contain it. Then something else my mother told me years ago, came to mind. "Son," she had said, "if you want to know the truth, search it out. Study until you understand. Whether it is in the actual experience or if it takes hours in the library, search until you know. Only then will you have the right to judge, if there is to be judgment."

Knowing my mother was right, I picked up the telephone book and looked up the address of the public library. Also knowing that I would be in rush hour traffic going into New

York, I decided instead to call a taxi and go the opposite direction and do some research.

George Bernard Shaw had made the comment, "Religion is the only real motivating force in the world." Was religion the motivating force in war? If it took me all day or longer, I was determined to find out for myself the foundation of the religions of the world and what part, if any, war played in their existence.

Traffic was light and the library was almost empty. I placed my bags next to a wide round table and went in search of books that would explain to me the things I needed to know.

After locating the world religion section where I found more than one hundred books on the subject, I narrowed my search to ten books about African, Native American, Hindu, Buddhist, Islamic, Jewish, and Christian beliefs.

The desire to understand the Islamic religion led me to open that book first. I turned to the section that discussed myths that surrounded Islam and began reading.

"So what is the reality of Islam? How does one dispel the myths that have been created and spread so viciously? The only way to examine Islam is to simply examine its belief system. Look at its sources and see what they have to say. This is the way to find the truth about what Islam says concerning terror, terrorism and terrorists. Anyone who is sincerely searching for the truth will do it no other way. The very name Islam comes from the Arabic root word, 'salama,' which means peace.

"If such a religion is based on the notion of peace, how is it that so many acts done by its adherents are contrary to peace? The answer is simple. Such actions, if not sanctioned by the religion, have no place with it. They are not Islamic and should not be thought of as Islamic."

The writer went on to explain that suicide bombing is not a part of the religion. Although some Muslims have taken suicide bombing as being a virtuous act by which one receives great reward in the afterlife, this could not be further from the truth.

"The Prophet has said," the writer continued, "'those who go to extremes are destroyed. Do not be delighted by the action of *anyone, until you see how he ends up.'* How can we be delighted with such an end? What really hammers the final nail in the coffin of this act, is that it is suicide; something that is clearly forbidden in Islam. The Messenger of Allah said, *'He who kills himself with anything, Allah will torment him with the fire of Hell.'"*

All other types of extremities such as hostage taking, hijacking and planting bombs in public places, are clearly forbidden in Islam.

If this is true, why is this called a holy war? This means it has been labeled a holy war by man, not by a religion. I wanted to believe what I had just read. I wanted to know the truth.

I felt a deeper desire now to understand the basic beliefs of the religions as they were explained in the books in front of me. I reached for the next book. As I opened its cover, a man sat down at the table next to me. I felt a little irritated because there were dozens of empty tables in every other corner of the room. Why did he have to choose the table right next to mine? He gave me a quick nod and then turned to the books in front of him.

Letting my mind concentrate once again on my purpose, I soon forgot he was there and began sorting and placing the books on the table side by side. At first I thought I would read through one book at a time, but I quickly changed my mind. I found myself wanting to compare the religions, so before long, I had opened eight books.

I quickly jotted down on a piece of paper the questions I decided would be relevant:

1. Do all of these religions believe in a supreme being or a God?
2. What is the philosophy of their beliefs?

That was good enough for now. I was anxious to move on to the research. I already had a basic understanding of the Christian religions in America. I knew that Christians believe in God, so I went directly to the religions whose beliefs I didn't know.

The *African* religion believes that "each individual is given a particular destiny by the creator before birth." They believe in God. They draw their strength, inspiration and wisdom from God. They believe that one person's well-being is important to the peace and well-being of the entire tribe.

The *Native American* (American Indian) worships an all-powerful, all-knowing Creator or "Master Spirit," or Great Spirit. They believe in God.

The *Hindu* religion scriptures say, "Man is a real living, growing entity while God is an ideal being. Man and God are identical in essence, but different in form." They speak of a God.

The *Buddhist* says we have to cultivate a consciousness in which the omnipotent Lord is the anchor. The fortieth chapter of the Yajur Ved states that we should build our lives around Him, as He is the only one who is eternal and would stand by us in every adversity. They believe in God.

A *Muslim* testifies that "there is no God but Allah" and "how merciful is Allah who has showed man, through *Islam*, how to lead a righteous life." They believe in God.

The *Jewish* faith is devout in their faith and belief in God.

"I don't mean to intrude, but I couldn't help noticing that you are studying several books at the same time," I heard the man from the other table say. "You seem rather intent, perhaps even a little disturbed."

"Is it that obvious?" I asked, a little embarrassed.

"Just a little," he smiled. "My name is Joshua Lambert." He reached out to shake my hand.

"I'm happy to meet you." I reached out my own hand. "I'm Jeremy Carter."

"I recognize two of the books, so I'm assuming you are studying religions."

I didn't know if I wanted to share with him my concerns but then decided it might be a good idea to discuss with another person what I had found.

"First, perhaps, I should explain," I glanced at the open books, "why I am sitting here studying eight different books on eight different religions at the same time."

He smiled. "I'm assuming it has something to do with the statement that has outraged so many Americans. The statement that 'this is a *holy war*.' Am I right?"

I nodded. "All the religions I've read about in these books, believe in a loving, compassionate God, not one who would condone such evil. Whether He is called Jehovah, Heavenly Father, Creator, Allah, Elohim, Lord Krishna, or simply Lord, He is one and the same."

"The foundation to all the religions is love, peace, purity, compassion, concern for fellowman, and living a good life. Is that what you also found?" Joshua asked as he set down his book and walked over to my side of the table.

"As I read about one religion, it blends in with another. What is written about one, also explains all others."

I showed him different passages I had read from each book as I continued. "Look — from this book it says, 'uprightness, physical cleanliness and sexual purity and non-violence. Purity of speech, including speech that does not hurt anyone, is truthful, kind and beneficial, as well as daily recitation of scriptures. The purity of mind comprises serenity of mind, gentleness, self control and inner purity.'"

Pointing to a paragraph in another book, he read, "'The believer cannot, therefore, be misled to do evil deeds, be unjust, dishonest, cruel, etc. How unjust to themselves are those who choose to neglect or purposely avoid this universal message.'"

"Listen to this one." I quoted: "'It is the mind that molds man's destiny, action being but precipitated thought. For, better than sovereignty over the earth, better than the heaven state; better than dominion over all the world is the first step to the path of holiness.'"

Joshua picked up the last book and let his finger run through the words until he found what he was looking for. "'Those whose minds are fixed on me in steadfast love, worshiping me with absolute faith, I consider them to be most perfect.'"

"Do you see what I mean?" I exclaimed as our eyes met. "And although none of these quotes are from a book on Christianity, they are the same as Christian text."

"That's because all religions come from the same foundation." His voice was firm and convincing as he spoke.

"For all the differences in religion, they are very much the same. They are just saying the same thing in different words or phrases. The differences are defined only in man's interpretation."

As he spoke, Joshua walked over to his table and picked up a small book. "This is a book entitled *To Te Ching*. I would like to quote some verses to you."

> *Through compassion, one will triumph in attack*
> *and be Impregnable in defense. What heaven*
> *succors, it protects with the gift of compassion.*

He turned several pages, then began to read again:

> *In a home it is the site that matters;*
> *In quality of mind it is depth that matters;*
> *In an ally it is benevolence that matters;*
> *In speech it is good faith that matters;*
> *In government it is order that matters;*
> *In affairs it is ability that matters;*
> *In action it is timeliness that matters.*

"It all sounds familiar, does it not?" he said. "The words may be different but the meaning is the same." Joshua closed the book, set it back on his table and picked up another one. "One more source before I let you get back to your own studies. From this source are words that sum up every religion that believes in God and brings them together as one religion just as it was in the beginning." He opened the pages of the large book he now held in his hand and began to read:

The Buddha's Words on Kindness

> *This is what should be done.*
> *Be the one who is skilled in goodness, and who knows*
> *   the path of peace:*
> *Let them be able and upright, straightforward and*
> *   gentle in speech,*
> *Humble and not conceited, contented and easily satisfied.*

Unburdened with duties and frugal in their ways.
Peaceful and calm, and wise and skillful,
Not proud and demanding in nature.
Let them not do the slightest thing that the wise
    would later reprove.
Wishing: in gladness and in safety, may all beings be
    at ease.
Whatever living beings there may be, whether
    they are
weak or strong, omitting none,
The great or the mighty, medium, short or small,
    the seen
and the unseen, Those living near and far away, those
born and to-be-born, May all beings be at ease!
Let none deceive another, or despise any being in
    any state.
Let none through anger or ill-will, wish harm
    upon another.
Even as a mother protects with her life, her child, her
    only child,
So with a boundless heart, should one cherish all
    living beings:
Radiating kindness over the entire world, spreading
    upwards to
the skies, And downwards to the depths, outward and
    unbounded,
Freed from hatred and ill-will, whether standing or
    walking,
seated or lying down.

I let the words I had just heard sink into my heart. These words expressed by one religion cover all religions. Though they differed in some things, these great religions of the world were united as they declared the great and wonderful things that were in store for humankind.

"There is a man by the name of John Hicks, a British philosopher, who has compared the different texts of Buddhism, Hinduism, Islam, Christianity, Judaism, etc.,"

Joshua said as he closed his book, "and he had found a striking similarity in scripture references of the different sects. From the Christian text, The New Testament, in the King James version of 1st Corinthians 2:9, it says: *'Eye hath not seen, nor ear heard, neither have entered into the heart of man, the things which God hath prepared for them that love him.'* This scripture is based upon Isaiah 64:4, a passage in the Old Testament or Hebrew Bible. And, in Islam, it is found as a *'hadith'* or tradition ascribed to the Prophet Muhammad. He terms this discovery as *'Cosmic optimism.'*"

"Do you think," I mused, "if we just took the time to understand another culture's religion, there would be wars? If even the Christian religions would study and understand each other better, would there be any reason for war?"

"A good question," Joshua said. "In religion there is only peace and love. War cannot come from peace. War cannot exist in love. There is where the answer lies.

"Thank you for your insight," I said as I shook his hand once again. "May I ask what made you sit next to me when there are so many empty tables and you could be alone to read?"

"I wish I could answer that question for myself," he smiled as he gathered up his books. "I don't even know why I came to the library today."

"I think I know," I replied, gathering up my own books. "Thank you again."

We shook hands as we went our separate ways, and in my heart I knew my prayer had been answered; for I had a greater knowledge now because of a man named Joshua.

It was noon before I hailed a taxi and headed across the bridge into New York. I leaned back on the seat, closed my eyes and let my mind replay the things I had learned. Then something hit me and I realized it wasn't only the religious barrier we had to break through, but racism was another hurdle to jump.

In our world, we take so much for granted. We judge others by their color or their culture, by their having or lacking education. I had been guilty of that myself, but now I began to wonder if I studied another's culture without bias, as

I had studied various religions, would I feel differently? Of course I would.

I could hear my mother's words once again: "When we are children we learn certain ideas that infiltrate and form our beliefs. If we accept those beliefs without studying to achieve our own understanding, and carry that concept with us for the rest of our lives, we jeopardize our own personal freedom. There are those who only listen to what they want to hear and read what they want to read in order to cement their beliefs, ignoring any information that might challenge their beliefs, change their view, or enlighten their minds."

I had a teacher once who would use objects to teach a concept so we would never forget the lesson. One day, in teaching about racism she used a prism to make her point. She explained that a beam of white light passes through a prism and then splits into a rainbow of colors. If we select just one of those colors, whether it is blue or red or yellow, it doesn't matter. What matters is that we ignore all the rest and look at life under that one color only. In our stubbornness we have lost an opportunity to see the whole picture, the beauty that the many colors reflect. The purpose of her lesson was to teach us that in the narrowness of our mind we refuse to see the beauty and goodness of a person of another color or creed.

I came to the realization that only the insecure need to have everyone believe as they do, so their beliefs will not be challenged. I also discovered that we should be constantly challenging our own beliefs, to see if they are still true.

American philosopher, William James said, "The best things are the more eternal things, the overlapping things, the things in the universe that throw the last stone, so to speak, and say the final word."

Through my thoughts, the taxi driver was telling me that because of the barricades in the road, this was as far as he could take me. I would have to walk the rest of the way. I gathered up my bags, climbed out and paid him. He smiled at me and wished me well.

I had worried about how I would feel coming back to the depressing sight before me, but now I felt useful. I was experiencing an inner strength I hadn't felt for a long time, and I knew why. I had let go of the pain and guilt that had eroded my heart and mind.

I didn't have to be here because I felt guilty. I could be here because I wanted to be. In the library, I felt excitement from the knowledge I had gained. Here I was excited about the experience and knowledge I could share.

I could hear Bob's voice calling me as I walked to the site, and I waved back, acknowledging that I heard him. I set my bags to one side and picked up my badge, hat and clothing I needed. Today, things were even better organized and volunteers were there, handing out food, water and supplies as they were needed. I waved back and walked over to greet him.

"How was New Jersey?" he asked, wiping the dust from his face.

As we worked side by side, I explained to him what I had learned about the Islamic religion, and as I talked I noticed my words were being overheard by two other workers. Work ceased for a few minutes as they stepped closer to hear what I had to say. As I spoke, they listened, nodding now and again in agreement. Without much discussion, four of us now understood a religion better, and with our education, we felt a little better because we were a little bit wiser.

"I saw you carrying your luggage when you came into the area. Need a place to stay?" Bob asked. "I've got a room if you need one. It's not far from here. My family is staying in my sister's apartment while I'm volunteering. She's out of town for two months, traveling with her husband. I'm only going to help a few more days. My company's found a make-shift office for now and I need to help set things up, but you're welcome to stay there as long as you want."

I felt grateful to him and accepted his offer. With that worry out of the way, I began to wonder if my nameless friend was still around. To my disappointment, I couldn't see him anywhere close by. I hoped I got to see him again before I had to leave.

A muffled sound brought me back to the present, and once again I felt my heart leap. I listened, thinking it was probably my imagination, praying it was not. Then I heard it again. I called to Bob and a man named Chris who was working beside him.

"Listen," I said quietly.

The two men stood silently beside me, their eyes wide, bodies tense. The three of us waited, hoping to hear something; then it came again. Without hesitation we were moving toward the sound.

"Keep talking," Chris shouted, "so we can find you."

"There," shouted Bob, "over there. See where the steel has been moved?"

Chris called for more help. We quickly surveyed the ground still cluttered with big chunks of concrete and noticed between two slabs a small opening. Once the steel beams had been lifted away, the opening would be visible if someone knew where to look. It would not have even been noticed if we hadn't heard the cry.

"We've found you," Bob was shouting down into the crevice. "Don't worry, help is coming."

Sobbing could now be heard from beneath the rubble. We were excited, yet apprehensive about how the rescue should proceed. Layers of concrete and rubble were around the pocket. The question was, which chunk of concrete was keeping the rest from falling into the hole? The miraculous thing was that the concrete had fallen in a way to form a pocket around the woman, and that after four days she was still alive.

"I've been praying that someone would find me," she gasped between sobs.

"Don't you worry now, ma'am, we'll get you out of there soon," Chris called down to her. "Are you injured in any way?"

"I think my left arm is broken, but I can move." She paused for a moment. "Please call me Matty."

"Can you tell me how big the hole is, Matty?" I asked. "Are you lying down or sitting up?"

"The hole is deep but narrow. I'm leaning against a large section of concrete. How long have I been in here?"

"This is the fourth day, you're a lucky lady," Bob answered. "Is there anything I can get for you while we wait for the equipment?"

"Could I have some water, please? I did have a bottle in my lunch bag along with a sandwich, an apple, and a few cookies. I was so thankful to have them, but they're gone now."

"One bottle of water coming up!" Bob shouted as he lifted one out of his coat pocket. "We can't get too close or it could cause the concrete to move, so as soon as the fire truck gets here, we'll use the ladder to lower it down."

We could hear the equipment coming behind us, with several men making their way toward us to offer their help. When the fire truck pulled alongside, we were ready to go to work. We opened the bottle and tied it to the small crane on the back of the truck with a string one of the firefighters found on the front seat. The ladder was stretched until the bottle dangled just above the opening of the crevice. Then the bottle of water was lowered until it disappeared into the slit between the concrete walls that surrounded it.

"I have it!" Matty's voice was hoarse as she spoke.

The large crane had arrived and was now in place. Our concern was how best to proceed at this point. We couldn't get near the pocket. Any kind of wrong movement could cause a cave-in, filling the crevice with concrete and ash and taking away the very life we were here to save.

As we debated we continued to assure her every precaution was being taken and she would be out within the hour. This was the second time I had helped rescue a woman. I thought about Shana for the first time since that day. I wondered how she was doing. Maybe tomorrow I would find out.

With the help of the firemen on duty, a cable was wrapped around a concrete slab and slowly lifted into the air. As it was lifted, the remaining slabs shifted and ash began sifting into the pocket. We knew we would have to hurry, but we still couldn't get close enough to the crevice. Some pretty heavy pieces of concrete had to be lifted away. The ash and debris were beginning to filter through the concrete polluting the air inside the pocket, and Matty began to cough as the air became almost impossible to breathe.

"Do you have something to cover your mouth and nose with?" I asked.

"Yes, but please hurry."

I had rescued a young man from a pocket crevice similar to this one and I knew how delicate the situation was. That time the dirt almost buried both of us before we could get him out.

"Can you stand up?" I asked, needing to know how quickly she could get out.

"I haven't dared move much, but I think I can stand," she answered, knowing exactly why I needed to know. As frightened as she was, she was still able to think clearly. I was thankful for that. One thing we didn't need was for her to panic.

"Thanks, Matty," I said, "for being so patient with us."

Finally, we could get close enough to see her, but with every step now, the sifting of debris into the pocket became greater. Then I had an idea. "Get a board and we'll lay it across, using the concrete on each side as braces." My mind was racing almost faster than my heart. "Then I can reach down from there and wrap the cable. We'll need two pieces of cable because both of the pieces of concrete that's covering the pocket will have to be lifted off simultaneously." Lifting one at a time would increase the danger of a cave-in. Once the concrete was out of the way, I had to get in and get her before the sides of the hole caved in around her.

Almost immediately a board was found and placed across the hole. Using it as a brace, carefully I made my way until I was kneeling directly above the hole. Two cables were hooked to the main cable on the crane. That way, with the pull of the crane, the concrete could be lifted together.

"Matty," I said, "we're going to lift these pieces of concrete now, and when that happens, the ash and debris may start to fill in faster. What I need you to do is, when I say 'now,' you reach up with your good arm so I can get hold of you and pull you up. Do you mind telling me your height and weight?"

"Not if it's a matter of life and death, I don't," she called. "I'm 5 feet 2 inches, and I weigh 115 pounds. Does that help?"

"Thank you," I responded. "It helps very much, and I promise it will be our secret."

"I'm sure you can get me out," she said in almost a plea. "I don't think I lived through all of this just to die now." I believed what she said.

I watched as the cables were lowered above me. As soon as they were low enough, I had them locked around the concrete.

"I've got the cable in place," I called to the worker who was standing close by waiting for my signal. "Are you ready, Matty?"

"Yes,"

"I'm signaling the crane now."

As the concrete moved, so did the debris and I wondered if there would be enough time before she was covered. Then I saw her arm come up. I extended mine down but I couldn't quite reach her. The hole was deeper than I thought. She realized the situation we were in even before I did. I could see her trying to lift herself up, fear showing on her face.

I knew instantly what I had to do. The rubble was filling the hole along with the ash. Using the board as a bar, I lowered myself into the hole, dropping down beside Matty. With every ounce of muscle I had, I wrapped my left arm around her waist and pulled her from the ash that had reached her waist. She moaned with the pain that engulfed her body, but she quickly placed her good arm around my neck to help me support her as we fought the ash and debris together. A feeling of dread came over me, and I felt a shiver. I couldn't even begin to comprehend the horror Matty had been through for the past four days.

The pocket began to fill in around us faster than we could move, but I knew I couldn't let anything else happen to her. I had to get her out, now. The debris that had fallen was sharp and several pieces had cut into our flesh as it tumbled down into the hole. Our eyes were burning from the ash and breathing became more difficult.

"Grab the ladder," someone shouted. "It's coming down right in front of you. Grab it, quick."

Though my vision was blurred, I could make out a fireman kneeling on the board above us holding a ladder. Even though the weight of the debris was dragging me down, I pushed Matty toward the ladder and she grabbed the side with her hand. By that time the fireman had started down and he was able to get a grip under her arms and lift her to safety. Knowing she was out, I began to concentrate on moving my feet under the weight of the dirt and getting out of there. As I looked up again through the dust I saw the familiar face of my nameless friend. I felt a sudden calm. My feet seemed to move freely. I found myself climbing the ladder, and it was over.

The cheers that now filled the air meant the danger was behind us. Once I got on stable ground, I felt the energy drain from me. I wanted to sit, but instead I found myself being congratulated by men with tears flowing down their dusty faces. The excitement of finding a survivor and experiencing the miracle of it all was an undeniable, humbling feeling. My excitement was shared by everyone around me.

I walked over to the ambulance where the EMT was attending to Matty's injuries. When she saw me, she reached out to me and put her good arm around me. We held onto each other and cried together.

"I can never thank you enough," she said through her tears. "I can't find words to express what I feel right now, but do you mind if I share with you what happened to me?"

Everyone wanted to hear her story so while the EMT took her vital signs, checked her bruises and cuts and placed her arm in a sling, Matty shared her story with us.

"I remember making my way down the stairs to the sixth floor," she began. "There were several of us who stayed together as we descended the steps from floor to floor. Then there was a rumble and the stairs began to crumble in front of us. That's all I can remember until I woke up and found myself enclosed in a cavern of cement. My head was pounding and I hurt all over. I couldn't move my left arm without feeling excruciating pain. I could see the light through a small opening between two steel frames. I could hear people and machinery, but everything was so loud above me, no one could hear me.

"I don't know how long I was unconscious, but it must have been several hours because before long it grew dark. I was so frightened I didn't dare move. I was afraid the concrete would fall on me before someone found me.

"As I lay there crying I heard my mother's voice saying to me, 'With God, nothing is impossible. Pray to Him, then leave it to Him. Whatever happens it is God's will. Don't be afraid.' So I prayed and I waited.

"After I had prayed, I realized I was still holding my lunch bag. I had water and I had food and I knew I would be found. God would make it possible."

As we stood there listening to Matty, we realized how precious her life was to all of us. In all this sadness around us, her life brought us joy. We wept as one, and the healing began. Whether her life was spared for us or for herself, I'll never know. I only know that because we had found her, faith was alive again.

After the ambulance left with Matty inside, I went to the Salvation Army camp and lay on my cot. I looked around to see where my friend had gone. When I finally found him, he was drinking from a bottle of water. Our eyes connected and he smiled as I came close to him.

"Come, sit here by your concrete bed and lean your head on your pillow of steel," he laughed, "and tell me about the experiences of your day."

"I've had an incredible day," I began as I eased my sore body to the ground, "and I need to tell you what I've learned, because what I see when I look into your eyes, tells me you will understand." I took a long drink from the bottled water that had been handed to me before telling my friend my story.

"Today," I began, "I learned that the best thing I can do for my country, at this point, is to educate myself so I can have a better understanding of what I am reading about 9/11 – what just happened to America. So I went to the library and opened the books that could teach me. I learned that all the world religions believe in goodness and compassion. They all believe in God and are filled with wisdom and love. Today, I learned that until we study and learn about another culture or race or religion, we cannot judge; we have no knowledge by which to judge. But I found that once we gain that knowledge, there is nothing to judge, only to understand. Today I learned that you can't blame the acts of one group on their religion."

I stopped for a minute and took another drink of water. My throat was so dry from eating dirt. I smiled as I continued. "I've also learned that my mother is a very wise woman because she taught me the things in life that count. And, my grandmother is a very wise woman. She told me a simple story that helped me through the struggles of my teenage years. A story I had almost forgotten. King Solomon, it seems, went searching for a magic ring that could make a happy man sad and a sad man happy. Soon he learned about a common merchant in his kingdom who had turned an ordinary ring into a magical one by carving these words around its circle: *"This Too Shall Pass."*

My grandmother's wisdom sustained me through high school, and because my grandmother taught me what was true, I know that all of this we are going through is temporary. This too shall pass. There is something else, not that I learned, but something I remembered. I remembered how precious a life is and how when we work together to save a life, we work as one. From that experience I learned if we are to save a constitution, we must work as one.

"May I share something with you, my friend?" asked the man.

I nodded yes and listened as he spoke.

"I share with you a bit of Celtic wisdom: *'May you recognize in your life the presence, power, and light of your soul. May you realize that you are never alone, that your soul, in its brightness and belonging, connects you intimately with the rhythm of the universe. May you have respect for your own individuality and difference. May you realize that the shape of your soul is unique, that you have a special destiny here, that behind the facade of your life there is something beautiful, good and eternal happening. May you learn to see yourself with the same delight, pride and aspiration with which God sees you in every moment.'"*

Author's Notes

What can I do for my country? In paraphrasing Patrick Henry, *the millions of people, in this country, armed in the holy cause of liberty, are invincible against any force that our enemy can send against us.*

If we are to be armed in the holy cause of liberty, we must have an understanding or knowledge of that which we must do. Not everyone can fight the battle on the battlefront, but there are other ways to help win a war, and everyone can do their part.

First we must educate ourselves so that we can give the cause justice. Knowing the truth is where true freedom lies. We take what we think we know and we begin to challenge its validity, to separate the truth from the fiction through experience, until we know what we know. Then we move forward.

It may be in the understanding of the truth of all religions and moving forward with that message of truth. It may be gaining knowledge that it takes many colors to build a beautiful and free nation, just as it takes many colors to form a beautiful rainbow. Racism degrades and injures a country. America was founded on diversity. Under the color of our skin we are all the same. We cannot judge another until we have the knowledge by which we can judge, and with knowledge we realize judgment has no place in our hearts.

With knowledge and understanding, we realize that our strength and our courage come with compassion and charity, two of the greatest weapons with which to win a war. Without them we are weak. It is the bravery of compassion that inspires us to put our lives in danger in order to save another. In saving just one life, emotionally or physically, we have helped save a nation.

If we can recognize within ourselves the power and light of our own souls by reaching within our being, we can find our true selves. When we allow all our fears to be wiped away, only then can we go forth and serve all others. If we can respect our own uniqueness and individuality and learn to see ourselves with the same delight that God sees us, then we will know that within our own life there is something beautiful, good and eternal happening.

Robert Frost said, *"In three words I can sum up everything I've learned about life — it goes on."*

Chapter Four

I Am My Brother's Keeper

The sun was setting and it was almost dark by the time I arrived at Bob's sister's apartment. I double-checked the address on the piece of paper he had written down for me before punching the security code to open the front door into the lobby. Bob had taken his family back to their home in New Jersey and would be spending the night there before returning to help in the morning. I was relieved to have the evening alone.

It was now the fourth day after the disaster. As I walked the five blocks to the apartment, the words of Celtic wisdom my quiet friend had shared with me continued to echo in my mind. I needed time to myself.

I unlocked the door of the apartment and stepped inside. It was so quiet I could hear a clock ticking in the background. The light from the street lamp filtered through a window, giving a soft peaceful glow to the room. In its light I could see a kitchen to the left and living room straight ahead. Without turning on the light, I made my way into the living room and stood by the window. The apartment was on the fourth floor, giving me a great view of the city at night. Yet without really looking at anything in particular, I stood there, holding my bags in my hand and staring into the night.

Suddenly I realized I still hadn't asked my quiet friend his name and he still had not offered to tell me, yet it seemed I had known him for a long time. "Tomorrow," I said to myself, "I've got to remember to ask."

I turned and looked around the room and noticed an overstuffed chair near the window. Dropping my bags next to the chair, I eased my tired body into it, letting my head relax against the softness of the padding. I smiled as I thought of the slab of cement and piece of steel that had become my resting spot at the site. This was much better.

I sat there for several minutes with my eyes closed, reliving my conversation with my friend. I had asked questions to which he seemed to have the perfect answers.

"How does a person recognize the presence of his soul?" That was my first question.

He answered with a question of his own. "You decided to go to a library so you could study and understand. What made you do that?"

"I don't know. It just seemed like the right thing to do."

"You recognized, then listened to the power within you, and that power directed you to the source of your knowledge."

For a moment I had to think about the answer he had given me as I tried to grasp the reality of it. "Why is the soul, with all of its power, so simple? Why is its presence so silent?" I asked.

"It was meant to be simple," he answered. "We are the ones who complicate our lives with expectations beyond that which we need for direction."

I knew his answer was correct. We all complicate our lives at one time or another. In fact, most of us complicate our lives on a daily basis.

"I understand what you are saying." I hesitated before continuing. "Can I ask you one more question?"

He smiled and nodded.

"Today, when I looked up from inside that hole, I saw your face. I didn't question, at that time, how you could be standing where I was able to see you when there was hardly room for the fireman. I just knew because you were there I was going to make it out. It seemed as if the weight of the debris could no longer restrain me, and I was able to move my legs toward the ladder. I had the strangest feeling that I was not alone. I felt the warmth of I don't know how else to explain it. I felt the warmth of another being."

"May you realize that *you are never alone,* my friend," he smiled as he spoke. "But now I have to go."

As he walked away, I wanted to call after him. I wanted to tell him I hadn't finished asking my questions, but instead I simply stood silently and watched him go. He had left me, once again to think for myself. But my brain had been too weary then to think. It seemed too weary now.

I brought my eyes back into focus as I turned on the lamp that stood next to the chair, and looked around me. Everything in the apartment was new and tastefully decorated. It reminded me of home and a wave of homesickness caused a tightening in my throat. I needed to talk to my parents and my kids. They seemed so far away, and here, in this room, I felt a quiet loneliness.

I reached inside my jacket pocket for my cell phone. It hadn't been recharged in four days and showed no signs of life when I turned it on, so I unzipped my bag and retrieved the recharger. Finding a plug-in on the wall by the kitchen counter, I set the phone in its cradle to recharge, then picked up my bag and went in search of a bedroom.

It was a large apartment but it didn't take long to find everything I needed. I looked at my watch. It was 9:15 PM. I'd give the phone fifteen more minutes to charge and then I'd make my phone call. I found a notepad and pen on the kitchen table and decided while I waited I would write down everything I could remember of the Celtic wisdom that had been recited to me. For ten minutes I sat at the table remembering and writing. I was surprised how much I could recall.

Bob told me he had stocked the fridge before he left. "I did it for you, Jeremy, so the only way you can pay me back is to eat everything that's there!"

Right now I was happy to oblige. My stomach was growling for food. Before opening the fridge, I picked up the remote and turned on the counter-top TV. I flipped through the channels until I heard the voice of the President. The screen showed his picture and the news channel was re-playing his taped radio message from earlier in the day. As I made a sandwich, I listened to his words.

"You will be asked for your patience, for the conflict will not be short. You will be asked for resolve, for the conflict will not be easy. You will be asked for your strength, because the course to victory may be long. A terrorist attack designed to tear us apart has instead bound us together as a nation. Underneath the tears is the strong determination of America to win this war."

I watched the picture of the President's face and listened to the sound of his voice, and for the first time, it really hit me... we are, indeed, at war. But the people responsible for fighting the war aren't only those wearing a service uniform. People like me, wearing a different kind of uniform, searching for survivors or bodies, also carry the responsibility. The volunteers standing shoulder-to-shoulder, passing buckets filled with the rubble from one to another until it was cleared away, feel the responsibility. The battle is also ours in defense of the hundreds of firefighters who died trying to save the thousands trapped in the Twin Towers and the Pentagon. As Americans, the battle belongs to us as we defend the thousands who died in those collapsed buildings, and those who were killed in the planes that were turned into weapons of war. The responsibility belongs to everyone who believes in freedom.

When the President talked of patience, resolve and strength, he was only asking for the things we already have. We may have to polish them a little so they'll shine brighter, but they are the very things that have made our country what it is.

The screen then shifted to a reporter, reading from a paper in his hand, that the number of people missing had increased by 200, bringing the total to 4,972. They had recovered 152 bodies including 18 firefighters.

Tears welled up in my eyes and the bite of sandwich I had been chewing on seemed to stick in my throat as I tried to swallow. I turned off the TV. I had seen and heard enough.

The cell phone's battery light was blinking, telling me it had power. Removing it from its cradle, I quickly punched the number of my parents' phone. After three rings, I heard the beautiful sound of my daughter's voice.

"Hello," she said brightly into the receiver.

"Hi Peaches, it's Dad," I said through my tears.

"Dad," she shouted. "Grandpa, it's Dad! Hi Dad, how are you? What's it like there? We've been so worried about you, when are you coming home?"

"Which question would you like me to answer first?" I laughed.

"I think the last one," she said softly. "I miss you so much."

"I'm only going to stay until the middle of next week," I reassured her. "I miss you too. How's school?"

"School's great. Everyone thinks you're a hero because you stayed to help. I'm so proud of you, Dad. And even though I miss you, I'm glad you're there helping to find those people who are lost under that building that collapsed."

I could hear my son's voice in the background. "Kyle wants to talk to you, so I'll say goodbye. Love you, Dad."

"Love you too, Kaylee." I heard her kiss against the mouthpiece of the receiver.

"Hey, Dad." My son's voice sounded so close, it was hard to imagine he was several thousands miles away. "All my friends think you're real cool. I've been watching a lot of the news channels hoping I'd get a glimpse of you, and there you were tonight on the six o'clock news, standing by an ambulance talking to a woman who had been rescued. It was so cool, Dad, listening to the reporter tell how you guys rescued her. Our phone didn't quit ringing for an hour!"

"I'll have to tell you all about it when I get home. Tell me about your football game last night. Did you win?" I wanted to talk about him.

"28 to 14." Then he proceeded to give me the highlights. "We're going to be tough this year. Hope you're here for the next one."

"I'll be home next week, I promise. Better let me talk to Grandpa and Grandma before my batteries die. Love you, Kyle."

"Love you, Dad. Here's Grandpa."

"How are you, son?" As my father spoke those words, I felt the comfort of his love. I recalled the words, *you are never alone,* and I was beginning to fully understand their meaning.

"I'm fine, Dad. I just needed to talk to family."

"Jeremy, are you alright?" Mom was on the other line. "You sound exhausted."

"I'll be sleeping in a real bed tonight," I assured her, "so I'll get a good night's sleep, I promise."

"I'll feel much better knowing that," she sighed.

With the minutes I had left before the phone lost its charge, I told my parents of some of the things I had experienced and seen. There was so much more I wanted to say but my cell phone began beeping. "I'll call you again when I get a chance,"

"We love you, Jeremy, please be careful."

"I love you too..." The phone went dead before I could say goodbye and the room was silent again.

As I placed the phone back on its cradle I wondered how many other firemen and volunteers had put their lives on hold while they searched and dug through the rubble. I wondered how many others had to say goodnight to their families over the phone as I had done.

Just as I was beginning to feel sorry for myself, a question surfaced. How could I be so ungrateful? Instead of complaining I should be thankful that I could say goodnight to my family simply by picking up a phone and pushing a few buttons. Had I not learned, in the past few days, how precious life is? I had taken so much for granted, expecting so much without recognizing the privilege of having so much.

For the rest of the evening, I suddenly found myself feeling grateful for the smallest things. I was grateful for hot water in the shower, and the bed I had to sleep in. I felt grateful that I could choose to put my life on hold for another day so I could be of service to other human beings. Most of all, I felt grateful to be alive.

At 11:30 PM, I turned out the light in the bedroom, and in the darkness I prayed that I might be more aware of the blessings in my life. Then I climbed into bed, pulled the covers close around me, closed my eyes and went to sleep.

In my sleep I began to dream. I was standing in a maze. The maze was a mass of vines. Stems, full of leaves, wrapped themselves around and around the vines, winding their way in and out until the thickness made it almost impossible to see what lay beyond them. Only tiny rays of light could make their way through. The height of the maze was high enough that I couldn't see over it. It was well manicured and the paths that led in every direction were meticulously trimmed.

I could hear the sound of a rhythmic breeze as it floated through the maze. The sound was hypnotic and as I listened to its rhythm, words began to form in my mind: *"Seek, and ye shall find."*

In my dream I asked, "Where do I seek? Which path do I take?"

"Look into your mind," whispered the breeze.

I looked and as I watched, my mind opened its doors to my view. In the shadows I saw what remained of the Trade Center. To the right the flag waved gently and gracefully. It was tattered now and dirty from the smoke and ash, yet it stood proud and protective over the broken concrete and mangled steel.

Once more the breeze whispered and I listened to the rhythm of its song. *"The flag has again been tested, but its pride and its strength are undaunted, for it is the symbol of freedom. It represents one nation, under God, indivisible. That is its strength. That is its glory. But if we turn our backs on our fellow men, we turn our backs on God, and if we turn our backs on God, we turn our backs on freedom. For are we not our brother's keeper? Is this not our pride, our glory and our purpose? Only when we forget our responsibility to God and to our fellowmen will our flag hang life-less and in shame.*

Then the air became still and quiet and I knew which path I should take. I turned and entered the one to the right of me. As I walked, light began to filter through the maze and the twisted vines withered and started to disappear until the maze was no longer there. Where the maze had been now stood a beautiful, dark oak table. It was round, about three feet in diameter, and approximately two feet tall. On the table was that same book with the white cover I had seen before in my mind. It was thicker now, but I knew it was the same book. The light around it was so bright I couldn't see the writing on the cover. What did the book represent? The light continued in its brightness and I woke up to the sun shining in my eyes.

I felt rested but disturbed over the dream. I wondered why I kept dreaming about a book. Did it have some significance in my life?

Looking at the clock, I realized I had overslept. I quickly dressed and ate a children's breakfast of sugar sweetened cereal, most likely left behind by Bob's youngest nephew. I washed the cereal down with a glass of orange juice, put my cell phone in my pocket, locked the apartment and started walking the five blocks to Ground Zero.

When I got to Liberty Street, just two blocks away from my destination, I slowed my pace as a dust-covered bicycle locked to a parking meter came into my view. A bouquet of flowers, looking as if they had been there for several days, was stuck in the rear wheel spokes. A feeling of incredible grief gripped me as I stopped to touch the handle bars. I removed a handkerchief from my back pocket and began to wipe the dust, first from the bars, then the seat, and finally from the fenders. I left the flowers untouched for fear they would fall apart. They needed to remain just as they were, for they represented love.

I passed the clothing store that had become a morgue the day after the attack, where workers brought any body parts they could find. I wanted to stop and shake the hand of the man who had so graciously opened his heart as well as his store to aid in the rescue, but the store hadn't opened yet, so I walked on.

As I got closer to the site, a cold haunting feeling caught me off guard. The air had a grayish cast from the pollution of the ash and smoke. There seemed to be an odor of death and a feeling of despair. Signs had been stapled to utility poles, with pictures and descriptions that listed the names, ages and addresses of missing persons. Below each description was the name and phone number of the person to contact. Small and large bouquets of once beautiful flowers were stuffed through the holes in the fences. I wanted to cry, but no tears would come. Only the pain of sadness filled me. I felt as if I was in a dream once again, but this time my dream was reality.

People were standing behind the yellow tape that had been placed around the huge gaping hole in the city. They looked as if they too, were dreaming, their eyes bright and glassy, their faces solemn. Some were crying, some stood silently. I could hear bits of conversation between strangers as they gave or sought comfort. One conversation in particular, caught my attention. About three feet from where I stood, two men were talking. "Instead of standing here watching this mess, I could be under it, along with several of my co-workers," one man was telling the other. "I've asked myself, over and over, why did I get out and they couldn't? Why was I given a second chance when they had to die?"

"I don't know if there's an answer to that question," the other man responded, shaking his head. "If there is, I hope you find it, if only to give you peace of mind."

They stood there quietly for a moment watching the equipment and men at work on the other side of the tape. Then the second man spoke again. "They call it 'survivor guilt,' you know, that feeling you have inside. That's why you keep asking yourself those questions. You feel guilty that you lived and they died."

A woman standing near them joined in the conversation. "My brother said that some of the 911 dispatchers are struggling with regret because they sent the firefighters who died into the towers. They had no idea the towers would collapse. They gave the instructions for them to stay in the buildings to continue the rescue mission."

"There's no way they could have known," remarked the first man.

"Yet they feel the same way you do," the woman said sympathetically. "There's no way you could have known what was going to happen, either."

The man was silent for a moment. "Perhaps the one good thing that has come from this, in my case, is that I've felt a sense of responsibility to those who died. I don't know if I can explain it so that it makes sense or not, but because the deaths seem so senseless, I want to make life more meaningful. I feel a responsibility to try to do something that will benefit other people, to think less of my needs and more of the needs of others. Does that sound corny?"

"Of course not," the woman said sincerely. "My sister's son was killed in the Oklahoma bombing and she wanted to come here to comfort those who lost children on September 11th. In the process of helping others, she's helping herself. She would tell you what you have already discovered. That whatever you do, don't feel guilty, just forget yourself and help someone else. That way you can heal yourself."

With tears in the man's eyes, he put his arms around the woman and hugged her. Then he thanked her for helping relieve the burden of guilt from his shoulders. As I watched, I was reminded of the words in my dream: *Are we not our brother's keeper?*

I turned to look at the mass destruction in front of me but my attention was drawn to the tattered flag that hung high and to the right of the bent and broken steel. The words of the Pledge of Allegiance came to my mind and silently I recited them. It hadn't occurred to me until I said the last word in my thoughts that the Pledge of Allegiance begins with the word "I" and ends with the word "all." I wondered if that was just a coincidence or if it was intentional to remind us that "I" pledge to be united with and responsible for "all"?

Freedom, in that case is not "free." It comes with a price tag. The cost is personal. It means that I have to take responsibility for my own actions and my own life. Only then can I reach out and take responsibility for the welfare of others. If I can't be responsible and accountable for me, how can I be responsible for my children? Hadn't I heard that the breakdown of the family structure would weaken the foundation of our country? Are we not, indeed, all our brother's keeper? Does it take a tragedy for us to remember our commitments?

"Good morning, Jeremy." The voice interrupted my thoughts and I turned to see Chris coming toward me. "Are you ready to get started?" he asked.

"Good morning, Chris," I replied, with renewed commitment. "I'm ready. I'm really ready. How are things going?"

"As well as can be expected." He looked at me with a look of humorous surprise. "But I think you *are* really ready to get started."

"It looks devastating, doesn't it?" I surveyed all that was in front of me.

"If you think this looks bad," exclaimed Chris, "you should see the scene a few blocks south of here. It's even more painful to look at."

"I don't know how it could be." I gazed over at the arched steel beams protruding out of the ground, gray from the ash. It could have been a set for the movie, *Planet of the Apes*, a picture made several years ago. What would have taken months and thousands upon thousands of dollars to create for a movie set, took two airplanes, some fuel and a few minutes to create for reality. Oddly enough, the site almost looked like it was in the process of construction instead of demolition.

Chris broke into my thoughts. "Matty stopped by late yesterday afternoon, with her husband and her eleven-year-old son. She was hoping to talk to you before they left. I looked for almost an hour but I couldn't find you."

"Matty was here?" I said regretfully. "I'm sorry I missed her. How was her arm? How did she look?"

"She looked a little peaked but good," said Chris. "Her arm was broken in two places. It's in a cast and will be fine. And she was sorry to have missed you too. Her husband was especially sorry, he wanted to thank you personally. He's taking her to see her folks in Portland, Oregon. He thought the change would be good for her."

"My concern is that she will be able to forget the ordeal she went through the four days she spent in that dark grave," I said. "I stood in it for less that five minutes and I wonder if I'll ever forget the feeling I had."

"I can only imagine," Chris said, his eyes looking into mine. "She left this card for you."

I reached for the envelope he held out to me. Inside was a large hand-made card showing a man in the body suit of silver armor underneath a fireman's jacket. On his head, instead of the headgear, he wore a fireman's hat, and his face was smudged. The face bore a remarkable likeness to me. She had written a verse beneath the picture:

One day, while the giant slept, an evil dragon came,
His eyes were cold with death. His mouth was hot with flame.

He cared not who he plundered, he thought only to destroy,
And he looked upon my tower as a simple child's toy.
With one sweep of a wicked claw, he reached into my tower
And destroyed its beauty and its grace, all within an hour.
Its broken walls began to crumble, its melting steel engulfed in fire,
While the evil dragon watched and laughed, from the safety of his lair.
Suddenly in a darkened tomb, I was frightened and alone,
Among the broken steel, imprisoned by the crumbling stone.
Surrounded by the horror, I closed my eyes and prayed,
And I heard a small voice whisper, "My child, don't be afraid."
Then you were there, and I could see the courage in your eyes.
A knight in shining armor, dressed in a fireman's disguise.
The dragon will not get his wish. His fire has no power,
For, in men like you, there will always stand a tower.

At the bottom of the page, a small note of thanks was written by her husband, Cliff and her son, Trend.

"I think I'll frame this," I said, holding back the emotion I felt inside. "I only wish I could have met her family and said goodbye before they left."

"She also wanted you to have this," Chris said, handing me a box. Wrapped in paper, inside the box was a sculpture of a fireman kneeling by a woman, her arm in a sling. It was sculptured in such fine detail I could even see the number on the fireman's badge. It was beautiful. The sculpture sat on a base of dark wood with an inscription that read, *A Knight in a Fireman's Armor.*

"You deserve that, you know," Chris said, as he admired the sculpture.

"You would have done the same thing," I responded.

"I don't know if I would have been as quick to think or act, if you want to know the truth." His eyes connected with mine once again. "You don't even realize what you did, do you? Your modesty becomes you," he laughed as he handed the sculpture back to me.

I re-wrapped it in the paper and carefully placed it back in the box. "I think I'll put this in the Salvation Army tent for now, so nothing will happen to it while I'm working."

I walked to the camp where the tent was located, on safe ground near the yellow tape. I explained to the volunteer what was in the box and asked if she would put it where it would be out of the way, yet safe. She promised she would protect it with her very life. I felt comfortable with that and left it in her care.

I was just heading back to my assignment when I heard a voice from behind me. "Sir, can you tell me if you've seen my brother?"

I turned to see a girl, about the age of fifteen, standing there with a piece of paper in her hand. On the paper was a picture of a young man. I walked over to her and took the paper she was handing to me. I looked closely at the picture.

"His name is Brad," she said anxiously. "Brad Timothy, and he's twenty-three years old. He worked on the 82nd floor of the South Tower."

I looked into the face of the young woman. Her eyes were tired from lack of sleep and swollen from crying. I felt helpless. With all of my heart, I wished I could help her.

"I haven't seen him yet," I said. "May I keep this picture so I can show it to everyone I talk to today?"

"Would you do that for me?" She cried with relief, and taking the paper, she quickly wrote her name and phone number on the bottom. "You can call me on my cell phone. I'll leave it on all day, just in case." She folded the paper carefully and placed it into my hand. "Thank you," she said. "Thank you very much."

In my mind I knew I would not find him, yet in my heart I prayed I would. And I did as I promised. I showed the picture to every worker on the site but no one recognized him. As the day wore on and the work became more difficult, I forgot about the picture. Over the past four days, several bodies had been carried out in body bags. My hope was that this girl's brother would be found among those who were still alive in one of the many hospitals in the area.

It was 3:00 PM when I finally took time to sit and rest. I found the slab of cement that had become my resting post and leaned my head, once again, against my pillow of steel. I drank from the bottle of water handed to me as I walked past the volunteer booth. In my other hand they had placed a sack with sandwiches, chips and cookies in it. I was thankful for the food. Breakfast had been hours ago.

"I knew I would find you here." Bob stood in the shadow of the sun so I couldn't see his face, but I would recognize that shape anywhere, and his voice was one of a kind. "Did you stay at the apartment last night?"

"I did," I replied, "and I slept like a baby and ate like a king. Thank you for your hospitality."

"Think nothing of it." He sat down beside me, opening a sack identical to mine. "One of these days let's eat where the chairs are softer. By the way, a very attractive woman by the name of Shana came here looking for you, not more than fifteen minutes ago. I told her to come back to this spot around 3:30 PM. I figured if you took a break this is where you would be, and you never take a break before 3:00 PM."

"You know me pretty well by now, my good friend," I laughed. A feeling of excitement shot through me at the mention of Shana, and it surprised me a little. The way Bob was staring at me, I think it showed on my face. I decided to change the subject.

"That reminds me," I said, probably not fooling him at all. "Matty came to see me late yesterday, she and her husband and son." I told him the story of how Chris had tried to locate me but was unable to find me in time, and that they were going to Portland for a while. As we ate, I told him about the card and the gift she had left for me. "I wonder how Shana knew I would be here. Did she say?"

"No, she didn't. She did say, however, that because you were a fireman, she knew they would need your help in the search and rescue mission. Maybe she found out through the department."

"I think I would like to get to know her better. What do you think?"

"How do you know she's not married?" Bob asked, a smug look crossing his face.

"There was no wedding ring on her finger that day. That's my only clue," I had to admit.

"Good luck, my boy." Bob was serious in his response, and he gave my back a friendly pat before he gathered up empty food bags, stuffed them into his lunch sack and headed back to pick through the rubble.

It was almost 3:30 PM. I poured some of the water left in my water bottle on the napkin that had been in my lunch sack and ran it over my face, hoping to wipe away the layer of ash and dust that had collected there. Then I poured a little water into my hands, rubbing them together to do the same. All the time I was doing this I felt a little foolish, not sure why it mattered that much to me.

Three-thirty came and went and there was no sign of Shana. I had just about given up on ever seeing her again when I noticed a redhead walking toward me. She was slim, about 5'6". So far she matched the description. She was wearing a dark green blouse and Levi's, and was carrying a jacket over her left arm.

"Jeremy... Jeremy Carter?" she said.

I felt a little nervous as I stood to greet her. I was thankful Bob had warned me so I could wipe some of the ash and grit from my face. "Shana Stewart, I hope." I smiled as she came nearer. As we shook hands, I was thankful I had taken the time to wash mine, as foolish as I had felt at the time.

"I'm so glad you decided to stay and help," she said. "I was afraid I would never see you again and I wanted to thank you in person for helping me that day."

"Just doing my duty, ma'am," I smiled at her. "What was the extent of your injuries? Did you have a concussion?"

"I did, and thank you for making me stay awake," she smiled back. "They also found a cracked cheek bone along with a few scrapes and bruises. Because the concussion was a few steps above mild, they kept me in the hospital overnight just to watch me, then released me the next day. I was pretty black and blue along the right side of my face for a day or two. Make-up is a great cover-up." She paused, then continued, "How long can a fireman from Missouri stay in New York City?"

"I'll be going home on Thursday. My son has a football game Friday afternoon."

When I mentioned my son, Shana seemed a little shaken and she dropped her gaze. "Oh, I see," she whispered. Regaining her composure, she continued, "How many children do you have?"

"Two. Kyle is sixteen and Kaylee is ten." I hurried on to explain, "My wife passed away two years ago, and we live with my parents." I was hoping the look I saw in her eyes was one of relief. I glanced at the third finger on her left hand. The finger was still bare, so I took a shot. "Do you have any children?"

"No, I haven't had that privilege." Her eyes met mine again. "I've never even been married,"

For the first time since Addie's death, I felt like I could really talk to another woman and it didn't feel too bad either. "What time do you usually get hungry?" I asked.

"Usually somewhere between 6:00 and 8:00 PM."

"I usually get hungry about that time too. There's a nice little restaurant about three blocks from here. Would you like to meet me there around seven o'clock?"

"I think I would like that." Her smile was reassuring. "I live about four blocks from here, and I know the restaurant you're talking about. It serves the best Italian food around. Do you like Italian food?"

"One of my favorites," I lied. Actually I'd never tasted it. I was beginning to feel like a high school kid again. I only prayed I wasn't blushing.

"I'll see you then, Jeremy Carter."

"I'll see you then, Shana Stewart." She reached out and shook my hand once again, then turned and walked away. I watched her until she disappeared from my view, my heart beating a little faster.

I had to get back to work. As I started walking toward my area, I reached my hand into my pocket and felt the sharp pain of a paper cut. I had all but forgotten about the piece of paper in my pocket with the picture. After rubbing the cut on my wounded hand, I removed the paper and unfolded it to look at the picture again. As I read the information one more time below the picture, I heard Shana's voice and looked up to see her hurrying back towards me.

"I almost forgot," she apologized, "I don't know who this jacket belongs to. At the hospital they said I was holding it when they admitted me. Does it, by chance, belong to you?"

I recognized the jacket. "It belongs to the other man who helped carry you away from the explosion. He placed it on the cement for you to sit on. He's been here every day since, volunteering. I'll make sure he gets it back, if you'd like."

"Would you mind?"

"Not at all." I was about to fold the paper and put it in my pocket when Shana reached for it.

"May I see that picture?" Before I could respond, she was holding the picture in both of her hands, staring at the face. "I've seen this man." Her voice was shaking. "We shared the same ambulance. I remember looking over at him. His face was all bloody and he was unconscious. I checked to see how he was before I left the next morning, but he hadn't regained consciousness. Each day I call the hospital to see if there's any change in him. They won't tell me much except that he's still unconscious, but in stable condition."

I could hardly believe my ears. I had my phone out of my pocket ready to dial the number on the bottom of the page before Shana even finished her story. "Would you do me a favor," I asked, and then explained to her why I had the picture. "This is not a coincidence. This is a miracle. I think you were supposed to come back so you could see the picture."

"What do you need me to do?"

"I'm about to make a very important phone call to a very worried young lady. Would you go with her and help her find her brother?"

"I would be more than happy to go." Her eyes filled with tears.

My hands were shaking as I dialed the number written on the paper. On the second ring the connection was made.

"Hello."

I looked at the paper again to see where she had written her name. "Janet," I said gently, "remember the fireman you spoke to this morning?"

There was a hesitation on the other end. Then I heard an intake of breath. "Yes, I remember." Her voice was barely audible. I could sense her fear, not knowing what I was going to tell her.

"I have some very good news for you." I tried to control my own emotion but struggled with the tears that filled my eyes as I said, "I've located your brother and he's alive!"

There was silence on the other end for several seconds while the words I had spoken were absorbed. Then I heard loud sobbing. "Where are you?" I asked. "Can you tell me where we can find you?"

She was crying so hard it was difficult for her to speak. Luckily she hadn't left the spot where I had talked to her earlier. I told her to stay where she was. Shana would be there in just a few minutes and would take her to the hospital to find her brother.

"I won't move," she sobbed into the phone. "I won't move, I promise."

I explained what Janet looked like to Shana. She listened carefully, her eyes sparkling through the mist of her tears. After I had finished, she wrapped her arms around my neck and gave me one of the most emotional hugs I had ever experienced.

"See you tonight," she whispered. Then she was off to help find a survivor. "Addie," I whispered, "what do you think of her?"

Maybe it was just my imagination but I thought I heard a voice whisper back, "I think she's perfect."

Author's Reflections

I pledge allegiance to the flag of the United States of America, and to the republic for which it stands. One nation, under God, indivisible, with liberty and justice for all.

To rephrase:

I have a responsibility to my country, to my flag and to my nation. I have a responsibility to God to unite with my countrymen to protect and defend the freedom to choose, the freedom to do and to be whatever I desire as long as I use fairness and correctness in my dealings with all others.

To rephrase:

I have the responsibility to be loyal to my family, my job, my community and my country.

I have a responsibility to respect and honor the flag. To stand up for, to fight and to live for the right to have the freedom it represents. The freedom to choose to do, to be whatever I desire.

I have a responsibility to be loyal to God, and to never forget the principles on which this country was founded. I have the responsibility to stand for God and country, for they cannot be separated. To do so would be to destroy the country.

I have the responsibility to protect the rights of others so that their freedom is not in jeopardy because of me. I have the responsibility to respect my fellowmen, to show compassion and justice to all.

The flag has been burned, spit upon, desecrated, ripped and violated by those who, in return, demand the freedom it provides. We seem to take so much for granted in our country, that at times we forget to be grateful. We forget to be responsible.

When we don't take responsibility for our country's freedom, we, by choice, must take responsibility for its decay.

The bent steel and broken concrete are evidence of ignorance, of knowledge untapped and of understanding left unopened. The broken bodies are reminders of the lack of compassion and the existence of evil.

Even as we mourn those who have died, we honor them as we unite and share the responsibility in defending their deaths. Every time we give of our time or our means, we take responsibility. Every time we listen with our heart and share the sadness of another, we take responsibility. George Elliot said, *"What do we live for, if it's not for helping each other?"* If this is true, we are, indeed, our brother's keeper.

We each carry within our souls a simple power so great that if we listen to it, it will guide us to all knowledge and all understanding. It lies there, silently waiting to be used. To ourselves we owe the responsibility to use that power.

Chapter Five

The Flight of the Eagle

We had recovered so many bodies and body parts by the end of the fifth day. I began to sense an emptiness within myself. As I tried to understand what it was I was feeling, I turned to Bob who was working beside me.

"What do you feel inside," I asked as we zipped up a body bag, "each time you uncover another body?"

"At first I felt shock," he responded. "Then the shock seemed to turn to a deep, painful sadness. Last night when I was driving home to Jersey, I told my wife that I felt like my mind and heart had shut down and I had become robotic. The sadness had reached a point, I suppose, where it could no longer stand the pain, so it closed its door and refused to let anymore in. Today there is a hollow feeling inside of me."

"Thank you." I felt relieved. "I needed to know that I wasn't alone with my feelings."

"Oh, I think most every person you see here today feels the same."

"It doesn't ease the anger though, does it? I can almost feel the anger swirling in the air with the smoke and ash. It's as if they're inseparable."

"Right now, I think they are," Bob answered. "Maybe that's a good thing for now. The anger keeps us connected."

"That and patriotism," Chris said as he dropped empty body bags to the ground. "Anger and patriotism are the two things I have seen today. Not only anger toward those who did this, but an anger toward those people in another country who would cheer this ungodly event, then burn our flag in front of TV cameras. The question, in most of our minds is, why do they hate us so much when they don't even know us?"

"Maybe for the same reason we hate a religion we don't understand," I said almost to myself. "Each time someone has expressed their hatred of the Islamic religion, I explain to them what I have learned in the library. Once they could understand that religion played no part in this tragedy, only the evil minds of men, their hatred of the religion seemed resolved."

"You think knowing us would change their minds? I don't think so. I think it's more than that," Chris said, his voice rising in frustration as he thrust his pick into the rubble. "We send food and clothes to them. It doesn't make any difference. They still hate us."

"Maybe it's because they have so little and we have so much," Bob answered simply. "Anyway, I don't think they all hate us, only those who have been taught to hate."

Before anyone could say anything more, however, music filled the air. Someone had brought a CD player and hooked it to amplifiers. The melody and words of "God Bless America" floated over the area like healing balm.

"I love America and I'm thankful I have so much." Chris looked at me, his voice mellow now.

The music filled the air with songs written during WWII. One song entitled "The Eagle," written by Hank Cochran, was cheered as it ended. Its words were inspiring.

Lord knows I am peaceful when I'm left alone.
I've always been an eagle. It's been awhile since I have flown.
My claws are sharp as ever, so's my eagle eye.
Something's gonna go to ground when the eagle flies.
Lately I've heard rumors that the eagle may be lame,
Just because I've been idle, don't mean that I'm tame.
You've jeopardized my freedom, my natural place to roost.
I can fly when I have to. They've turned the eagle loose.
So lay all your doubts aside when you go to bed tonight,
My feathers are all ruffled now. I'm ready for a fight.
Just because I took awhile to fly, don't mean I don't care.
When you feel the shadow crossing, the eagle's in the air.

The music lifted us and the mood shifted to one of resolve, giving us the strength to work beyond our own capacity. The feeling was dynamic.

"Inspiring music is the healer, the instructor. It reaches into the mind and weaves its way into the heart and the soul until it fills the whole body with its beauty and its message," my grandmother used to say. My grandmother had a lot of faith in the power of music. She trusted its ability to lift and to inspire. However, she warned me about hard rock and the message it delivers to the mind and the heart.

"Trust yourself to good music and no other," she reminded me as her fingers touched the keys of the piano, filling the room with soft soothing music. I believed my grandmother then, but today as I watched the men around me put their trust in music to lift and move them forward in their task, I knew my grandmother was right.

I had decided I would leave at 6:00 PM so I could get back to the apartment, shower and be at the restaurant before Shana arrived. The closer it got to the time to leave, however, I found it difficult to stop and leave those who tirelessly picked and shoveled through the rubble.

When I finally gathered up my tools, I looked around me. Does music heal? Just ask any of those men who listened to the songs, "God Bless America," "The Battle Cry of Freedom," "Praise the Lord and Pass the Ammunition," and "You're a Grand Old Flag," as they dug into the rubble and swept away the ash. Things haven't changed in all the years since those songs were written. Our ideas haven't changed. We still feel the same sense of devotion to our country. Courage and bravery will always be our strength and freedom will always be our cause.

"God Bless the USA," written by Lee Greenwood, was playing over the loudspeaker as I walked to the Salvation Army tent to pick up my statue. I could hear a hundred voices joining in on the chorus:

*And I'm proud to be an American where at least I know
    I'm free.*

And I won't forget the men who died who gave that right
    to me,
And I'll gladly stand up next to you and defend her
    still today,
'Cause there ain't no doubt about this land,
God bless the USA!

"God bless the USA," I prayed silently in my heart as I asked the woman standing near the Salvation Army tent wearing the Salvation Army insignia if I could retrieve my box from their tent.

"Only if you will show me what's in it," she joked. But I was happy to show her. As I took the statue from the box and unwrapped it, she started to cry. She took it in her hands and carefully examined it up close. "It's beautiful," she sighed. "It's simply beautiful."

I took the time to explain its significance to her before I wrapped it and put it back into the box. As I turned to leave, the woman shouted, "Wait, you forgot your jacket. I slipped it into a plastic sack so it wouldn't get so dusty."

"Thank you. I'd hoped to see my friend, whose name I've yet to learn, during the day so I could tell him about his jacket. But he didn't seem to be anywhere around." I'll bring it back with me in the morning, I thought to myself, and hope I'll see him sometime tomorrow.

I had less than an hour before I was supposed to meet Shana and I still had five blocks to walk. I found myself humming the tune and singing the words to "The Eagle." It had captured my soul. *"You've jeopardized my freedom, my natural place to roost. I can fly when I have to, they've turned the eagle loose... Just because I took awhile to fly, don't mean that I don't care. When you feel the shadow crossing, you know the eagle's in the air."* I really like that song.

Once I got to the apartment, I set the box with the statue in it on the table by the front room window and laid the jacket over the back of the chair. I didn't want to forget it in the morning when I left. My next stop was the shower. By the time I had finished showering and dressing, I had ten minutes to get to the restaurant. I arrived with three minutes to spare. When Shana walked through the door I had a table by the window facing away from Ground Zero.

I watched her walk toward me. She had a graceful way of moving, her chin tilted slightly upward. Her dark red, shoulder-length hair was pulled up except for strands here and there that were left to fall around her face and neck. Her dress, teal in color, was neither too tight nor too loose; not quite casual, but not dressy either. It was perfect. It had been a long time since I'd looked at a woman in the way I was looking at her. It caught me off-guard. I wasn't prepared for what I was experiencing. As I held her chair for her to sit down, I caught the scent of her perfume. It was neither too light nor too heavy. It was perfect.

"Thank you," she said softly, as I moved her chair closer to the table. I think she was as nervous as I was.

"You're welcome," was all I could think to say as I sat down across from her. I was thankful the waiter was there to hand us our menus so we could discuss food.

"Since you've been here before," I suggested as I browsed through the menu, "why don't you order for both of us?" In truth, the closest I had ever been to Italian food was spaghetti.

"We could start with an Italian salad bowl. Oh, and they make the best lasagna. Would you care for lasagna?"

I nodded.

"Then for dessert, you'll want to try the spumoni."

The waiter took our order and left us alone, neither one of us knowing what to say to each other without our menus.

Finally, to get the conversation going, and simply out of curiosity, I said, "I've never eaten spumoni. Tell me what it is."

"Spumoni," she explained, "is vanilla ice cream with rum flavoring, pistachio ice cream, maraschino cherries, pistachio nuts, whipped cream, and raspberries. I hope you like it."

"Sounds delicious," I lied. I hate pistachio nuts, which means I hate pistachio ice cream.

The waiter brought the salad to the table and set an empty bowl in front of each of us. Once we had the salad transferred to our bowls and began to eat, I felt miserable. I didn't know how to eat in front of a woman I hardly knew. "Come on, Jeremy," I said to myself. "Relax. This is a simple salad in front of you. You've eaten a salad thousands of times. This time is no different."

I looked at Shana and she was smiling at me. "Tell me about your children," she said. That was a safe subject, I thought. I could do that.

"Kyle is sixteen and stands an inch taller than me. He has dark brown hair and hazel eyes. He's an athlete, plays football, basketball and runs the hurdles in track. He wants to be a doctor so he's also studious. He's a good kid.

"Kaylee is ten going on eighteen. She loves dolls and books. She is her grandmother's joy and is as beautiful as her mother." I didn't mean to say that, it just slipped out. I didn't want to talk about Addie in front of Shana. It wasn't the thing to do at this point. Even I knew that. My eyes met Shana's and she smiled again, that understanding smile I had seen once already in the half hour we had been together.

"Tell me about your wife,"

"I don't know if I can," I said honestly. I didn't think I could trust myself to say what I felt about Addie and not offend Shana.

"That's OK, I understand." Shana took another bite of her salad. Had I offended her, I wondered, by not wanting to talk about Addie? She looked so beautiful sitting across the table from me. How did I look to her? I hope I wasn't making a fool out of myself.

"Tell me about yourself," I asked, hoping to release any tension I may have caused.

"Well," she said as she wiped her mouth with the napkin, "I'm a CPA for a firm that right now has no place to call home. I've been with them for fifteen years. I worked part-time while I attended college and then they offered me a place in their company once I graduated. My life has been my work..." She stopped talking and her eyes started to mist. "I'm sorry, I didn't mean to get emotional. It's just that I don't know who I am without my work, and right now I have nowhere to go to work, and it may be several months before that changes. I'm frightened, I guess, because I feel like I have no identity."

The waiter came with our lasagna and garlic bread, and two glasses of lemon water, took our salad bowls and left us alone again. This time we were happy to see him leave.

"My wife's name was Addie," I said, not knowing why I was saying it. "She was my life. She was my inspiration and I lost her to cancer. I lost her and I lost myself until I came to New York and witnessed the most horrible event I could ever imagine. I've spent eighteen years fighting fires, seeing death, going in and removing burnt bodies from homes. I won't go into any more detail, but nothing prepared me for what I have seen and done over the past five days, and I've changed in a way that makes me feel so grateful. Am I making any sense here?"

"Since September 11th, I've had to reevaluate my life as well," Shana said. "At first, when it happened, I was stunned. Then I was angry. When the anger started to subside, I started to think about what I had really accomplished in this life. I never married because I didn't have time for marriage. I didn't want to complicate my life with children. I couldn't trust myself to let anything get in my way for fear I would lose all that I had worked for. I had prestige and money and I thought I was happy. I pretended to be anyway, and convinced myself that I was.

"Nothing prepared me for what I found when I looked inside myself and found nothing but emptiness. As tragic as this attack has been, it made me look at my life for what it is. Through it all, I've changed in a way that makes me feel so grateful. Yes, Jeremy, you are making complete sense."

"How can something so good come out of something so bad?" I asked. "Over the past five days the country has seen so much good that has come out of so much bad. We are more patriotic. We are more caring and loving. We are more compassionate and less tolerant of crime and destruction. And, like you and me, we are more aware of ourselves and what is really important in our lives. We have become more responsible people."

She lifted her glass to me, and I, in turn, lifted mine. "To a new kind of faith, not only in the nation and the men who lead us, but more importantly, faith in ourselves."

"To faith and to the trust it inspires." I clicked my glass to hers.

We drank our toast. Then as she set her glass down, Shana asked, "Do you know what trust is?"

"I think trust is having faith that something or someone you care about will always be there for you," I responded without thinking.

"And that you will always be there for yourself?" she asked.

I nodded. "Trust is having the faith in yourself to move on in spite of what has happened, I suppose. It is knowing that whatever is behind you has fed you with wisdom and that now you can go on with life and what it brings. But, first, you must allow trust to be a part of your life."

"And can you do that?" Her gaze was intense as she searched into my eyes.

"Can you?" I sensed there was more to her story than she had been willing to share. "You must have been hurt pretty deep to have stopped trusting love," I said gently. "Please, will you tell me what happened?"

"It was a long time ago," she hesitated to go on, but I reached across the table and slipped my fingers through hers.

"Please," I prodded.

She must have found, in my eyes, what she was looking for because I felt her fingers relax in mine. "We met in college," she said as she gazed at our hands. "He was working on his law degree. He was good-looking, intelligent and a liar." She almost laughed and brought her eyes back up to meet mine. "For two years he told me all the things I wanted to hear. Then on the day he graduated, he simply emptied my heart and walked away. I had never loved anyone that much and I couldn't replace the part of me he took with him. I hid the pain behind my career and hid my trust away, inside my empty heart. You're the first person I have shared this with. Can I trust you with my secret?"

"You can trust me with your life," I responded.

"I already did," she said softly as she lifted her fingers from mine and placed her hand over my own. "I already did."

I'm not sure what passed between us at that moment, but I knew we had found the answers to the questions we had inside and, once again our lives were changed.

I watched Shana's face as we finished the main course and talked. Her intelligent green eyes were large and round, her lashes were long and dark. Her nose reminded me of Addie's in its shape and her lips were full. She was taller than Addie and not as attractive in a physical sense. But she reminded me of Addie in her ability to see the truth. Her honesty and insight were also Addie's strengths. I knew I shouldn't sit here and compare, but I couldn't help myself.

By the time we got to the spumoni, I had forgotten that I hated pistachios. I ate it without tasting them. I only tasted the raspberries and whipped cream.

As I walked Shana home we soon fell into step and I found her hand and held it in my own. We walked silently, not wanting to break the spell. I wanted to kiss her goodnight, but my grandmother told me once that you never kiss a girl on the first date because it shows lack of respect. Standing on the steps to Shana's apartment, I wish my grandmother hadn't been so free with her advice. I wrote down Shana's telephone number and promised I would call the next day to make plans for the evening. We said goodnight in a way that my grandmother would have been proud of me. Then I made my way back to Bob's sister's apartment and Bob.

I stood by the window of the apartment in the darkness and thought about Shana and how she had touched my life so quickly. I smiled as I thought about the spumoni and how, even with all of its flavors, I had only tasted the two that I enjoyed, the raspberries and the whipped cream. I decided if you could forget what you hate in life and concentrate only on what you love, then life would be just like dessert. All you have to do is ignore the pistachios of life and concentrate on the raspberries and whipped cream.

"Home so early?" Bob asked as he came into the front room, not bothering to turn on the lights. "It's only 11:00 PM. How was the evening?"

"I'm sorry, did I wake you up?" I turned to look at him.

"Naw, I wasn't really asleep. Tomorrow will be my last day here. I have to be back to work on Monday to start putting together my makeshift office. I hate to leave, you know?"

"Yes, I know, and I'll be sorry to see you leave."

"When do you have to get back to being a fire chief?" he chuckled.

"Next Thursday, so I'll leave Wednesday afternoon."

"At least you've got a good place to stay until you have to leave. Now back to your evening. Did it go as planned?"

"You mean does she like me? I think so." We stood together looking out the window as I told him about the evening and Shana and how I felt. I even told him about the spumoni.

"Must be love," he laughed. "By the way, what's in the box on the table?"

I switched on the lamp, then picked up the box and once again carefully unwrapped the statue inside and handed it to him.

"Let me guess," he said in awe of what he was holding. "This statue is from Matty, am I right?"

I nodded.

"Did she sculpt it herself?"

"I don't think so," I replied. "Her arm is still in a sling."

"Well, whoever did this work is a master."

I agreed. The details of the sculpture expertly and sensitively portrayed an emotion of life. It was a masterpiece.

Bob searched the bottom of the statue for a signature but to his disappointment, found none. "I'll have to get in touch with Matty when she gets back and find out who did this. Do you know Matty's last name?"

I reached in the box and found the card Matty had given me. On the bottom where she had signed it, she had also written her last name. "McCort."

"Matty McCort," Bob repeated. "A fine Irish name, to be sure. Let me write it down on a piece of paper so I won't forget it."

The bed felt good when I crawled in. As soon as my head touched the pillow I was asleep. I didn't move again until I smelled the aroma of bacon and the sound of Bob's booming, base voice singing, *"And I'm proud to be an American where at least I know I'm free. And I won't forget the men who died who gave that right to me. And I'll gladly stand up next to you and defend her still today. 'Cause there ain't no doubt about this land, God bless the USA!"*

"Good morning," I shouted above his voice.

"Didn't mean to wake you," his laugh was hearty.

I looked at him. "I find it hard to believe your story about the 'Bob' you were before September 11th, when I see this 'Bob,' an apron wrapped around his middle, flipping pancakes, singing patriotic songs and laughing like Santa Claus."

"You know what?" He stopped laughing and his eyes grew serious. "I'm glad you never had the opportunity to meet that 'Bob.' This is the real me you see, after I shed that heavy facade that I covered myself in for so many years." Then he burst out laughing again. "It weighed more than I do."

I sat down to a breakfast of bacon, eggs, hotcakes, and juice. I hadn't eaten this well since the first day of the firemen's training meeting in Jersey. But more important, I sat down to breakfast with a good and kind friend whom I'd miss after today. I could already feel the void of his friendship.

"I'm grateful you sat on the cot next to me that day," I grinned as I buttered the hotcakes he had just flipped onto my plate. "I'm grateful you shared your story with me and that I got to meet the real you. I'm going to miss you," I filled my mouth with a bite of one of the most delicious pancakes I had ever eaten, "especially tomorrow morning when I have to fix my own breakfast!"

"I'm going to miss you too," he smiled. "As we looked out the window together last night and you told me about your evening, I realized your friendship is a priceless gift. A gift that will never tarnish, break or become outdated. One I can take with me wherever I go, because it fits perfectly in my heart. Yes, my friend, I will miss you, too."

Bob chewed and swallowed slowly, his eyes growing tentative. "Last night I couldn't sleep, so I found some paper and began writing down all the things that have happened since that day. As I put the words on paper, they began to remind me of another time and place. My grandfather served in WWII and he used to tell us stories. I said to him one day, 'How did you do it? How did you make it from day to day not knowing if you would be alive tomorrow? How did you survive the horror of it all?'

"He looked at me with love in his eyes, put his arm around me and said, 'Bobby, you do it because it has to be done. When you are in the trenches you are fighting, not for yourself, but for your children and your grandchildren. It is their freedom that becomes more important to you than your own, and that knowledge gives you strength you didn't even know you possessed. If you have to die to preserve their freedom, then so be it. That is your motivation, dear grandson. That is your motivation, and you have preserved freedom for one more day.'

"I'd forgotten those words until I began to write my own story of war and devastation. I now know how he handled the death around him as he fought on. He did it because it had to be done."

"He sounds like a remarkable man," I said.

Bob nodded and smiled as he poured more coffee into his mug. "He was all of that. I remember once when I was complaining about the Vietnam War and the Gulf War, he looked me in the eye and said, 'War is a part of life that keeps beginning and keeps ending. Today, it may be fought in someone else's country and you can sit back and criticize its purpose. But what happens there may affect your very future because tomorrow it may be fought in your country, if the battle is not won in theirs. Either way, life goes on. Be it free or be it in bondage, you help to make that choice. Trust in your country, Bobby,' he said to me. 'Trust in the principles it was founded on. But most of all, trust in God and know that He will not let this country fall until we who live here lose our love for it through our own disrespect.' My grandfather died shortly after that." Bob's eyes misted over.

"I wish your grandfather could have met my grandmother," I said in all sincerity. "They sound like they were molded from the same pot of clay."

He chuckled, "Everyone should be blessed with grandparents who understand what life is all about. Maybe the blessing is in the heeding of their wisdom. I wish I would have had the foresight to thank him for his. He believed in this country with all his heart. Why it took me so long to catch on, I don't know. It's interesting that his words are so sharp in my memory right now. I'm surprised I even remember them. I was such an arrogant teenager who grew up to be an arrogant man. I was too young for the Vietnam War and too comfortable with my life to become part of the Gulf War. I think I was a disappointment to my grandfather in that respect. Maybe that's why I regret that I can't stay and see this clean-up through to the very end. I feel I owe as much to him as I do to this country."

Bob began clearing the dishes from the table and I put them in the dishwasher. He had opened his heart once again to me and I felt honored to have his trust. "Did your grandmother give you a lot of advice?" he asked

"Enough that I didn't dare kiss Shana on our first date," I laughed.

"Same pot of clay, you said?"

"Same pot of clay," I nodded.

Making sure we had everything we needed, we left the apartment and started walking toward Ground Zero. Bob was telling me about his first day of work at the Trade Center. While he talked, I couldn't help feeling I had forgotten something. Then I remembered.

"I forgot the jacket!" I stopped Bob in mid-sentence, startling him.

"You what?"

"Wait for me, I'll be right back. I forgot the jacket." I handed my hat and coat to him and ran back to retrieve what I had almost forgotten. When I returned, he was staring at me.

"You think you're going to be needing that today?" He couldn't help but chuckle at the vision of me in my fireman pants and a sport jacket.

"I'll explain it to you while we walk," I responded with a chuckle of my own. When I had finished my story Bob looked at me.

"Sounds to me like this jacket has played a part in bringing you and Shana together," seriousness entering his voice. That had never occurred to me and I fell silent. I needed to find out more about the owner of the jacket.

When we came to the bicycle, without a word passing between us, we each took our hand and removed the dust that had collected on it over the last twenty-four hours. We then walked silently past the hundreds of picture posters stapled to the poles. The gray polluted air carrying the smell of death and devastation reached out to us as we crossed over the yellow tape. We picked up our assignment that sent us in separate directions and waved to each other, promising to meet at 3:00 PM in the place that had become our retreat. It all seemed so normal now, as if this were a daily part of our lives.

I passed the workers who were coming off-shift. The ash that covered their hats, their faces and clothing still circled in the air around them as they walked, making them appear almost ghostly. But in their eyes reality was stark, and on their faces fatigue, both physical and emotional showed itself without mercy. They would nod as they passed me. Some would murmur a good morning or words of encouragement, but mostly, they were even too tired to talk. They had been through another excruciating night. There was no other way to describe it.

I found my area and unloaded my gear. The six men who had arrived before me were already at work. Pausing only long enough to wave a greeting to me, they went back to what they were doing. The sounds of the picks combined with the noise of the huge equipment in the background scooping up thousands of pounds of broken concrete, created an eerie mood.

"Ten big trucks brought in more equipment," one of the workers motioned to the row of trucks behind us. "That should speed up removal of this blasted rubble."

We all agreed.

"They buried Father Mychal Judge yesterday," said a fireman, standing beside me. "He's really going to be missed."

"I'm sorry," I replied. "I'm not from here. Who is Father Mychal Judge?"

"You've asked the right man." He smiled wistfully. "I know all about him. He was an Irish priest known as the Fireman's Friar because his first concern was the welfare of every firefighter in New York City. His next concern was everyone else in New York City. He'd been a Fire Department chaplain since 1992, and had a knack for telling stories and jokes like you'd never heard before. He had a reputation for holding Mass in a firehouse just as if it were the church — which caused a lot of concern among his peers. But it didn't stop him. He had the trust and love of every firefighter in the city. They knew he would always be there for them and that day was no exception. He *was* there for them and now he is there with them. I think that's how he would want it to be."

"He died in the Trade Center?" I asked.

"Someone had told him that firefighters were trapped in the towers. With no concern for his own safety, and in concern for the last rites of any who might die, he was seen running into the lobby of the tower I was in. There were six of us at the tower's emergency command post, in that building, waiting for instructions when the whole building began to shake. The lights went out and a booming sound surrounded us. The pressure was sucking out the windows. The smoke became so thick we couldn't see or breathe. The only thing we could do was take hold of hands and together find our way back through the lobby. That's where he was lying, right there in the lobby. He wasn't buried under any rubble but he was dead. We picked him up and brought him out.

"Chief Ganci, our Department Chief and First Deputy Fire Commissioner, Will Feehan, died that day too. They were all buried yesterday."

"My name's Jeremy Carter," I said as I reached out to shake his hand. "I want you to know that I share in your loss. I'm also a firefighter."

"Tad Allen." He clasped my hand in a firm handshake. "I see by your badge you're from Missouri."

A truck and loader pulled up close to us as I was explaining to Tad how I happened to be there. We watched as the scoop dug up pieces of concrete, lifting them into the air and dumping them into the bed of the truck. We carefully looked for anything unusual with each scoop, but there was nothing.

"Do you know a firefighter named Lenny Roberts?" I asked, as we watched the loader do its job.

"Sure do, in fact he's right over there." Pointing to the right of us, Tad raised his voice to be heard over the loader. "Hey, Lenny!" One of the men turned his head in our direction. "Someone here wants to talk to you."

As he got closer, I recognized him. "How are you feeling, Lenny?"

Lenny looked at me for a minute, then a smile began to spread across his face. "I don't know your name, but your face, I'll never forget. When I woke up you were gone and I didn't know who you were or if I would ever see you again. I wanted to thank you."

He walked over to me, put his arms around my shoulders and gave me a hug. "Thank you for being there, for listening and caring about a fellow firefighter."

"It's not often a tough fireman like Lenny gives anyone a hug," Tad chuckled. "Consider yourself lucky."

"I was just checking to see if he was an angel," Lenny said in a mocking tone, "but he's just a mortal after all."

"I hope that doesn't disappoint you?" I joked.

"Not at all." Then he leaned closer and whispered, "I hope I can trust you to keep our secret about me crying like a baby and everything."

"You have my word," I whispered back. Then, raising my voice, I reached out my hand, "My name is Jeremy Carter."

"Very happy to meet you, Jeremy." He shook my hand.

The loader stopped suddenly and a volunteer shouted, "I need help here."

Everyone dropped what they were holding and went to the volunteer's side. We knew he had found a body. We knelt down and began to move the rubble from the form. As we did, the arm and shoulder of another body appeared.

"Dear God," Lenny's voice was barely audible, "they're holding hands."

I felt the emotion of tears as I saw the two hands clasped together. No one moved. We just knelt there on our knees, staring, not wanting to disturb the one thing in this whole mess that had any meaning.

"May I help?" I recognized the voice immediately. It was my friend whose name I had yet to learn.

He knelt beside the clasped hands and began to carefully move the debris from around the heads of a young man and woman. Then he gently brushed the ash and dust from their broken faces as we watched. Slowly, the feeling found its way back into our arms and legs and we began to help. Lenny and I removed the rubble from around the mid-point and Tad worked at the base. It took several minutes to clear away the debris. From the condition of the bodies and the way they were lying, it was obvious they had jumped from one of the upper floors. Even though the sight in front of us was one of broken, decaying bodies, we couldn't feel revulsion. It was as if our hearts had taken over, covering our minds with a vision of a young man in a light shirt and colorful tie and a young woman, dressed in a navy blue suit, holding hands while they waited. What they were waiting for we didn't know, but we knew that what we saw represented love and trust in true form. We could only kneel there and watch over them until the body bags were made ready.

"How can we part them?" asked Tad. "It almost seems irreverent."

"I don't think they would mind now," the quiet voice of my friend said.

"I wonder if they were in love?" Lenny's voice was also very quiet.

"Maybe they were married," Tad whispered. "Or perhaps they were just friends."

"Whatever their relationship was," I said, "their trust in each other is undeniable. They apparently knew that death was certain, whether they chose to stay and die in the fire or jump to their death, which probably came even before they even hit the ground. I think they put their trust in God as well as in each other. Then, taking hold of each other's hand, they jumped."

"I think they must have loved each other very much to have that much trust." Tad's face was solemn as he spoke. "I only wish it could have had a better ending."

Author's Notes

On every coin and piece of currency that we carry in our wallets is written these words: "In God We Trust." In 1861, Chief Justice Chase of the Supreme Court wrote a letter to the Director of the Mint. In this letter he stated: "No nation can be strong except in the strength of God, or safe except in His defense. The trust of our people in God should be declared on our national coins."

On September 11, our strength was challenged and we learned something valuable about ourselves as individuals as well as a people united. We learned that we had not lost the patriotic courage on which our nation was founded. The events of that day changed our lives, altered our beliefs and demanded our respect and our anger. This tragedy asked for our humility and our patriotism. It cried for our integrity and our honor. It asked that we put our trust back in God.

The question, "Can anything good come out of something so bad?" has been answered with an undeniable "YES." We only have to look at ourselves, reevaluate our lives and see our future with more mature eyes. We have felt a kind of fear that our generation has never had to deal with, the fear of freedom lost. Out of that fear, we must learn to trust ourselves so that we can trust our fellowman. Next, we must be able to trust in God so that we can trust in our country. Our trust then becomes our right and our responsibility to defend that which we believe in, and to do it with integrity and honor.

Then we can take that trust and mold it until we have created a sense of courage and patriotism woven so tightly, it will be impregnable. We can redefine "trust."

Trust is not only what we have but what we give,
It is not only in our hearts , but in the way we live.
Trust shows itself through honor and through selflessness,
It gives itself to honesty, to loyalty and truthfulness.

Trust is found first in self, then shares itself through unity
And embraces those who give their lives to secure our liberty.
Trust is faith that freedom rings with the sound of every voice,
And the belief that God and country will always be our choice.

John F. Kennedy said, "Let every nation know whether it wishes us well or ill, that we shall pay any price, bear any burden, meet any hardship, support any friend, oppose any foe, to assure the survival and the success of liberty."

Chapter Six

Thank You for Being My Friend

As I headed back to my assigned area, I looked around me and wondered how long it would be before the people of this city could walk along the sidewalks of this street without feeling the traumatic loss of what was once a part of their world. The devastation in front of me I could not describe. There was no combination of words that could adequately define the picture. Even the old saying, *you've got to see it to believe it,* didn't apply here. In this case, seeing made it even more unbelievable.

Daily, people walked along the edge of the yellow tape, hoping to find a way to grasp the reality of this nightmare. Some stopped and placed flowers at the edge of the rubble while others just stood and gazed for a while before silently moving on.

Sometimes I would overhear conversations in which one person would share with another their experience of that day because they were either near or in the building when all hell broke loose. All of them, in their hearts, wished everything would go back to the way it was before the morning of September 11.

The scene behind the yellow tape was a picture of fire-fighters, police officers, iron and construction workers and volunteers, working together with blowtorches, picks, shovels, buckets, ropes and other equipment, in an effort to close the wound. The picture included huge trucks filled with broken slabs of concrete and long thin pillars of steel, inching their way along self-made roads. Beyond them, enormous cranes with their long, extended arms repeatedly reached into the rubble, lifting bits and pieces of the Trade Center out of the ash. The picture was ugly but it was also accurate. In this grayish background, one thing stood out: the red, white and blue of a tattered and dirty flag that moved with grace in the folds of the breeze.

The flag had been pulled from the rubble by a search and rescue specialist. A steelworker taped it to a piece of wood and mounted it on the tower's antenna. In my mind, the rips in its cloth represented battle scars, and only added to its dignity. The dirt that soiled its stripes of freedom represented the evil that had tried to destroy something that was indestructible. In its attempt, it could only brush the surface but could not penetrate the shield; for the shield is the power of freedom.

"This is not the first time the flag has been attacked," a voice behind me said.

"I turned to see an elderly gentleman sitting on a broken steel beam that was lying sideways across the bits of rubble.

"I didn't realize my thoughts were so loud," I laughed.

"Let me tell you a story." He motioned for me to sit down beside him. "In the summer of 1813, America was fighting for her independence. Maj. George Armistead, a commander at Fort McHenry, asked for a flag so big, the British would have no trouble seeing it from a distance. Four hundred yards of wool bunting were handed to Mary Pickersgill, who was a 'maker of colors,' and her thirteen-year-old daughter, Caroline, with instructions to make the biggest flag they could out of it."

"Four hundred yards of material?" I repeated, amazed.

"Not just any material, my dear boy," he corrected, "but four hundred yards of the best wool bunting money could buy.

"They proceeded to cut fifteen stars, each measuring two feet from point to point. Next, eight red stripes and seven white stripes were cut, each two feet wide. By August the flag had been sewn together. It was 30 feet by 40 feet, and cost $406.90. That flag was raised at Fort McHenry and on September 13, 1814, after a day and night of heavy artillery firing, silence erupted just before dawn.

"Francis Scott Key waited anxiously from the deck of the enemy's ship for the first light of day to see if the flag was still there. With the dawning of the morning light, he strained his eyes and looked into the distance and there, amid smoke and ash and destruction, he saw that magnificent flag. Undaunted by the enemy, she waved her colors proudly, high above Fort McHenry. She may have been a little dirty and there may have been a few holes in her, just big enough for the light to flicker through, but she was there. She was there because she stood for justice and perseverance. She was there because she stood for courage and freedom. She was there because she stood for purity and innocence.

"Key was so inspired by the sight, he immediately sat down and wrote a poem on the back of a letter he had in his pocket."

"The Star Spangled Banner," I said.

"Exactly, son. And I know there are those who think it shouldn't be the National Anthem, but let me tell you something. Those words were inspired for a reason. Maybe they are to be a constant reminder of what it took to preserve our freedom. Maybe God, in His wisdom, knew as this nation grew more prosperous, we would forget unless there was a reminder, and the best reminder is one that you can sing."

As this man, aged in wisdom himself, expressed his feelings about the flag and the song, I, too, began to consider the words and their meaning as well as their purpose for being sung as the National Anthem.

"Thank you," I said as I shook his hand. "Every time I salute the flag or sing the National Anthem in the future, I will remember our conversation, and I will do those things with more gratitude and respect."

"I watched the attack on September Eleventh from the window of my apartment," the man went on to explain, "and every day since then I come here just to sit for a few minutes and look at the flag. Today I crossed the yellow tape for the first time because I needed to be closer to her."

"I understand."

"Well, I had better be on my way, I have a son who worries too much about me. Glad I met you, son."

"Jeremy."

"Glad to have met you, Jeremy," he smiled as he shook my hand again. "My name is Sam."

"Sam, can I ask you one question before you go? Why was he on a British ship at the time the British were firing on Fort McHenry?"

"Francis, you mean?"

I nodded.

"He had gone aboard to make a prisoner exchange and wasn't allowed to leave until the battle was over. But that's another story. Takes time in the telling and you haven't got all day to sit around and listen to stories. You've got work to do and I had better let you get to it. Maybe we'll be looking at the flag at the same time again on another day." He waved as he turned to follow the only path that existed in this maze of stone and ash.

I turned in the direction where no path existed. I took a chance with every step, hoping I wouldn't cut myself on a jagged pipe sticking out, or worse, fall into a pocket formed underneath the rubble. Sometimes I even had to teeter on unstable slabs of concrete.

As I made my way, I thought about my dream in which I was standing inside the maze, not knowing which way to turn to find my way out. The only difference was, in the maze the way was smooth; there just wasn't a destiny. Here the way was dangerous but at least I could see where I needed to go.

The thought occurred to me that there might be some meaning to this but I didn't have time to sort it out right now. I was too busy concentrating on my footing. There had been a lot of injuries during the clean-up. Some of the injuries required stitches, others required hospitalization. It was not safe work; it was treacherous at times and everyone there knew it. But like Bob's grandfather had said, "*You do it because it has to be done,*" and there were hundreds willing to step up and do the job.

When I got back to the work site, Lenny was helping the driver of a loader parked in front of them. They were pulling pieces of loose bent steel out of the way so the loader could move in a little closer. I pulled on my gloves and stepped in to help.

"Thanks, fellas," the driver of the loader called out as we finished clearing a path for him. Then he climbed back onto his equipment and began to move forward. We waved to him and moved back so he could do his work.

"Have you noticed," Lenny chuckled as he leaned on his shovel, "that even with the most sophisticated equipment they've got here, it still takes the sweat of the brow, and a pick and a shovel, to prepare the way for them?"

"I don't think you'd get too far with a pick, when it comes to breaking through the thick concrete," I suggested, and he agreed.

We talked as we worked, clearing and chipping away and shoveling, making little progress in the vastness of the rubble. Nevertheless, we did make progress, and that's what mattered. It mattered, to us, that we were there.

"Did you know that Afghan's opposition leader, Ahmed Shah Massood, died yesterday?" Lenny said. "He was a victim of a suicide bombing a week ago by two men posing as television journalists. A spokesman for him claims that Massood had warned the world about the threat of terrorists but the world didn't listen. I think they're listening today." There was sudden anger in his voice. "Why did it take something like this to make the world stop and listen?"

"Sometimes I think the world is too busy talking to listen," I answered. "There can be no peace in the world when countries are unwilling to listen and learn about each other. There can be no foundation of trust when propaganda spreads lies and half-truths. There can be no structure of compassion when people remain ignorant and unaware that we are all the same. If only all countries would communicate on a level of honesty and integrity, there would be no room for hate."

"I can't even imagine a world like that," Lenny muttered as he stopped working and looked at me. Then his eyes narrowed. "Last night I watched the late news and I saw groups of refugees from one of the villages in Afghanistan, fleeing their homes. They had only what they could carry on their backs for food and clothes, and I thought to myself, 'How are they going to survive?' Seeing the little children made me want to cry. Here I was, sitting in my home, my big screen TV in front of me, my fridge full of food and my children sleeping, each one in his own bed, in his own room. Their closets are filled with clothes, shoes, and toys.

"I felt a deep sadness as I watched the refugees walk down that dusty road, not knowing what was ahead of them, and only too aware that there was nothing behind them but war. They have never tasted freedom. They have no idea how sweet the flavor is. We take so much for granted, Jeremy.

"As I watched them on the TV screen, I said to myself, 'These are the people you've been hating for six days now, Lenny. How can you hate people who live in constant fear for their lives and the lives of their children? People who have had their homes destroyed and their futures jeopardized.' This isn't their war. They are the victims just as much as we are."

He took a deep breath in an effort to gather his composure before going on. "I got up and turned off the TV. Then I walked into the bedrooms of my children and knelt beside their beds and simply watched them sleep for a while, not really thinking anything, just feeling. Feeling gratitude and love. It was so peaceful. I carried that feeling back with me to the family room. I turned off the lamp, and in the dark quiet of the room I knelt and prayed. Even though I am well acquainted with prayer, I very seldom take the time to kneel. It seems I'm always too busy. Most of the time I pray in my mind and heart and count that as a sincere prayer. This time, however, I felt such gratitude and humility, I had to kneel and speak with my voice so I could appropriately express my thanks and my thoughts to God.

"I thanked Him for the simple blessing of letting me be who I am. I thanked Him for sight and sound, for a body that is strong and a mind that is healthy. I thanked him for the books and the music that touch our lives and educate us. I thanked Him for my home and my job. Then I thanked Him for the most important things in my life, my wife and my children. And I thanked Him for allowing us to live in this country. As I prayed, I began to understand that I had everything in this world that mattered. I had my health, a family that loved me, a home that was comfortable, and I had freedom.

"I stayed on my knees then, and I prayed for the people in Afghanistan who have to live like they do because of those who control them. I prayed for their little children, that they might not go hungry and might know, someday, the warmth of a home and the peace of freedom. I prayed for those who died that day in the Trade Center and the Pentagon. I prayed for the people who have to go on in life without them.

"Finally, at the end, I prayed that I could let go of the guilt I felt inside because my comrades died performing their duty while I lived. When I finished praying, I felt I had matured beyond the man I had been before I knelt. I was wiser now. The hate I had felt an hour ago was no longer a part of me."

He laid his shovel down, sat on a piece of concrete, and was silent for a moment. Then he spoke again. "Before I could lift myself up off my knees, the answer to my request to be released from guilt was answered and I felt it being lifted from my heart." He raised his hand up into the air and spread his fingers. "Just as I feel the breeze flow through my fingers now, I felt the guilt flow from my body. And in an instant, it was gone, and I felt tremendous peace."

His eyes met mine. "I don't know how else to explain it," he sighed. The emotion had drained him.

"I think your explanation is perfect." I felt as if I have just heard the most beautiful sermon ever taught, about gratitude and appreciation.

I sat down next to him. "Yesterday," I said, "I overheard a volunteer talking with one of the truck drivers about the firemen who had died inside the towers. He, along with a group of people, were working their way down the smoke-filled stairs. The fear they felt, he said, was intensified as the smell of jet fuel became so strong they began to feel light-headed. They knew they had to get out of there but still had about thirty floors yet to descend. It was at that point that they saw the firefighters moving up the stairs, quickly, in spite of the fact that they were loaded down with gear.

"I listened as he explained to the other man that he had never really met a fireman before that day, and probably wouldn't have paid much attention if he had. In his own words, he said, 'I didn't feel that we traveled in the same circle. I was in finance. They were in the fire station downtown. But that day, they were angels from heaven and their concern was for a group of frightened people trying to get out of a burning building. They took the time to make sure everyone was okay before moving on. They were some of the most compassionate and gentle men I had ever met, and we all felt the reassurance of their presence.'

"I had to smile when the truck driver looked at him in a stern sort of way and said, 'You sound surprised as you use those words to describe the firemen.'

"The man seemed a little embarrassed but went on to explain that if he would have been asked to describe a fireman a week ago, those two words would not have even been considered. But that day, he said he had met at least thirty of them and they were all the same. They were all compassionate, gentle and brave beyond any doubt. He explained that he couldn't describe what he saw in their faces as they moved up the stairs. He only knew what he saw was not fear."

Tears began streaming down Lenny's face as he listened.

"I read an article once, written by Ernie Pyle, the great correspondent in World War II," I continued. "In the article Mr. Pyle was describing the atmosphere of a room where thirty-five men were seated and being briefed on an assigned bombing mission. These men knew how dangerous this assignment was and knew the odds of their returning. In this article he talked of what he felt in that room, or rather, what he felt in those men sitting in that room.

"'What I felt,' he wrote, 'was *a profound reluctance to give up the future.'*

"That's what the man saw in the faces of those firefighters; a profound reluctance to give up the future. That's what I see in your face, Lenny, and you had to live because your work was just beginning, while they were finishing theirs."

"Thank you for telling me that." His voice was sincere. "You will never know how much your friendship means to me." He wiped his eyes with a red dotted kerchief and I wiped mine with the back of my hand.

"Anybody here?" shouted Chris's voice from behind a pile of rubble.

"Only us firemen," I shouted back, as Lenny quickly smudged his face with his dirty glove, trying to cover up any clean streaks that might have been left by the tears.

"Do I look okay?" he asked quietly.

I had to laugh. It was almost comical. He was concerned that he should look as dirty and smudged as possible, a complete contradiction to the term, *do I look okay?* "You look great," I told him, and I meant what I said.

"You probably really think I'm a big baby by now," he scoffed.

"I think you are just what you are supposed to be. That's what makes you such a good firefighter. If you become calloused and indifferent then you are no longer effective, and that's when it's time to hang up the hat. I think you have a long career ahead of you."

"It's almost 3:30 PM, guys. Are you going to take a break?" Chris asked.

I looked at my watch, amazed the time had gone so quickly. "I promised Bob I would meet him at 3:00 PM. It's his last day here. He has to be to work tomorrow. Talk to you two later."

Carefully I made my way back to the area where Bob and I were supposed to meet but he wasn't there. I picked up a bottle of water and some snacks from the table by the tent and sat down to wait for him. My feet were beginning to get sore from rubble jumping so I took off my boots and set them to the side. My feet instantly felt relief. My body simply felt fatigue.

"Mr. Carter!" I heard my name called and looked in the direction the sound had come from. A little girl was waving her arm. The beautiful smile on her face told me it was Shellie, the little girl who had lost her doll. I waved back as I stood up and walked over to greet her.

She held up the doll. "See my new doll, Mr Carter!" Her excitement was evident as I crossed the yellow tape and knelt down beside her. She wrapped her arms around my neck, accidentally pushing my hat back off my head, and gave me a little girl hug. I was touched.

"What a beautiful doll. What is her name?" I asked as I picked up my hat and placed it on Shellie's head.

"I didn't forget, Mr. Carter," she giggled. "Her name is Addie. She likes her name very much. She wants me to thank you for helping me buy her."

"You're welcome, Addie," I said, touching the doll only lightly, not wanting to get it dirty.

She giggled again, then took her small hand and placed it on my cheek. She looked me in the eye and said, softly, so only she and I could hear, "My other doll was named Sarah and she is in heaven now. She's just fine, so you don't need to worry about her anymore. Thank you, Mr. Carter for being my friend, and thank you for Addie." Then she leaned forward and gave me a kiss on the forehead.

"Thank you for being my friend, too, Shellie. I know someone in heaven who loves dolls named Sarah. I'll bet Heavenly Father made sure they got together."

"Do you think so?" Her eyes were wide with excitement.

"Yes, I think so."

Just then, Shellie's mother walked over to join us. I noticed a camera in her hand as I stood up to greet her. "Would you mind if I took a picture of the two of you together while Shellie still has your hat on?" she asked.

"Not at all," I grinned, kneeling down beside Shellie.

"Put your arm around her and bring your faces a little closer together," she suggested.

Trying hard not to get Shellie's clothes too dirty, I put my arm carefully around her. She was less afraid of getting dirty. She put her free arm around my neck and we smiled as I heard the snap of the camera.

"One more," said Shellie's mother. "This time look at each other." Shellie giggled and I smiled. We looked at each other and the camera snapped again.

"Thank you for taking this time for us. Shellie wanted to come and show you her new doll and to let you know that she named her Addie. She insisted that she talk to you, by herself, and I'm just glad we found you so she could."

"How did you know my name?" I asked, knowing we hadn't exchanged names that day, except for Shellie's.

"Your fire department business card was caught in the fold of one twenty-dollar bill," she explained. "I was so happy to see it because I had failed to ask your name when we talked and I knew Shellie would never be content until she could see you again and introduce you to Addie."

I didn't usually put my cards in the pockets of my pants because they get bent, but somehow, for some reason one was there and found its way into the money clip.

I've often wondered if destiny is a part of life. Perhaps Shellie needed to come back and we needed to talk about dolls and friendship, not only for her but also for me.

"I'm glad you brought Addie to meet me," I smiled at Shellie. "And, thank you, Shellie's mother, for bringing her here."

Shellie began to laugh. "Her name is Adrianne, not Shellie's mother. But she is my mom."

"I'm so sorry, I was so concerned about learning your name I forgot you didn't know mine either," Adrianne said. Then she went on to explain a little about herself.

"My husband worked in the Trade Center, on the main floor. He wasn't there that day because he had just had back surgery two days before. He was still in the hospital or I think he would have been right there making sure everyone else was out before he thought of himself. One of his best friends who was a police officer, was killed. The officer had wrapped his arms around two people, protecting them from the debris as he led them to a safer place, and then he told them to hurry out of the area. He made sure they were on their way before he turned back to do his job.

"One of those people whose life he saved was my brother. I don't know why I was so lucky but I'll always be grateful." She smiled through her tears and shook my hand. "Thank you again for all you've done for Shellie. You didn't need to but you did, and I will always be grateful to you for helping a little girl you didn't even know, through a real crisis in her life."

"I only ask for one favor in return," I said. "When you get those pictures developed, will you give me a print of the two you just took? I want a picture of the little girl who helped me through my crisis too."

"I'd be more than happy to do that. We're going to the hospital to visit Shellie's father right now and I'm going to drop these off at the store on our way. He wants these pictures so we can frame them and put them on Shellie's wall in her bedroom."

They waved goodbye as they turned to leave. Then Shellie turned back and waved one more time. She reminded me of Kaylee when she was that age and I suddenly felt a twinge of homesickness. I turned to see if Bob was at the "retreat," knowing he could cure my ailment. But the slab of concrete sat vacant. I checked my watch. It was 4:00 PM.

I decided while I waited I'd give Shana a call. I had memorized her number so all I had to do was find which pocket my cell phone was in and then dial. She answered on the second ring.

"Hello,"

"Hi." I never was good at talking to girls on the phone when I was a teenager and I hadn't improved with age.

"You sound tired,"

"I feel better now that I'm talking to you." That seemed to go all right. Maybe if I talked to her long enough I'd catch on. "Do you think you'll be hungry about eight o'clock tonight?"

"I think eight o'clock would be a good time to be hungry. Why don't I take you to an American restaurant that serves the best steak you've ever eaten?" I liked her suggestion.

"Do we have to wait until eight o'clock to get hungry if we are going to have steak?" I asked, my mouth watering already.

"We could make it seven-thirty."

"Sounds good, I'll pick you up. See you then, bye."

"See you then." The phone went silent as Shana hung up on the other end. I left my phone on for a few minutes, holding onto the feeling that made me tingle when I talked to her.

I was just putting the phone back into my pocket when I heard the sirens in the background. I watched the ambulance as it passed and continued on in the direction that made my heart jump. That was the direction Bob had gone this morning. I quickly pulled on my boots and followed the ambulance's trail as it made its way through a rough road that had been crudely cut by the trucks and heavy equipment. As I got closer I could see the EMT's leaning over a large man lying on a stretcher. Blood was running down his face. His coat was torn and covered with blood along with the right leg of his pants.

"Stay with me now, I'm going to give you something intravenously to relieve the pain," one EMT was saying, "but I need you to stay awake, OK?"

The other EMT was reporting back to the hospital by the small walkie-talkie connected to his shirt. "The patient is approximately forty years old, 6' 4", two hundred and eighty pounds. First examination shows a head injury, cracked ribs, evidence of a broken right leg, and right hand. Vitals are erratic due to signs of trauma." He proceeded to report the blood pressure and heart rate and that they had begun an intravenous pain medication.

"I'm a friend of his," I told the EMT, "and I've had training. Is there anything I can do to help?"

"Keep him awake for us, he's got a concussion and we need to try and stabilize him before we transport."

"His blood pressure is dropping and his heart beat is becoming more erratic. He's going into shock. Let's get him out of here," whispered the other EMT.

"Bob," I said gently, "we're going to take you to the hospital. Everything's going to be all right, buddy, just stay awake and talk to me."

"Can't talk," he whispered, "hurts too much." The perspiration of pain was evident in his face.

"OK, I'll do the talking. You just blink your eyes once in awhile. The rest of the time keep them open."

We got him into the ambulance and hooked up to the machines. The EMT's made him as comfortable as possible, turned on the sirens and headed for the nearest hospital. I talked and Bob dutifully blinked his eyes. I told him about the man I'd met earlier and repeated to him the story that had been told to me. All the time I talked, I watched the machine as it recorded his vital signs. His blood pressure was still shooting up and down because of the trauma to his body. His heart rate had stabilized slightly.

"His right leg has a bad break just below the knee cap." The EMT directed my eyes to the swollen and distorted leg.

"How bad we won't know until they x-ray."

A voice, coming from the walkie-talkie, then drew his attention away from the conversation. He pressed the button and gave the hospital our expected arrival time which was about five minutes, and updated the information on Bob's vital signs.

By the time we got to the hospital, the medication had kicked in and Bob was feeling less pain.

"Call my wife, Jeremy." His voice was strained. "Number's in my wallet."

They stopped me at the "No Admittance" door and wheeled him through to surgery. I needed Bob's wallet so I could get his phone number. I hurried back to the nurse's station and explained my problem. Within two minutes I had Bob's wallet in my hand. I found the card with the information I needed. I took out my cell phone and started to dial. Before I had finished, the two EMT's came through the "No Admittance" doors. They stopped long enough before climbing back into the ambulance to thank me for helping, reassuring me that his condition wasn't critical.

A nurse then appeared with Bob's clothes in a hospital bag. "Mr. Goldberg is in surgery, but we need a release form filled out by a family member. Have you contacted his wife yet?"

"I'm doing that right now," I said. "But before I push 'send,' can you give me any information on his condition? I don't want to alarm his wife unnecessarily."

"If they don't find anything unexpected, he should be just fine. He's a healthy man. I think you would be safe to tell her he is going to be all right." She smiled and left me in charge of Bob's belongings.

It dawned on me that I didn't even know Mrs. Goldberg's first name. Inside the wallet I found a very nice picture of her, but no name. I decided *Mrs. Goldberg* would have to do for now and I punched "send." The phone rang four times. On the fifth ring, the answering machine picked up.

"Hello, you have reached the Goldberg residence, please leave a message."

"Where are you, Mrs. Goldberg?" I said under my breath. At the sound of the beep I recited all the information she would need, to the answering machine. As I hung up the phone I turned the card over and on the back was written, *Nadine's cell phone number.* I prayed her cell phone was turned on. I dialed and waited.

"Hello,"

"Mrs. Goldberg, this is Jeremy Carter..."

"Well, hello Jeremy, Bob has told me so much about you... Jeremy, is something wrong?"

"Bob has been injured and he's in the hospital. He is going to be fine so you don't need to worry..."

"Which hospital, Jeremy?" Her voice was shaking.

I gave her the name and address.

"I'm only about ten minutes from there. Wait for me, I'll be right there."

"I'm not going anywhere. Just come through the emergency entrance doors. I'll be here."

"Thank you, Jeremy." The phone went silent as she hung up.

I made one more call to Shana's cell phone and left a message, at the sound of the beep explaining the situation. I asked if she would meet me at the hospital, pushed the "one" key to save, and the pound key to disconnect. It's a complicated world we live in.

Nadine was accurate when she said she was ten minutes away. Precisely ten minutes from the time she hung up her phone, she walked through the emergency doors. Her shiny, black hair was much shorter than it was in the picture, but I recognized her face immediately. She was at least 6 feet tall and carried herself as if she were proud of that fact. Her long legs were accentuated in the pantsuit she had on. I could tell by the cut of her clothes that they were expensive but she wore them as if it didn't matter. Nothing fancy, just practical. I wouldn't call her attractive as much as striking. Her face showed deep concern as she reached out her hand. "Jeremy Carter?"

I nodded.

"I'm Nadine Goldberg. Thank you for waiting. Any word yet as to Bob's condition?"

"Nothing yet," I answered.

A nurse who was waiting for Nadine's signature, interrupted before I could say any more. She explained the forms to us and indicated where they needed to be signed. Gently she led Nadine to a chair where she could sit and fill them out. Then she gave her a sympathetic smile. "I'm sorry. I know this is the last thing you want to be bothered with at this time, but it's necessary. I'll be back in a few minutes to pick them up."

"I hate filling these things out," Nadine grimaced. She looked at the forms for a minute, then gave a deep sigh. "How bad is it, Jeremy? Tell me what to expect."

I offered her a chair. "Expect that he will be OK. He was in a lot of pain until the pain medication went to work. His right leg is broken just below the knee and, possibly, his right hand. There may be some cracked or broken ribs and he has a concussion."

Nadine sat silent for a few minutes, letting what I had told her register. "At least he's alive," she said finally. "And, right now, that's all that matters. I can handle the rest."

I knew she could. I watched as she filled out the necessary forms and concluded that she was a woman of strength. Yet under the surface I could tell she was frightened.

It was almost 6:30 PM when the Doctor came out of surgery. His cap was wet with perspiration and his gown slightly spattered with blood. "Well," he smiled, "he's all put back together. He's going to be just fine."

Tears of relief flowed freely from Nadine's eyes. "How broken up was he?" she tried to smile back.

"He has a slight concussion which means he has a hard head. He took quite a blow. His right hand is in a cast. His right leg is in suspension for a pretty bad break just below the knee. He has four cracked ribs, but his sense of humor is intact. You can visit him now, if you like. Don't be too shocked when you see him. He has a swollen eye that will be black and blue by morning. He's pretty bruised up and sore tonight, but tomorrow will be the worst day. After he gets through tomorrow, he'll show a lot of improvement. They will be moving him to a room in a few minutes so you can tag along. Then you'll know where to find him for the next few days."

"Thank you Doctor," we both spoke at once.

"Let me tell you," he chuckled, "under the influence of local antiseptic, that man kept us all in stitches, using medical terms, of course. I'll check on him again in about an hour. Right now I think I'm ready for a steak." He waved and was gone.

The clock on the wall indicated it was 6:35 PM. I had a date for steak at 7:30. I thought of canceling, then decided to wait until I saw how Bob was doing.

The nurse motioned for us to follow her. She took us to a small cubicle where the curtains were drawn. We stepped through.

"Hi guys," Bob said with a slight slur in his voice. "The room is a little small but the drinks are on the house." He gazed at Nadine. "Hi baby doll, you are sure a sight for a sore eye."

"I think you are going to be just fine," she smiled as she leaned over the bed to give him a kiss.

"Where are the kids?" Bob asked.

"I was already in the city," Nadine explained as she held his hand. "I called your mother to let her know about the accident. She offered to go sit the kids until I got home. Which reminds me, I need to call her back." She pulled the phone out of her purse and began dialing a number. She got the answering machine, so left a message, letting Bob's mother know how he was and said she would call back when she had a room number.

"Your mother probably took them out for pizza," Nadine chuckled. Then her voice grew serious. "How did this happen, Bob?"

"Not sure. One minute I was moving some pieces of steel from the rubble and the next minute I was looking at stars, and my whole right side was in excruciating pain. He looked at his wife. "Does this mean I can't go out and play tomorrow?"

"Correct statement," she replied. "How do you feel? Are you in any pain?"

"He smiled. "Just don't tell any jokes. If I laugh it hurts my ribs. How do you like my new leg swing? It's non-refundable, so we have to keep it."

A nurse opened the curtain and stepped in to check him. "Between the pain medication and the local stuff they gave him," she said, "he has been one happy guy. It'll wear off by tomorrow so enjoy him while you can. We're going to move him upstairs to room 304 now, if you would like to follow us."

The male nurses prepared the bed and patient for transport and I stepped out in the hall to pick up the bag holding Bob's clothes. My cell phone rang while I was in the hall.

"Jeremy? It's Mom. I just called to see how you're doing."

Hi, Mom. I'm glad you called. I'm fine, but I'm here at the hospital with a friend of mine who was injured today."

"Very badly?"

"Bad enough, but it could have been much worse." I explained his injuries to her and told her how tough he was. Then I found myself telling her about the whole day. I told her about Shellie's doll and Mattie's statue. Most of all, I needed to tell her about Shana. I told her how we met and how wonderful she was.

"Mom, I think I'm in love with her." I hadn't realized how important it was for me to share my feelings for Shana with my mom until I had done so.

"Oh Jeremy, I'm so happy for you. She sounds wonderful. Will we get a chance to meet her soon?"

"I sure hope so, Mom. How's everything going there?"

"Everything is just fine. We'll be glad when you come home. Kyle took Kaylee to the movies and Dad is out in his workshop. I've thought about you every minute today, until finally I just decided if I was thinking about you so much then I must need to call and find out why. Now I know, you needed to tell me something very important."

"I'm so grateful that you're my mother." I knew she couldn't see my smile through the phone, but maybe she could after all. The emotions of the day were catching up with me, and somehow, my mom always knew when I needed to talk to her. "Thanks for always being there for me."

"Love you, Jeremy."

"Love you, Mom. Tell the kids and Dad 'hi' for me. See you in a few days."

The sound of my mother's soothing voice had always brought a feeling of calm when there was turmoil in my life. Bob's accident had affected me more than I realized.

I smiled to myself as I made a mental note to recharge my phone when I got back to the apartment. I just might need to talk to Mom again. I wonder if men ever outgrow their need for their mothers. I hope not.

By the time I got to the room, Bob was looking fairly comfortable. And, to my surprise, Shana was there. She and Nadine were talking as if they had known each other forever.

"Glad to see you could make it." Bob's booming voice had been demoted to a soft tone. "We went ahead and started the party without you."

Shana reached out and took my hand in hers. "I'm glad you could make it, too."

We talked for a while and Bob seemed to be getting sleepy. He needed to rest so I asked Nadine if there was anything we could do for her before we left.

"No, I think I'll get a taxi and go as soon as Bob goes to sleep. Then I'll come back tomorrow when he's grumpy," she laughed, the signs of emotional fatigue showing on her face.

"Jeremy," Bob said, half asleep, "I need you to put Nadine safely in a taxi for me."

"I'll do that right now. You go ahead and go to sleep."

"Thanks buddy, goodnight," and he was asleep.

I called two taxis from Bob's room and by the time we were at the entrance of the hospital they were waiting in front. I made sure Nadine was in her cab. We waved goodbye, then climbed in ours.

"Where to?" The taxi driver asked.

"I don't think they will let me in the restaurant looking like this," I laughed, and gave the taxi driver the address to my apartment.

"While you shower and change, I think I'll just sit by this beautiful window and relax," said Shana, as we entered the living room of the apartment.

When I came back into the room less than fifteen minutes later, she was sitting in the chair looking longingly at the statue she was holding in her hands.

"It's beautiful. I wonder where they got it?"

"It's mine," I answered. Then I told her the story.

"It's a true story with a happily-ever-after ending," she sighed. "The statue only adds to the wonderment of it all."

She set the statue down gently on the table and reached out to me. Putting her arms around my neck, she pulled me close and looked into my eyes. "You are my hero, Jeremy Carter," she whispered. Her lips met mine with a sweet and tender kiss… a kiss that lingered. I didn't want to let her go but my grandmother's wise advice, given to me long ago, on the respect of womanhood, disrupted the mood and I reluctantly broke the connection.

"I think we should call for a taxi now," my voice sounding a little shaky.

Shana smiled, picked up the phone and dialed. We only had to wait a few minutes for the taxi to arrive. She gave him an address and he delivered us to the restaurant that served the best steaks in New York City, according to Shana. I paid him and we walked into the restaurant an hour and a half later than we had planned. For all that had happened, that wasn't too bad.

After we were seated and had ordered our steaks, I told Shana about my mother. I explained about my mother's wisdom and insight. Then I told her that my mother would like to meet her soon. Did she think that could be arranged? My heart was pounding.

"I think I would love to meet your mother." Her smile was soft and her eyes so clear I could see my reflection in them.

We talked about life and coincidences. We wondered if Bob's life had a purpose beyond what we could see. It was the second time he had escaped death. We discussed fate and destiny and if it had played a part in bringing us together. We talked about Kaylee and Kyle. We talked about my grandmother and her advice. Then we talked about love.

"I had a lovely evening, once again," Shana said as I walked her back to her apartment. "I also think you had a very wise grandmother,"

"I don't think my grandmother would mind if I kissed you tonight," I said as I brought her close and kissed her gently, but with the warmth of passion that stirred inside of me.

When I looked into her eyes, I could see love there, and I was happy.

When I climbed into bed, I lay there for a long time just thinking about the day. A lot had happened since this morning. I remembered Lenny saying that after his prayer he felt wiser and older. I remembered something my mother had written on a note and placed in my room when I was seventeen. *You can learn knowledge, but wisdom cannot be taught. It can only be experienced to be understood.* It was great advice then and it is great advice now. Its concept doesn't change with time, only the depth of its meaning.

The events of the day had instilled in me a wisdom that overshadowed all education. A wisdom that brought with it gratitude and peace of mind, just as it had for Lenny.

When I closed my eyes, I saw the white book again. This time it didn't seem to trouble me. I just accepted the fact that it was there. It was lying on a beautiful white doily that covered a small, round, mahogany table. I could tell that more pages had been added to its thickness. It was close enough for me to almost reach out and touch it, but it wasn't time yet; and I fell asleep.

Authors' Notes

On September 11, we were reunited with humility. That day we renewed our feeling of love and respect for God and each other. Sometimes we are so busy looking out there beyond ourselves, we miss the opportunity to look within. It isn't until something stirs our senses that we begin to appreciate the priceless gifts of freedom and country. With appreciation comes gratitude. Gratitude is a gift we give to God when we acknowledge what He has given us.

I know of a young woman who lives with a rare skin disease known as E.B. (Recessive Dystrophic Epidermolysis Bullosa). Her fingers and toes have become crippled as well as webbed together. Her skin cannot repair itself. The disease causes deformities and scarring in the mouth and throat. Her esophagus scarred shut and was replaced with a piece of her colon when she was a little girl. Because she no longer has a stomach valve, reflux is causing her vocal chords to slowly erode. Her tongue is so scarred, she cannot lift it, so it is difficult for her to enunciate her words. But with hard work and determination she has learned to sing, at least for now. She has a beautiful high soprano voice. When she sings, her voice is angelic in its purity and sweetness.

There are no words that can adequately explain the feeling that comes over an audience when she sings. But when her song is finished, it is an emotional audience that rises to their feet to applaud her.

What impresses me most about her is not the fact that she can sing in spite of all the physical reasons why she shouldn't be able to, but how grateful she is for that one gift that she has been given. She has the ability to see far beyond the disease that causes her physical pain and limitations. She doesn't dwell on what has been taken away from her but what has been given to her. Gratitude has brought her peace of mind and heart.

Gratitude is a sign of humility and recognition of the gifts we have been given. It is appreciation and respect. It shows itself in service and selflessness. A grateful heart is felt not only by the person wearing it, but by anyone standing nearby.

People who live without gratitude are unhappy people. Nothing can please them. They will never be happy with what they have and they will never have enough. They are selfish, disrespectful and arrogant. They are miserable and miserable to be around.

You don't have to look far to find something to be grateful for. Just look inside yourself. Then, look around you. Then look at the world.

We have a country that gives us the freedom to be whatever we want, if we want to put forth the effort. When we do, we show gratitude.

We have the freedom to live our lives in any way we choose. When we choose to live a life of service and find joy in giving, we show gratitude.

We have the right to build our own future, to be successful and prosperous. When we do so with integrity and honesty, we show gratitude.

We have the responsibility to protect, defend, and honor our country. When we do so with courage and bravery, we show gratitude.

We have the privilege of owning property. When we show respect for this land, we express gratitude.

We have the gift of family. When there is love in our home, we are showing gratitude.

In our country we have so much to be grateful for. In our lives we have so much to be grateful for. God has given us everything. It's a waste of life to be ungrateful.

Those who walk with gratitude
walk in peace and harmony.
Their path is paved with kindness.
Their journey filled with joy.

Chapter Seven

Step into the Arena

When I opened my eyes Monday morning, my first thought was of Bob. It was 7:30 AM. I wondered if they let visitors in around 8:30 AM.

Breakfast was a quick glass of juice and a slice of buttered toast. Anxious to get on my way, I was dressed and in the taxi at 7:45 AM, a bag with my firemen's clothing in my hand. I thought of John's jacket still lying on the back of the chair in the apartment, only after it was too late to go back and get it. I would have to take care of that tomorrow.

The halls of the hospital were empty when I arrived. Relieved, I quickly stepped onto the elevator without being seen and entered Bob's room at 8:30 AM. He was sound asleep. I sat in the chair next to his bed and waited for him to wake up.

He was a pitiful sight. His eye had turned dark purple and was even more swollen than it had been the night before. New bruises had appeared along the right side of his face. He looked like he had been in a fight. He moaned as he shifted his weight. Then his body relaxed again and he snored on.

As I watched him sleep, my thoughts went back to the day he'd sat next to me on the cot in the Salvation Army tent and told me his story. I couldn't imagine him being the arrogant man he had described to me that day. I made a mental note to ask Nadine. The Bob I knew was caring and kind with a sense of humor that delighted everyone around him. And he was genuine in his friendship.

The door opened and a nurse came in to take his vital signs. She was startled to find a visitor sitting at the bedside of her patient.

"I didn't expect visitors so early in the morning!"

"I'm sorry if I frightened you," I apologized, "but I wanted to see how he was doing before I went to work. How is he?"

"He's doing better than he should. He was really banged up. Look at the bruises along the side of his face. That's the way he looks down the right side of his body. He's lucky he has so much muscle. He's lucky to be alive."

"Has he been in much pain?" I asked.

"He has a pain pump so he can administer his own medication as needed." She showed me how it worked. "As you can see, he has used very little. I think today that will change." She proceeded to write on Bob's chart the information she was gathering as she checked him. When she touched the area around his eye, he moaned and his eyes opened. "Must be time for breakfast, you after my blood again?"

"Not this time, darlin'," the nurse laughed. "Got enough from you last time to take me through lunch. I'll bet you're hungry though."

"Not if the only thing on the menu is blood, I'm not."

"How about some juice, coffee, a boiled egg and some toast?" she asked as she carefully laid his arm by his side.

"Well, if that's all you have, then it will have to do," he gave her a wink.

"You have a visitor." She motioned to me, smiled and left.

"I hope you're feeling better than you look," I greeted him.

"I was hoping I looked better than I feel," he moaned. "I'm glad you're here, Jeremy. There's something I've got to talk to you about while we're alone. Well, actually two things. It's just that one is more important than the other."

I pulled my chair up close to the bed so he didn't have to move his head to look at me. "What is it that's so important?" I asked.

"First, they came in twice during the night and drew blood from me. I asked myself, why would they need to draw so much blood for treatment of an injury unless, in their initial draw, they found something? I need you to do some snooping around for me, OK?"

"I'll see what I can find out." My stomach tightened as I spoke. I didn't want anything else to happen to him. I wanted him to have a good long life. He deserved it. It was probably nothing anyway, just a precaution because of the extent of his injuries.

"The next thing I want to talk to you about may sound strange, but it happened and I need to tell you. Yesterday, when I woke up and found myself on the ground in pain, a man was there beside me. He told me not to be afraid, that in spite of the pain I was in, I would be all right. I felt his hand on my forehead and I looked into his eyes. Almost immediately I felt a peace come over me. A peace I've never felt before. And I knew I could handle the pain until the medics got there. Do you know what I'm saying here?"

I nodded. "What did the man look like?" I asked, knowing all the time in my heart who he was.

"Let's see, he was about your height. He had a slim build, dark wavy hair and dark eyes. There was something about his eyes. Calmness is how I would explain it. Gee, Jeremy, I know it sounds crazy. I mean if I hadn't experienced it myself, I would think it sounded crazy. But I did experience it. I just wish I could understand it."

"I think you understand it well enough. Don't try to analyze it, just allow what happened to be remembered in your heart."

Nadine came striding into the room just then, bringing with her a basket of fruit and two teenage boys. They had to be twins and looked about the age of Kyle. Behind a huge bouquet of flowers a younger version of Nadine made her way to the small table by the bed and carefully set the vase down. Then she reached over and gave her father a kiss just above his swollen eye.

"Good morning Dad," she said, tears gathering in her eyes. "How are you feeling? You look... well, let's just say you've looked better."

The two boys stood silently. Their faces had paled visibly at the sight of their father.

"Did you sleep well last night?" Nadine asked as she kissed him gently, then ran her fingers through his hair in an attempt to smooth it down.

"I'm afraid I was much too popular to get any sleep, baby doll," he smiled with effort. "Why don't you introduce Jeremy to our children."

"Jeremy, I'd like you to meet our daughter, Tracee. She is nineteen and going to Harvard. She's going to be a lawyer and I think she'll be a credit to the profession."

Tracee blushed as she shook my hand. "I'm glad to meet you Jeremy. You'll have to forgive my mother's introduction. It's the only one she's memorized so far." Tracee had her father's sense of humor, but her mother's striking looks. She was dressed in Levi's and a sweatshirt. Her intelligent face showed no signs of makeup except for a little lipstick.

"Derek and David, meet Jeremy Carter, a good friend of your father's. Jeremy, these are our sons. They are seventeen and will, one day decide what they're going to be when they grow up. But, for now, their lives revolve around basketball, which, by the way, they are very good at."

Derek and David each shook my hand and smiled the same smile. "Which one is which?" I asked. I looked from one to the other. They were identical. They, too, resembled their mother, handsome boys with black hair and dark eyes.

"The one in the blue sweater is David. The one in the t-shirt is Derek. That's how we tell them apart," laughed Tracee. "David has a more refined taste in clothes."

"What she doesn't know won't hurt her," whispered David, or Derek, in my ear.

"Thanks for being there to help our dad," one of the twins said. Then he turned to his father. "And you tell us not to fight."

"You should see the other guy," Bob remarked. He tried to shift his body, but moaned in pain at the attempt.

"Are you all right?" Nadine cried as she rushed to his side, not knowing what to do for him. His children gathered quickly around him.

"Are you in a lot of pain, Dad?" Tracee's face was tight with worry.

"Just when I try to move or breathe." Bob's voice was strained. Beads of perspiration appeared on his forehead. I watched as he pressed the little button on the pain medication tube that was attached to the needle in his arm. "But don't worry, it'll feel better when it quits hurting."

"The doctor said this would be your worst day," Nadine consoled him. "Just close your eyes and rest, we're not going anywhere."

"I'll check on you later, buddy," I told Bob, wiping the perspiration from his head with my hand. The pain medication was beginning to take effect and his body was relaxing. He gave me a weak smile.

"Don't wait so long to come around, next time."

"I'll be back this evening," I promised.

As I walked into the hall, Nadine followed me. "I can't thank you enough for what you have done," she said as she put her arms around me and gave me a hug. I felt her body go limp and she began to cry. I just held her and let her use my shoulder. After a few minutes she stepped back, wiping her face with her hands. I handed her my handkerchief.

"I don't usually do that," she admitted, gratefully accepting the handkerchief to wipe away the evidence of tears. "I can't tell you how much it has meant to me to have you here. I don't know if I could have handled it without you. Your friendship for Bob has reached out and touched his family. Thank you, Jeremy."

"It's Bob you should thank for our friendship," I replied. "He is the most genuine person I've ever met. Can I ask you something?"

"Of course."

I repeated to her the story Bob had told me about himself. "Was he really that bad?"

"He wasn't always that way. When I first married him, he was the man you met that day on those cots. But he soon forgot that part of himself as he climbed the ladder to success. I watched it happen and I could do nothing about it. He became obsessed with making money and the status it brought. In the attempt to give his family everything, he almost lost them." She didn't say anymore; she didn't have to.

"I understand," I said, giving her another hug. "I'll be back this evening."

I pushed through the doors of the hospital just as Shellie and her mother were stepping out of a taxi.

"Mr. Carter," shouted Shellie with glee, "What are you doing here? We have your pictures for you. They look really good, too. We're going to show them to my daddy now. Do you want to come and see him with us?"

"Please do," echoed Adrianne. "He would want to meet you. Are you visiting someone here?"

"A friend of mine was injured yesterday at Ground Zero, but he'll be fine," I answered. "I'd like, very much, to meet your daddy, Shellie. Show me the way."

She took hold of my hand and together the three of us walked back through the doors and to the room where a man lay in traction. "You didn't tell me it was this bad," I whispered to Adrianne.

"It isn't as bad as it looks," she whispered back, "but it's bad enough." She introduced me to her husband, Clint, a warm and friendly guy in spite of his present predicament. I could see where Shellie got her bright blue eyes and sandy hair. I sensed a special love in their relationship as a young family. There were several flower arrangements and plants decorating the room which told me he was either very well liked by friends and co-workers or they came from large families; or maybe it was both. "Three more days and then he can come home," Shellie boasted as she sat her doll beside her father on the bed.

"Not that she's counting," Clint smiled. "Today I'm supposed to be released from bondage here and if all goes well, I'll go home Thursday."

"Clint was in a car accident two weeks ago and the crack along his spine wasn't picked up in the first x-ray," said Adrienne. "A week ago yesterday, when he tried to get out of bed, his legs wouldn't hold his weight. They did emergency surgery that afternoon. If he had moved just right he would have been paralyzed for the rest of his life. They didn't want to take any chances."

We talked for several minutes more before Adrianne remembered the pictures. She took them out of her purse to show us. Then she reached into a bag she had carried in, and pulled from it two framed 5"x7"'s. "These are for you. This is so you will never forget us. We will never forget you."

I looked at the two pictures and I knew they would always be a reminder of a most extraordinary experience in my life. Shellie reached up and taking my hand, pulled me down so that we were eye to eye. "Put them where your heart can always see them," she instructed. Her voice was soft and filled with a child's emotion.

I gave her a gentle hug and answered, "I promise I will." Then, before my own emotions could surface, I thanked Adrianne for the pictures and wished Clint well in his recovery. I explained that I needed to get back to Ground Zero. They thanked me once again and I left.

It was 10:30 AM before I reached Ground Zero. I changed and stored my good clothing in the tent, then made my way to the area where Bob had been injured. I asked one of the workers if he had been there when it had happened.

"I was," he explained, "but I really didn't see it. My back was turned to him. It was the strangest thing, though." He set his shovel down and walked to within a foot of where rubble was stacked on top of more rubble. "The force of the blow knocked him from where he was standing, about in the middle of all that you see in front of you, to where I'm standing now. And almost immediately, the very spot where Bob had been working, caved in, taking with it several tons of concrete and rubble. Had he not been knocked out of the way, he would have been crushed under all that mess."

I stood there motionless, my spine tingling.

"I know what you're thinking," he said. "In a way, it's a testimony to us that we're being watched over while we work. Let me tell you how committed Bob is. As soon as he regained consciousness, he was determined to get up and get on with his job. If it hadn't been so serious, it would have been comical." He stopped talking for a minute and looked around him. Then he nodded, "There were eight of us working here when it happened. How many do you see working today?"

I counted. "Seven, with you."

"Right. Everyone just went right back to work, after Bob was safely in the ambulance. We all know that at any given time, the concrete and rubble could shift against the broken beams. We don't know if we will uncover a body or get injured ourselves, but the commitment to get rid of this reminder of September Eleventh is greater than our own safety." He paused and looked at me, then smiled. "But, of course, I'm not telling you anything you don't already know, am I?"

I smiled as our eyes met. "Did you, by chance, see another man; tall, dark wavy hair, with Bob right after he was hurt?"

"Now that you mention it, there was. He knelt beside Bob and talked to him. His voice was so quiet I couldn't hear what he said, but Bob seemed to be less anxious after the man touched his forehead with his hand. The man stood up then and walked away. That's strange, I'd forgotten that until you mentioned it just now."

I thanked him, we shook hands and I let him get back to his own work.

The rest of the day as I worked, I paid more attention to the faces of the men around me. I watched Chris and Lenny and all the rest of the faces. What I saw was that same determination and commitment I had witnessed earlier in the faces of another group of men. We all wanted the same thing — to eradicate all the evidence that was a continual reminder of the horrendous crime committed against America.

Three small experimental robots, about the size of shoeboxes had been brought into the area where we were working. They were lowered into the gaps between collapsed buildings in search of bodies. Each robot carried a camera and specialized sensors that could detect body heat or colored clothing through the coats of gray dust. They could move through the broken glass and twisted steel to reach areas that were too dangerous for rescue workers or the rescue dogs to try to reach. We waited and watched, but during the six hours we were there working, they had found no bodies. It was disappointing for all of us.

"We have seen probably the smallest, most sophisticated piece of equipment that can be used in this search and rescue," Chris said solemnly, "with the ability to reach into the unreachable crevices, to find the unfindable, if there is such a word. Yet, they're coming up with nothing. Where are the bodies? Why can't they locate them?"

"Yesterday I was talking to a demolition worker," Lenny commented. "He told me that he and the rest of the members of his local worked around the clock, the first day, to remove a bridge between the two towers. They're still here, working every day helping to recover the bodies. He told me they're able to lift the steel and remove the debris. With each body they find, they stop and call in the police. One day they found twenty bodies. They're finding some, Chris." He put his arm around Chris's shoulder as he talked.

"I don't think they'll ever find all of them, there are so many hidden under thousands of tons of concrete and metal," I concluded.

It was 5:00 PM when we finally stopped for a break. While I walked toward a cool bottle of water and my slab of cement, I made a quick phone call to say hi to my kids. Kyle answered the phone. The sound of his voice reminded me how homesick I was. I had to make our conversation short because I had forgotten to plug in my cell phone again last night. He brought me up-to-date on life at home, then handed the phone to Kaylee before we lost our connection.

"Oh Dad," she said, "don't you wish you could have eyes that had x-ray vision so you would know right where to find those people who are still buried under all that stuff? I think about them all the time. There are still so many yet to find."

My phone began beeping. "You're cutting out, so your batteries are going. It's kind of creepy, Dad. When your batteries die, we'll be disconnected and not know what's happening to each other. And even though I know you're there, I can't talk to you again until your batteries are recharged and you can call. It makes me feel very lonely for you. Bye, I love you."

"I love you, Kaylee."

I put my phone back into my pocket, picked up a bottle of water and a snack. I found my "retreat," sat down and watched the cranes and bulldozers. They seemed small among the mounds around them. Above me a search dog was being transported from his search area across to the rest area. One end was attached to a stationary rope by two pulleys. The other end was threaded with a second rope that propelled the net into motion. The German Shepherd sat steady on the net as it moved through the air. The dog had just finished its twelve-hour shift and was going to the main tent for some rest.

His handler was there to greet him as he limped off the net once it reached ground level.

"Come on boy," he said gently, "time for a rest. We'll get some ointment on those paws and you'll feel better." He then lifted the dog into his arms and began to carry him.

I was touched as I watched the love and concern the exhausted handler had for his dog. I walked over to him, introduced myself, and asked if I could pet the dog.

"Sure," he said. "Hundreds of firefighters come up to us just to pet the dogs. I think it's their way of showing respect for the work these dogs do here every day."

"Flint, this is Jeremy. Jeremy, meet Flint, one smart German Shepherd. And I'm Allen."

"How do you train them?" I asked. As I ran my fingers through the dog's thick coat, I could sense the fatigue in him.

"Come with me. I'm going to get Flint some medical attention and something to eat. Then I'll tell you how it works."

As we walked, Allen explained that the dogs were.... being housed in the aircraft hanger of a convention center. "Crews have come from as far away as Florida and Puerto Rico to help search for survivors." He motioned me to one of the many tents that had been staked for the dogs. Flint found a spot and lay down. I could see the bottom of his one paw had been burned.

"That's from the heat of the steel," Allen said as he pointed to the paw.

One of the vets who had volunteered his services set food and water in front of Flint, then lifted his leg.

"How was his paw today?" asked the vet as he inspected the sore paw. "Looks raw again. I think we'd better keep him in tomorrow." He ran his hands over Flint's legs and belly for any sign of new injuries. Next he checked his nose.

"We see a lot of cut paws and noses as well as cuts on the legs," the vet explained to me before inserting the needle into Flint for a re-hydration drip. "We may treat as many as a hundred and fifty rescue dogs in one day because of the rough terrain they have to tread."

"The keen noses and acute hearing of these dogs will locate a survivor long before any of that high tech stuff they have," Allen explained. "They're trained to seek out the scent of a living person. They penetrate into the rubble as far as they can. Then they bark if they've picked up the scent. As you can see, they work without the respirators or masks so their eyes and noses have to be flushed out on a regular basis. Then we have to keep the dogs re-hydrated with saline. I'll share an interesting fact with you," he continued as we walked from the tent. "These dogs are trained to find survivors. They haven't found any. They sense the mood and become very stressed when they aren't successful, just like we humans. When that happens we have to get them away from the pile and play games with them. They don't like to be held in even for a day, injuries or not. They want to be out there searching. They want to find someone alive just as much as you and I do."

I had watched the dogs from day to day as they'd sniffed among and through the rubble. Not once had I even imagined their emotions. Not only had I not considered their emotions, but I hadn't realized their commitment or thought about the danger they were being placed in as they searched. If only there were more robots to help.

I told Allen about the robots. He had already seen them at work and was grateful they could reach places he didn't dare let the dogs venture into. But he made one comment that held true concerning their limitations.

"The robots will never replace human rescuers or the dogs, for that matter, in one very important aspect of rescue. They have no warmth, no feeling. Sometimes it's the human touch that makes the difference in the victim's chance of survival. It's the dog, once he finds the victim, then barks for help and stays by the victim's side until help comes, that inspires the will to live. It's a psychological thing that can't always be explained.

But, as human beings, we tend to need that warmth of touch, that sense of affection to survive not only in this situation, but in everyday life, it seems."

I agreed with him. I had seen proof of what he had just told me, many times. I thanked him for taking the time to talk with me and for giving me a deeper appreciation for the dogs who spend twelve hours a day without any protection, doing the job they had been trained so well to do. I shook his hand and let him go so he could get some well-deserved rest himself.

I thought about Bob's rescue and John's touch that had given him the strength to withstand the pain until the EMT's could get there. I needed to go to the hospital and check on a friend. Gathering together my gear, I set it in the tent until tomorrow. I picked up my bag of clothing, made sure the two framed pictures were still there, and left Ground Zero.

As I passed the bicycle, I paused and thought how Bob had helped me yesterday morning. Tonight I dusted it alone. Brown stems were all that was left of the flowers. I made a mental note to pick up some fresh ones and place them there in the morning.

When I arrived at the apartment, I removed my dirty clothes and threw them in the washer. They were so dirty they could stand up by themselves. I showered and dressed, plugged in the cell phone to recharge and took time to sit in the chair while I arranged the two pictures around the statue. Suddenly I felt very tired, not only physically but emotionally and mentally as well. I wanted to close my mind to this small world I had been living in for seven days, just for a few minutes. But I couldn't shut it out.

I hadn't listened to the news the past few days. I didn't know what was going on with the war against the terrorists except the little bits of information I heard at Ground Zero. I didn't know what was happening in the rescue attempts at the Pentagon. My mind was so filled with all that was happening here, it seemed like there was no room for any more. My head ached and my eyes felt like they were full of sand. I just needed to close them, but I couldn't even do that.

I reached over and picked up the picture of Shellie wearing my hat, her arm around my neck, both of us smiling at the camera, and I wanted to cry. I picked up the statue that Matty had given me and the tears began to flow. I let them fall freely, unable to lift my arms to wipe them away. I just sat there, the picture in one arm, the statue in the other, and cried. When I was finally able to release the emotion I had carried with me all day, I stopped.

I called for a taxi, then called Shana to tell her I would pick her up in five minutes. She seemed relieved to hear my voice. I wondered why, until I realized I had forgotten to call her earlier. The taxi was waiting as I hung up the phone.

Five minutes later the taxi stopped in front of Shana's apartment and she was standing there, waiting. I apologized immediately as soon as she got in. She kissed me lightly on the lips and said she understood. I really think she did.

I looked at her and asked, "Can I kiss you now?"

Her laugh was like soft, soothing music and I took her in my arms and kissed her, then I kissed her again. I felt the stress drain from my body as I held her and my world expanded just a little. I leaned my head back against the seat and closed my eyes and let the world move around me.

"You look so tired," she whispered in my ear. "Are you all right?"

"Now I am," I whispered back. "Thank you."

As we rode the elevator to the third floor, I explained to Shana Bob's concern about the extra blood they had taken during the night, and that he wanted me to do some snooping. "I wonder if his chart would show anything? Where do you think we would find it?"

"At the nurse's station, probably," she answered, a mischievous grin appearing on her face. "Shall we snoop?"

The elevator doors opened and we peeked out into the hall. "All clear," Shana spoke quietly out of the side of her mouth. "Look, there's no one at the nurse's station."

"This is too easy." I couldn't believe we could just walk up to the desk and steal a patient's chart without some resistance. "What the heck, let's go for it." We moved quickly toward the desk. Then, while Shana watched the hallways, I began looking for charts.

"I'll be with you in just a minute." A voice was heard from the other side of the counter facing away from us. Startled, we looked but still couldn't see anyone. Shana walked around the counter and there on the floor, on her knees, was a nurse. "Be careful," she said anxiously, "stay right there, I've lost my contact lens right around here." She made a circular motion with her finger.

"Let me help you," Shana said quickly as she dropped to her knees and started feeling the floor with her hand. While they searched, Shana asked the nurse what had happened, keeping her involved in conversation while I did the detective work. I found the chart just as the nurse cried with relief, "I found it! Thank Heaven I found it!" She stood, and finding her purse, reached in for the solution for her contact lens while I looked through the information on the chart. Just before the contact was popped back into her eye, the file was placed safely back into its slot.

"Now, what can I do for you?" she asked, blinking her eye in an effort to stabilize the contact.

"Just checking on a room number. Bob Goldberg?" She had already helped us more than she knew.

"Just to your right, room 304." She smiled so sweetly as she pointed, I almost felt guilty for what I had just done.

"Was there any information on the blood tests?" Shana whispered as we made our way to room 304.

"It's all in coded script, I swear," I said, "but I did see something I recognized. I think it has something to do with his white blood count."

"That could be serious." She stopped and looked at me.

"Then, maybe it's nothing," I said hopefully. I took her arm and guided her to Bob's room.

"I was just telling Nadine," Bob chuckled as we walked into the room, "that you are more aware of time than anyone I've ever met. And even though you didn't give me a specific time, you are always on auto-drive and you should be walking through the door just about now."

"He's telling the truth," Nadine laughed. "I swear!"

"I can't help it if I like knowing what time it is any given time of the day." The serious tone of my voice was mocked by the humor in my eyes. "How are you feeling?"

"Much better tonight, thank you. I've had to push the pump a little bit more today, but the nurse convinced me it would help my body heal faster if it didn't have to work with the stress of the pain. I think I believed her."

We spent the next half hour talking about the power of family and friendship, how the heart never stops growing as it fills with love, or shrinks and becomes cold when love is not present. Then I told Bob what I had found out about his accident. Nadine gasped and tightened her hold on Bob's hand. However, Bob didn't seem to be at all surprised.

"You are meant to live for awhile yet, good friend," I told him. "There is something important you have yet to do, apparently."

"One thing I needed to do was to refill my heart with love. I couldn't see what I was doing to myself and my family until a week ago when I began to see the me I had become. In saving my life, God saved a family. I have been warned and I have committed myself to be a kinder, gentler person. I have committed myself to love more and give more freely, to care less about success in my work and more about success in my family. Oh, and one more thing — to always have you as my friend. How am I doing so far?"

"I think you're doing just fine," I replied. I took his hand and held it for a moment, bonding a friendship that would last beyond life.

I decided not to say anything about our adventure to find Bob's chart. He seemed to have forgotten about his quest for the time being, and I couldn't give him any real answers to his question anyway. Shana and I promised to come back the next evening. There were hugs all around and we left Bob and Nadine alone to spend some time together.

"You look exhausted," Shana said when we were back in the hallway. "Let's just grab something in the hospital cafeteria and then I'll drop you off at your apartment and let you get some rest."

"I look that bad?"

"I'm afraid so. Even the cafeteria food will look good next to you." She punched the elevator button and, once we were on the first floor, she took my arm and led me through the doors to the cafeteria.

The food didn't look that bad. We had a pretty good selection. It actually tasted reasonably good.

"My boss called today," Shana said between bites. "The company has found a building in which to set up the business again. They've been able to locate temporary equipment for now and want me to start back to work tomorrow. For the first week we'll just be putting things in order, but by the end of October they plan to be fully operational again."

"How do you feel about that?" I asked.

"I'm not sure. It isn't the same as it was before. I don't have the same game plan I had before the attack." She paused for a moment before going on. "My mother tells me I've changed. My father hopes I've changed. I feel like I've changed."

Shana had never mentioned her parents to me before and I had never thought to ask. "Tell me about your parents," I said.

"Well, they live in upstate New York. They are very loving parents who worry about me constantly. I have two brothers, both younger, both married with families. The two of them have been on a personal quest, for the past five years, searching the kingdom, high and low, for a knight in shining armor who will rescue me from the evils of spinsterhood."

"Odd you should say that," I teased. "I have been knighted in porcelain, would that qualify me?"

Shana laughed. "I don't think they would even question authenticity of qualifications if they approved of the man. I think you are far above their expectations."

The conversation gave the cafeteria food the touch of a gourmet.

As tired as I was when I climbed in bed, sleep eluded me. I found myself sitting in the overstuffed chair in front of the living room window, staring out into the night. Life sometimes presents us with so much to think about in a day, it takes time to put it all in order. With all that I had seen today, I was able to take the meaning of commitment to a new level of understanding. It gave my purpose a deeper meaning and I closed my eyes, knowing I was where I needed to be for now.

Just before I went into the unconsciousness of sleep I saw the white book of my prior dreams waving in the air as if it were a flag. The pages flipped open and closed. Once again it had grown in width as if more pages had been added. Before I could even wonder why it represented itself as a flag, I was sound asleep.

Tuesday morning I woke with a desire to be at Ground Zero as soon as possible. For the first time I felt a need to be there. I had been able to bring into focus the level of commitment of the people I worked with that allowed them to put their lives on hold for days, even weeks. This task took priority over all else in their lives.

As I walked out the door I remembered to fold John's jacket, put it in a sack and take it with me. When I reached Ground Zero, the bitter, electric smell of smoke burned my nostrils. I thought of the dogs working without masks, sniffing through the acrid smoke with such a keen sense of smell, they could pick up another scent beneath it.

A fence company truck was parked next to the Salvation Army tent where some men were unloading chain-link. It looked like they were getting ready to construct a fence beyond the police barricades, closing access into the area, to protect... to protect what? It almost seemed ironic, I thought to myself as I watched the chain link being unrolled. It was a little late for protective fencing. I couldn't help but wonder where the chain was linked in the Intelligence Department to connect it with high-tech equipment that was supposed to prevent the very thing that had happened here. The comparison could have been amusing, but not today.

After I stored the jacket in the tent and picked up my gear, I asked a volunteer if there was any chance I could help with the dogs.

"You can check with one of the handlers in the K-9 tent and see," the volunteer at the assignment tent said. I thanked her and walked to the tent I had been in the day before.

I could see Flint sitting on a pad next to the vet. I walked over to him.

"How's the paw doing?" I asked as I stroked behind his ears.

The vet turned and recognized me. "Hi, back for another day?"

"I was hoping I could help with the injured dogs. I'm a trained EMT, if that qualifies."

"It does as far as I'm concerned." He handed me a tray full of medication packets. "We have forty dogs right now that need treatment. Check their legs for lacerations and their paws for cuts or burns. Check their noses while you're at it, and thanks for caring."

I spent the morning with the dogs, talking to them, caring for them and becoming their friend. By 1:00 PM I had the forty dogs in my care, medicated and soothed. It was a rewarding job. Flint was still on his pad when I finished, so I shared some lunch with him. His paw looked much better today, but not healed enough for him to step into the battlefield yet. "Maybe tomorrow, Flint," I comforted him. "Maybe tomorrow."

Before I left the K-9 tent, I had made forty new friends. I can see how victims could survive if they had the companionship of one of these gentle dogs to sustain them while waiting to be rescued.

I needed to get back to my area. Chris and Lenny would begin to wonder where I was. I made my way through the rubble where a sign of a path was beginning to take shape, which would make the walk less dangerous. The flag waved gently in the breeze overhead as I passed the spot where I had talked to Sam yesterday. I glanced over to see if he was there. The beam he had sat on was empty and I felt a twinge of disappointment.

"Ahoy there," a familiar voice called from behind me. "I thought it was you, so I quickened my step to catch up."

I turned to see Sam, a big grin on his face. He had quickened his step to a pretty good speed, I thought, for his age.

"I thought I had missed you, Sam," I said. "I'm glad I didn't. Do you have time to tell me about Francis Scott Key?"

"Do you have time to listen?" he responded.

"I think so,"

"Good." He motioned me to sit down as I had yesterday, and then he continued with this story. "Francis was a respected young lawyer in Georgetown. That's where he lived when the

British were over here causing so much trouble. They had entered Chesapeake Bay on the 19th of August, in the year 1814. Before the day had ended on August 24th, they had invaded and captured Washington. They set fire to both the Capitol and the White House. The flames could be seen 40 miles away, in Baltimore. But you know what? A thunderstorm hit about dawn and put out the fires. The next day, more buildings were burned and again thunderstorms put out the fires. Now, isn't that interesting?"

"More than just a mere coincidence, you think?" I asked.

He nodded, then continued, "In the meantime the British had managed to capture the town physician, Dr. William Beanes. He was an elderly man and the people were concerned for his safety as well as his health. They asked Frances to find a way to get him back.

"Now, Francis was an ingenious man and was quick to respond by arranging to have Col. John Skinner, an American agent for prisoner exchange, accompany him.

"On the morning of September 3rd, he and Col. Skinner set sail aboard a sloop flying a flag of truce. On the 7th, they finally found the ship named the *Tonnant*, which was the name of the ship Dr. William Beanes was being held prisoner on, by the way. On that ship they bargained for the release of the doctor and two other prisoners. Like I said, Francis was an ingenious man. He had, in a pouch, letters written by wounded British prisoners saying how well they had been treated and the excellent medical care they had received from Dr. Beanes. After reading the letters, the British officers told them they could have their doctor back, but would not allow the men to return until the attack on Baltimore was finished. They placed them under guard, first on the *H.M.S. Surprise*, and then moved them onto the sloop where they remained until the battle was over. That's why, my dear boy, Francis had the view he had."

"Can you tell me if that flag is still in existence?" I asked.

"It is. Its home is now in the Smithsonian Institute's Museum of American History. It is in very delicate condition, so much so that they keep an opaque curtain over it to shield it from the light and dust. It can only be viewed for a few minutes once every hour."

"I think my children need to see that flag."

"It will bring tears to your eyes when you take them to see it," Sam said, his eyes misting at the thought. "You'll stand there for those few minutes and you will feel such pride in your heart that you'll cry. I can guarantee you that. It's a fragile flag now, but it refuses to give in. In a way it reminds me of the flag you see hanging up there. It refuses to give in. Just like these people who come here every day. I watch them and I feel such pride in my heart and I cry. I don't want to forget what these people are doing here to preserve a nation."

We sat there on the steel beam, quietly looking at the flag for a minute. "Tell me," I asked, "how the flag was designed."

"It was done in 1777. The Continental Congress passed the First Flag Act, on June 14th. The Act states: "Resolved, that the flag of the United States be made of thirteen stripes, alternate red and white; that the union be thirteen stars, white in a blue field, representing a new constellation.""

"I'll bet you can tell me the years and the changes since that time," I laughed.

"That I can," he smiled proudly. "In January of 1795, it was changed to 15 stripes and 15 stars. In 1818, there were thirteen stripes and one star for each state.

In 1912, President Taft presented an executive order that established proportions of the flag and provided for the arrangement of the stars. They were placed in six horizontal rows of eight each, a single point of each star to be upward.

"President Eisenhower, in 1959, changed that executive order so that it provided for the arrangement of the stars in seven rows of seven stars each, staggered horizontally and vertically. In that same year it was changed so the stars were arranged in nine rows, staggering horizontally and eleven rows, staggering vertically. Anything else you need to know about the flag?"

"I think you've just about covered it," I replied with deep respect.

"One more thing you might want to know," he said while rising from the beam. "The star is the symbol of the heavens and the divine goal to which man has aspired from the beginning of time. The stripe is symbolic of the rays of light cast from the sun. I think that should cover it." He smiled as he took my hand and gave it a strong shake. "You're a fine young man, Jeremy. I'm proud to have met you. Go on now and get back to work. Maybe we'll meet another day."

"And I feel honored to have met you, Sam. I hope we meet again before I go home. You've been a great teacher and I'll always remember what you've taught me. There's one more question I would like to ask you, if you don't mind."

"A good student always has a lot of questions." Humor showed in his eyes.

"What is a sloop?"

Sam laughed, "I wondered when you'd get around to asking that question. In those days a sloop is a small warship just big enough to have guns on the upper deck." He winked, then turned and walked away. As I watched him I had the feeling this would be our last meeting. I missed him already.

"What do you know about the flag?" I asked Chris later, when we stood back to let the robots do their job.

"I guess what everybody knows,"

"And what's that?"

"That it represents freedom and liberty. The stripes represent the thirteen original colonies. The white stripes stand for purity, the red stripes for bravery, and the blue stands for justice. That Betsy Ross made the first flag. Things like that." He looked at me. "Is there something else I should know?"

After I explained to him what I had learned, Chris didn't say anything. He just looked at me and then looked up at the flag flying above us. His eyes were thoughtful. When he spoke again, he did so in a quiet tone. "When you look at that flag and you know the story behind its creation, when you know what it represents, can you doubt that it was divinely inspired? Have you ever noticed when it is flying with all the other flags of the world that none of them compare to its beauty? Can you question your commitment to a flag that is threaded with so much inspiration?"

I smiled at him and shook my head. No, I could not question my commitment to the American flag. Nothing more needed to be said. Chris had expressed it all and done so with eloquence.

That evening Shana had to work, so I went to the hospital alone. Nadine had gone to buy Bob a chocolate shake, which meant he was feeling much better. His color was good, especially the black and blue of the bruises.

We talked about Ground Zero. Because Bob had nothing better to do, he was up-to-date on the latest news concerning the terrorists, bin Laden and the war against them.

"They're comparing this attack to the one at Pearl Harbor. A total of 2,390 died at Pearl Harbor. When they add together the 266 who died in the planes, those they can only guess who died at the Pentagon and the World Trade Center, the numbers tally over 5,000. More than twice as many lives were lost last week in a fraction of the time, and the only casualties on the side of the enemy were the hijackers.

"Remember the *Titanic*? Well, 1,500 people died when the *Titanic* sank. When you add that to the number of lives lost at Pearl Harbor, you come up with 3,890. Does that give you a grasp on the reality of what has happened?"

"I don't know if I'll ever have a grasp on the reality of what has happened," I replied.

"There is a good side to this," he continued. "Someone had written an article in the paper. Let me read it to you. 'Out of every great tragedy, there's a paradigm shift. Pearl Harbor put an end to the Depression and to isolationism. Fort Sumter put an end to the idea that slavery was negotiable, or a thing that could be compromised.'" He set the paper aside. "And we are seeing the good that has come and will come from this tragedy. We are remembering who we are and how we got here. We have brought bravery and patriotism back to the surface. We feel a loss as a country that can't be recovered by sitting back and letting someone else take care of it. We are in this together."

"I worry," I said, "that we'll forget what we've learned through all of this. In six months from now, will our commitment level be the same as it is today? Will we still be willing to make the sacrifices necessary to preserve our freedom?"

"I've thought about that, myself," Bob admitted. "Today I want nothing more than to keep the promises I made, not only to my family, but to myself as well. When I'm back on my feet, will I be as strong in my commitment as I am right now? Believe me, I've thought about that and it concerned me until I could define it to my understanding. In my own definition a commitment is a promise you make first to yourself, and it has to come from the heart or it is of no value. If you break that commitment, then you break your heart as well. If I can keep my commitment to myself, then I have kept the commitment to my family, to my nation and to God. Does what I'm saying make any sense to you?"

I nodded. "You're telling me that it all begins with self. First we have to be committed, from our hearts, to be the best we can be. If we can do that, our commitment to others becomes a natural act."

"Bingo!" He sighed with relief.

"You're an incredible guy, you know that?" I said. "Just when I think you've reached your best, you take one more step forward."

"One thing I've learned," he laughed, "is you never reach your best. It's always out there somewhere waiting for you to get a little closer. Now go home and get some rest. I'll even call you a cab. I know tomorrow's your last day, but I expect one more visit before you head back to Missouri."

Author's Notes

We the people of this United States, in order to form a more perfect union, establish justice, insure domestic tranquility, provide for the common defense, promote the general welfare, and secure the blessings of liberty for ourselves and our posterity, do ordain and establish this constitution for the United States of America.

To rephrase:

We the people who enjoy the freedoms of the United States, in order to make our country a better place to live, must commit *ourselves to be just, to be honest, to do our duty, to be tolerant of all races and religions, and protect the rights of liberty, do support and sustain, by our actions, this constitution of the United States of America.*

To rephrase:

I, who enjoy the freedoms of the United States, in order to preserve the freedoms I expect, must commit myself to live my life in a way that would make this country a better place to live for all my neighbors. To show courage, to be just, honest, and patriotic, to be accepting of all races and religions, and to protect their rights of liberty. I must commit *myself to live by these principles that shall preserve the United States of America.*

Never think that just one person's commitment or promise or pledge to do or to be, won't make a difference in this world. Think about Thomas Edison, Albert Einstein, Henry Ford and Alexander Graham Bell. They each believed they could make a difference. With that commitment they moved forward.

Margaret Mead said, "Never doubt that a small group of thoughtful, committed citizens can change the world. Indeed, it is the only thing that ever has."

With commitment comes peace of mind. Peace of mind is power. A power that overshadows all things that may come against us.

Theodore Roosevelt spoke these words:

It is not the critic who counts, not the man who points out how the strong man stumbles or where the doer of deeds could have done them better. The credit belongs to the man who is actually in the arena, whose face is marred by dust and sweat and blood, who strives valiantly, who errs and comes up short again and again because there is no effort without error and shortcomings, who knows the great devotion, who spends himself in a worthy cause, who at best knows, in the end, the high achievement of triumph and who, at worst, if he fails while daring greatly, knows his place shall never be with those timid and cold souls who know neither victory nor defeat.

Chapter Eight

When We Are One

Before leaving the hospital I stopped in the gift shop and bought a small bouquet of flowers to place in the spokes of the bike on Liberty Street. As I climbed into the back seat of the taxi, I gave that address to the driver. I didn't want to wait until morning to leave the flowers; it had to be done tonight.

After I paid the driver and he drove away, I turned to the bike and dusted the handlebars and fenders. Then, I knelt down beside it to wrap the stems of the flowers around the spokes, talking to it as if it could respond. "I wonder who you belonged to?" I asked as I looked for a nameplate of some kind. There was none. A chain imprisoned the bike to the metal bar with a lock that had no key. It stood as if it were a memorial to those who lie beneath the rubble.

"I don't think your owner is coming back to get you," I said, wiping the dust from the seat. I felt a sadness come over me. The bike looked so alone. It could have stood as a memorial to those who now had to live without the love of those buried beneath the rubble. Both were imprisoned in chains with locks that had no key. I sat down next to the bike and leaned my back against its rail.

"A lot of people died last week," I continued. "There's a different feeling at Ground Zero than there was a week ago. We've given up trying to find survivors and just hope we can find most of the bodies. I hope somebody finds you and takes you home soon."

I stood and looked at my watch. It was 9:50 PM. My cell phone rang, startling me. I reached in my pocket and grabbed it before it rang again.

"Hello," I said into the receiver.

"Hi Jeremy, it's Shana."

"Hi there, how was your day?"

"Long and lonely," she replied. "I just got home. Where are you?"

"On Liberty Street, talking to a bike."

"What?"

I laughed. "I missed you tonight. What's your tomorrow going to be like?"

I have to be to work at 8:00 AM. But I told them I needed the afternoon off. What time does your plane leave?"

I had changed my return ticket but I still had to verify it in the morning. "The flight is for 7:00 PM, but it's not a sure thing yet. I won't know until tomorrow if its going to take off or be cancelled."

We spent the next hour talking to each other through an invisible airwave. I walked back to the apartment as Shana told me about her day. I fixed a sandwich, stacked the plate with chips and opened a pop while I told her about mine. She asked about Bob. I sat in the chair by the window and ate while we talked about Bob. Then I asked her if she would like to come to Missouri and meet my family after she got settled at work.

"If I come," she said, "I have to know that you are really ready for something to happen between us."

"I didn't think I could ever make that commitment to anyone else accept Addie," I responded, "until I met you. I've learned this week that love is a strange thing. Once you open your heart and allow it in, it expands and begins to fill all the empty places within, created when you shut it out. It doesn't mean I have to quit loving Addie in order to love you. It only means I can expand my love to love you also. I need you to know that before you accept the invitation."

"I wouldn't want you to forget your love for Addie. You need that love always inside of you so that you will know how to love me." There was wisdom in her words as she spoke.

My hope was that she could apply that same wisdom when it came to trusting herself to give her love away. I had to find out, so I asked, "I think I need to know," I chose my words carefully, "that you are ready to let go of the hurt you have carried inside for so many years, so you can love me without doubting."

There was silence on the other end of the phone and my heart dropped. Then her voice came through the airwaves into my ear, soft and emotional. "The hurt was lifted from my heart when I sat in that huge chair by the window in your apartment and you told me about the statue. That night my heart was so full of love for you, not only a physical love but a love that goes much deeper. A love I didn't know existed. Once I had experienced it, I was afraid you wouldn't be able to love me as deeply as I loved you."

This was not a conversation to have over the phone. I wanted to take her in my arms and hold her. I wanted to see the love in her eyes and feel the love in her touch.

"I hope there is no doubt in your mind right now." My voice was urgent as I talked into the receiver. I wondered if my grandmother had anything to do with this. She would not be pleased with my thoughts right now, but she would be pleased with my actions.

"There is no doubt." Her words were all I needed to hear and I could live through the night knowing there would be a million tomorrows for us to be together.

It was 11:30 PM. when we finally said goodnight to each other. Shana's words, there is no doubt, played themselves over and over in my mind. I began to understand that there is no doubt when love is real because love brings with it its own kind of courage as it takes away the fear. In all that love does and can do, it remains one of the great mysteries to man.

I thought back to the first day I saw Shana and the tragedy that had brought us together. I wondered how much I had changed. The man I was before September 11 would have stayed to help, I don't doubt that. That part of me was the same. But would I have taken the time to study another culture or religion to help me understand another people? Would I have been able to feel the love of a close friendship or, for that matter, would I have been able to fall in love? What had changed was my ability to love again. That thought contradicted itself. I had felt love. I loved my parents and my children. I had friends. But, if I had loved before, why was I so miserable?

"Because you quit loving yourself." Startled, I turned to see who had spoken those words, but no one was there. The words, however, seared my mind and I knew I had the answer to my question.

I set the cell phone in its cradle to recharge, and turned out the lights. In the back of my mind something told me I had, indeed heard a voice, one that was familiar to me. It wasn't until I remembered that I had left John's jacket in the Salvation Army tent that I recognized the voice. It was John's voice. As ridiculous as that sounded, I was convinced it was true. I hadn't seen John for two days. That wasn't unusual because there were so many people working at Ground Zero. Tomorrow I would look until I found him.

I was tired but I didn't want to go to bed yet. This was my last night here and I was beginning to feel a little melancholy. My intention, when I came here, was to spend a day walking the streets and feeling the life of this beautiful city. Instead, I got to know the heart of New York City and suddenly I didn't want to think about leaving. The chair felt warm and comfortable as I eased my tired body into its softness. I recalled doing that same thing not too many nights before. I laughed to myself as I compared the chair to Kaylee's security blanket she carried around with her until she was almost five years old. It seemed to comfort me when I felt sad and wrap me in its arms when I cried. Tonight, it welcomed me once again.

As my eyelids closed I saw John standing beside me and I asked him, "Did you come to get your jacket?"

He smiled. "You can keep it one more night."

"I've looked for you, but I haven't been able to find you," I heard myself say. "My friend, Bob, told me you were there when he was injured and that because of your words and your touch he was able to stand the pain until help arrived. Will you tell me why?"

"Would you not have done the same for him?" asked John.

"How could I?"

"Don't you love your friend, Bob?"

"Of course I do, but I don't understand." My mind was becoming confused with his questions.

"I touched him with my love, just as you have touched him with yours," he replied.

I thought of that day in the hospital when Bob was in so much pain. I had taken his hand and he seemed to relax. I thought the pain medication was starting to take effect. Was it, instead, the transmitting of love from one soul to another?

"Inside of you dwells the power of generous and healing love. When you allow the path of your spirit to open, you can bring this power to the world. Think of what you have learned about love tonight. Think of the power it carries. Let these thoughts be your dreams."

He turned to leave. "Wait, don't go, there is so much I have to tell you."

"I will see you tomorrow, my friend." He spoke these words, then he walked away. I wanted to turn and see where he went but the chair was so warm and comfortable.

When I woke up it was 3:00 AM. Once again John had invaded my dreams, yet it seemed so real, I found myself walking through the rooms just to make sure I was alone.

When I left for Ground Zero the next morning, I did three things. First I called the airport to see if my flight was still scheduled for departure at 7:00 PM. The voice on the other end explained that the flight still showed up on the computer but the schedule was changing from hour to hour because of the present situation. Would I mind calling back periodically through the day and get an update. I packed everything in my suitcase, hoping there would be no cancellation.

Second, I made a phone call to Missouri to talk to my family. I knew it was early but Mom and Dad would be up. I was right. Mom answered the phone on the first ring.

"Hello, Jeremy," she said in her early morning cheerful voice.

"How did you know it was me?" I asked, never doubting for a moment that my mother was psychic.

"I could tell it was your ring," she laughed. "You're not calling us to tell us that your flight has been cancelled, are you?"

"I won't know until later today. I have to call through the day for updates. How's everyone doing?"

"We're fine. Kyle had an early class this morning. He'll feel bad he missed your call. Kaylee isn't feeling well today. I think she's worried about you flying home, but she'll be fine as soon as she sees you. Right now she's asleep. I think I'll just let her stay home. How is Shana? How is Bob?"

"Bob is doing well. I think he'll be able to go home in a few days. His broken leg is the main problem. Bob is one special guy, Mom. You and Dad would really like him. I'm going to invite him and his family to come for a visit whenever they can." I decided to tell her about the blood test report I had seen on his chart.

"That's what you get for prying into things that are none of your business. See how much worry you have caused yourself." She paused. "Now I'll worry too. I only hope it's nothing serious. I hope you have some information before you leave."

"I'll ask until I find something out," I reassured her.

"I know you will. Now, tell me about Shana." I could hear the concern in her voice. "Are you going to invite her to come for a visit also?"

"You will be happy to learn that I already have and she has accepted. I think you and Dad are going to love Shana. Have you said anything to Kyle and Kaylee?"

"I think that is your department. But if you feel the way you say you feel about her, I can believe they will be happy for you." I heard a sigh of relief through the receiver.

"I'll call you as soon as I find out the details on the flight. I love you, Mom."

"I love you too, Jeremy, and I pray that your flight will be on schedule."

The third thing I did, after hanging up the phone was to make sure everything in the bedroom was in order. I took the sheets off the bed, but didn't know what to do with them so I placed them in the hamper along with the towels I had used.

While I ate breakfast, I turned on the TV.

"… The Vice President said in an interview," the reporter was speaking into his microphone. "…that many of the steps we have now been forced to take will become permanent in American life. These steps will represent an understanding of the world as it is, and dangers we must guard against."

Behind him the breeze had gathered some ash, sending it whirling through the air, giving an eerie touch to his next comment. "The war on terrorism is not going to be over quickly. We will need to dig in and prepare for the long term. We will need, as a people as well as a nation, to be on a much higher alert, perhaps for the rest of our lives."

I watched as the reporter paused and walked toward the camera for dramatic effect. Then he continued, "One important lesson the American people learned on the morning of September 11th was that we are not untouchable, that our lives can be and, in fact, have been forever altered in just a few short minutes. We will never be so innocent again. We will be suspicious and prepared. We can no longer sit back and ignore the rest of the world. Maybe that's a good thing."

The cameraman moved around the reporter. What remained of the Trade Center could now be seen in the background. "One important lesson the terrorists have learned from all of this is that freedom can't be brought down, like a building, once it has been born. Perhaps their biggest mistake was to believe that it could be. In their attempt to crush a city they only brought that city closer together and made it stronger. And behind that city stands a whole nation. Back to you…"

I wondered how freedom was viewed from abroad. How do you explain to a child in Afghanistan what freedom represents? The words to the song "God Bless the USA" came to mind and I began to sing,

> If tomorrow all the things were gone I'd worked for all
>   my life
> And I had to start again with just my children and
>   my wife…

I turned off the TV and picked up the sack of clothes I would need for the day.

> *I'd thank my lucky stars to be livin' here today*
> *Cause the flag still stands for freedom and they can't*
> *take that away.*

I locked the door to the apartment, walked down the steps onto the sidewalk and started toward Ground Zero.

> *And I'm proud to be an American where at least I*
> *know I'm free,*
> *And I won't forget the men who died who gave that*
> *right to me.*

I crossed to Liberty Street, stopped and adjusted the flowers woven in the spokes of the bicycle.

> *And I'd gladly stand up next to you and defend her*
> *still today,*
> *'Cause there ain't no doubt I love this land. God bless*
> *the USA!*

Ground Zero was just ahead of me. I could see the devastation as I repeated the last lines of the song:

> *And I'd gladly stand up next to you and defend her*
> *still today,*
> *'Cause there ain't no doubt I love this land.*
> *God bless the USA!*

I could see several hundred feet of chain-linked fence beginning to enclose the area. Handmade signs with quotes had been hung on the fence along with pictures of people yet to be found. I stopped and read a quote by W. Paul Jones: *"While the hero is acclaimed by others, courage entails a steadfast 'in spite of' – a self-confrontation in which we put ourselves on the line in an act of 'nevertheless.' Courage, then, has less to do with accomplishment than with the way we approach life."*

It was a perfect definition of the character of these people who come here every day and put themselves on the line in an act of "nevertheless."

On another sheet of paper, attached to the fence, was a quote by John Holt: *"The true test of character is not how much*

*we know how to do, but how we behave when we don't know what
to do."*

I read the quote again and I thought of the people who had
reached out their hands and their hearts to others who needed
help to reach safe ground, the morning of September 11. "Mr.
Holt," I said out loud, "You should have been there to see it."

I didn't want this to be my last day at Ground Zero. I think
I would have given almost anything to be able to stay. I
watched one of the dog handlers as he knelt by his dog to
check one of the paws. "Do you think you can go out there
today, boy?" I heard him ask the dog. The dog gave a soft
bark and licked his master's cheek. "Your paw looks pretty
tender, maybe we'd better wait until tomorrow." The dog, in
response, gave a sharp bark. The handler wrapped his arms
around the dog's neck and held him for a minute. The scene
in front of me was so touching I couldn't take my eyes away.
I heard the click of a camera. The Salvation Army volunteer
had taken a picture.

"I have to leave to go back to Missouri tonight, but if I gave
you my address and money to pay the costs, would you send
me a copy of that picture?" I asked.

"I'd be happy to," she replied. "In fact I've taken dozens of
pictures of moments just like this one. If you would like, I'll
send you copies of all of them."

This woman had just given me something to help me
remember this past week and I felt a little better about having
to leave. She handed me a pen and paper. "Just write your
address on this paper. That will be all I'll need." She smiled.
"Your money could not be accepted in this exchange. Strange
words coming from the mouth of a Salvation Army
Volunteer, right!"

I laughed as I wrote my name and address on the piece of
paper she provided, and then I thanked her for her kindness.
She looked at my name and her eyes began mist. "It is you who
needs to be thanked, Mr. Carter." She took my hand. "It was
my nephew's picture on the leaflet that was handed to you that
day. You were kind enough to help a young girl locate her
brother." She reached up and kissed me on the cheek.

"Janet, right?" I said. I hadn't forgotten that experience. It was one of the many that had not been mere chance. "Her brother's name was Bryan. No, Brad. How is he doing?"

"Brad lost the sight in his left eye and his memory has some huge lapses but the doctor said in time, he should have a full recovery. I can't believe you remembered their names."

"When you send those pictures," I asked, "could you include one of Janet and Brad?"

"I know that sending these pictures won't begin to repay you but at least it will help me feel like I've scratched the surface."

I assured her that the pictures would more than repay me. I explained that I was struggling with the fact that I had to leave, and just knowing I would have pictures to remind me of my experience here had helped me. "You see," I told her, "you are just returning the favor."

How small the world really is, I thought to myself as I gathered up the gear I might need. One life connects to another, then to another until, in some way we all begin to connect together as one. I tried to imagine a world where there was no need for religion because all believed as one. I tried to envision a world where there was no division between cultures. A world where the color of the skin only added to the beauty of the rainbow. Is that what Heaven is, earth with no thought to race, religion or color? Is Heaven earth without hate where the only law that exists is the law of love? I think when I find John I will discuss the subject with him.

I didn't need much gear because my day would be spent saying goodbye to friends. I checked to make sure John's jacket was still in the tent, then made my first stop at the K-9 tent. My love for these dogs was unquestionable. I was excited to see Flint resting on his pad. I walked over and sat down beside him. His paw had been wrapped and I wondered if he had been out on an assignment. He looked tired and his food had hardly been touched. I remember Allen saying that it is as stressful on the dogs as it is on humans when they can't search out the bodies beneath the rubble.

"Good morning, Flint." I reached over and scratched him behind his ears. "Tough night out there?" He stared up at me through big, sad eyes without raising his head off the pad. I took a piece of meat from his dish and held it out to him. He sniffed it for a few seconds, but didn't seem to have the appetite to eat any of it.

"I know how you feel, boy. It's not easy to keep coming up empty-handed." I rubbed his side. "There's nothing you want more than to find something down there. We've grown from this experience, you and I. We've learned about life and its commitment. We've experienced sadness and the need to overcome it. We've seen death and it makes us more appreciative of life. We've found new friends that we will keep in our hearts forever. But most of all, we have experienced love for those who have died and for those who have survived. We've felt love for each other as volunteers. All of these things are important, Flint. All these things become part of who we are and they bring depth to our character."

Flint was watching me now with more intent. He raised his head, tipped it to one side as if he were listening with interest to what I was telling him. I continued to stroke him. "I want you to remember that while you're resting. I want you think about the greatness in you. Remember one more thing. Remember that you will always be my friend."

Flint's eyes were bright now and his bark told me he understood what I was trying to tell him. He licked my hand and accepted the meat I again held out to him. "I have to go back home tonight so I probably won't ever see you again, but I hope you won't forget me." I slipped my arm around him and gave him a hug.

"You are going home today." It wasn't a question but an observation. I looked up to see John's clear eyes looking down at me. "He's a beautiful dog, isn't he?"

Flint stood and walked over to John. He waited for John to kneel beside him and pet him. When he did, Flint licked his hand. It was an exchange of tenderness I witnessed between the two of them.

"I was hoping I would find you this morning, I have your jacket. It is in the Salvation Army Tent."

"I appreciate the fact that you've taken such good care of it," he smiled as he continued to pet Flint. "I detect a feeling of sadness in you in spite of the fact you are going home."

"It's a strange feeling, I don't understand," I said. "I miss my own family, yet I feel like I'm leaving a family behind. I want to go home but I don't want to leave here."

"It's a natural feeling. Don't try to analyze it, because you can't analyze love. You just accept it. Love sometimes makes you sad. It isn't always a happy feeling but it is a true feeling, and it brings with it a joy that doesn't always connect with happiness at a precise moment. Think about it. Do you not feel a joy within you because of the friendships you have made? Isn't there joy in your heart because of the work you've done here?" John stood and motioned for me to follow him as he walked away from me.

It seemed that he was always walking away from me. "I had a dream last night," I said, catching up with him. "You were in it. It's not the first dream I've had this past week that you've invaded."

"I hope they were pleasant dreams then." He looked at me with those ever-calm eyes.

"I guess they were pleasant enough, but more important, they were full of questions. Even in my dreams you answer my questions with more questions," I chuckled. "Provoking questions that make me search inside to find the answers, if I can find answers."

"Do you think the answers are already inside you and my presence in your dream just represents a way of bringing them to the surface?"

"There you go asking another question!" I enjoyed talking to John. Maybe it was because he made me think. "There was one thing you did say to me, in my dream, that was not a question. You said that inside me there is a power of generous and healing love and I just have to allow the path of my spirit to open to bring this power to the world. If you were to say that to someone walking beside you, right now, what would you mean by that?"

"If I were to say that to you right now, I would mean exactly what I said to you in your dream."

"Tell me, please," I begged.

John stopped and looked at me. "In you," he said, "there exists a love so powerful, it can bring comfort, ease pain, bring happiness, erase anger, and even heal. All you need is the faith to believe you have it within you. Everyone is given the power of love as a gift but few bother to open the package. It's there, in your heart. The path to that power is right before you. Just let it lead you. Tell me, what have you learned about love this past week?"

I thought for a moment before replying. "I learned," I said, "as I began to recognize the acts of love, that I don't have to know someone to feel love for them. I simply love them as a human being. I felt such love for the man I found that day in the rubble. Even though he was dead, I loved him and I mourned for him. I could see a little girl who needed reassurance and an elderly man who needed comfort. And it moved me to action."

"It moved you to love," John said quietly. "You will probably never know the effect you had on one elderly man, but you know what your love has done for a little girl and her family. You healed a heart."

"Did my love ease the pain of a friend?" I asked.

"Did it?" he responded.

"I think so."

"So it did. But what did you have to learn about love before you could recognize your love for others?" he questioned.

"You know the answer to that one," I smiled. "I heard your voice last night just as clear as I hear it today. I don't know why or how, but you seem to know me better than I know myself. You seem to enter my dreams when I have questions and you seem to be there when I need to talk to you. You avoid talking about yourself and I keep forgetting to ask you to tell me about yourself. Today, I haven't forgotten. Will you tell me about yourself?"

"What do you want to know?"

"Why you enter my dreams. How do you know what I'm thinking and even what I have done before I tell you? Why are you here and what do you do for a living? And, how come you know all the right answers, or maybe I should say, the right questions to ask? Simple things like that."

"I'm here, just like you are, to help in the search and rescue of those bodies that lie beneath the rubble. My life's work is counseling and asking questions."

He looked at me and then his gaze followed one of the broken steel beams that still reached into the sky. "See that beam?" he motioned with his hand. "It stands as a monument to those who lost their lives. It's a reminder that while love has been forgotten in one part of the world, it has been remembered and renewed in another part. With its renewal, love has brought power. If I enter your dreams it is because you desire it. If I know your thoughts, it is because you share them without speaking. If I ask the right questions it is only because you desire to know the answers." He smiled again. "There, have I answered your questions?"

"I think that you talk in riddles, but you make sense in a strange sort of way," I admitted.

"One more thing I must tell you about love before you go to the hospital to say goodbye to your friend. Once love is given, it begins to mushroom until it is once again returned. I hope to talk with you one more time before you leave, however. Would you meet me by the Salvation Army tent this afternoon around 2:00 PM?"

"I would like that," I answered. I watched him as he walked away one more time. Then it struck me too late, how did he know my next stop was the hospital?

By the time I got to the hospital it was 11:00 AM. I stopped by the nurse's station to inquire about Bob's blood test. How I was going to explain that I had seen the chart, I didn't know yet. At this point it didn't really matter; I just hoped for some answers.

"I think I recognize you," the nurse at the station said. "Weren't you the one who took two years off my life the other morning in Bob Goldberg's room?"

"I'm afraid so," I said, feeling lucky she was the nurse at the station. "Since we know each other so well, may I ask you a question?"

"Shoot," she smiled.

"Bob was concerned that so much blood had been drawn that first night. He asked if I would check into it and see if you really needed that blood for lunch or if there was a problem. With luck on my side, I was able to read on his chart that the white blood count was high. What I want to ask you is, is there a problem?"

"More like a miracle." Her eyes looked steadily into mine. "More like a miracle, that's all I will tell you. The rest you will have to learn from the man of the hour." She pointed in the direction of Bob's room.

"Before I let her go I asked if she could check on Clint. I explained I didn't know his last name but his wife's name was Adrianne and he had a young daughter named Shellie. Once I mentioned Shellie's name she smiled, picked up the phone and punched a button. After waiting for a response she asked for the condition of Clint Swenson. She listened for a moment, then hung up the phone.

"Clint is doing very well. He is out of the brace and will go home tomorrow. When you mentioned Shellie, I knew who you meant. Shellie has found a place in the heart of every patient as well as the staff on that floor. She has a doll named Addie that she takes to visit the patients and she lets them hold the doll. I can't tell you what it has done for some of the elderly patients. When she walks into a room, it automatically lights up."

I remembered John's words, "Once you give love, it mushrooms until it returns to you once more." I now understood what he meant. I also began to realize the power of love.

I felt a pang of homesickness as I took out my cell phone and punched 'redial.' I got a recording at the airport telling which flights were cancelled, on schedule or delayed. So far my flight was on schedule.

Bob was waiting for me as I entered the room. "Boy, am I'm glad to see you. I was afraid you wouldn't be able to make it."

"I wouldn't leave without saying goodbye to a good friend," I laughed. "Besides, my mother wants me to invite you to come and visit us whenever you can. She would be very upset with me if I didn't deliver that invitation in person."

"Your mother is a very wise woman, but then we already knew that, didn't we?"

"How are you doing?" I asked. He looked good. The bruises were much lighter and he seemed to be able to move without wrinkling his nose in pain.

"One more day and I'm out of this high rise leg swing," he joked. "Not that I haven't enjoyed lying here with my leg in the air. Once my leg is down, they won't be able to keep me here. One turn of the nurse's head and I'm out of here."

I pulled a chair up to his bed and sat next to him. "So, what do the doctors really say about you?" I was hoping he would offer to tell me the miracle, but he wasn't ready yet.

"They say I'm in good shape and the healing process is moving along very well, thank you. How's Ground Zero?"

"It's going as well as can be expected," I replied. "But there is so much to do, it'll take months. They've found so few bodies.

"I was watching the news this morning," Bob said. "The people want immediate retaliation, but the President is holding back for more information. There are those who are critical of him while other applaud him. I remember my grandfather telling me how concerned Churchill was that the United States would pull out of the war against Germany in a quick retaliation against Japan right after the attack on Pearl Harbor. Churchill's worry was that the United States was going to wage the wrong war, at the wrong place, at the wrong time, against the wrong enemy.

"Roosevelt, however, did not give in to the popular public cry for quick retaliation but instead, listened to the wisdom of his Chief of Staff, George C. Marshall and held to the original plan of vanquishing Germany first. The idea was that the defeat of Japan would contribute little to the defeat of Germany, while the defeat of Germany would be Japan's swan song. Roosevelt had to convince the public of that fact, and in time he did. The rest, as they say, is history.

"Roosevelt commented that *'we have learned that we cannot live alone, at peace; that our own well-being is dependent on the well-being of other nations, far away. We have learned that we must live as men, and not ostriches, nor as dogs in the manger. We have learned to be citizens of the world, members of the human community.'*

"I would like to impress you with the idea that I could remember that quote, verbatim, on my own, but it was my grandfather who quoted it to me several times so that I wouldn't forget it. I would like you to be impressed that I remembered it, however."

"I am impressed, I'm impressed that you know the history," I remarked, because I was truly impressed.

"So, you see," he continued, "the President must wait. He must know how to fight an enemy that no other leader has had to contend with. He can't wage war on a country; there are no countries involved — only enemies inside those countries who are also enemies of those countries. He needs the support of other countries. He needs to evaluate and listen and learn all that he needs to know before he can even consider fighting this enemy. This war will probably last longer than WWII, and it will not be fought with the same strategy. But, I believe if we wait until the right time, the success will be effective and we will have the support of many nations. What do you think?"

"I think lying in this hospital has given you the mind of a strategist. Once again, I am impressed. I wish they had you sitting with them at the conference table, or wherever they sit."

Bob's laugh was stronger today, which meant his ribs were healing. I could see, however, that I was going to be the one to bring up the subject of the miracle. "Tell me about your miracle," I said without any further discussion of war.

Bob's face went sober and he looked at me for a long time. "I wasn't going to tell you about that. How did you find out?"

"Remember, it was you who asked me to check it out, which I did." I told him how Shana and I had achieved the information and the nurse told me I would have to hear the story of the miracle from the man of the hour.

He smiled at me. His eyes blinked several times before he could speak. "I've got leukemia, Jeremy. The miracle is that they caught it early. They caught it even before there were any symptoms. With medication they think they can put it into remission. If the break in my leg wouldn't have been this severe, they wouldn't have done the blood test that showed the abnormality. Because they tested for bone fragments that may have gotten into the blood stream, my life has been extended.

"I'm not one to go to the doctor, Jeremy. I'm one who believes that sickness is in the mind. What if this hadn't happened to me? By the time I would have decided to get a doctor's opinion it could have been too late. The miracle is also in the extent of the injury. Can you believe that?"

It took me a minute to realize what he was telling me. At first I wanted to scream, "But it isn't fair to save your life so you can die of leukemia." Then I remembered the words of my grandmother's wisdom. "Life isn't fair, Jeremy," she had said when I was 17 years old and didn't make the soccer team. "You're not always going to get exactly what you want every time. Sometimes you get what is best for you. In the meantime you learn character." What I saw in Bob right now was most definitely character.

"I'm so sorry, Bob. I wish I knew what to say to you right now." Everything I wanted to say wasn't written in the script I had to follow now.

"Don't feel sorry for me, Jeremy, be happy for me. Just think, I have more time to spend with my family than I would have had. I have more time to enjoy life than I would have had. I'm grateful for this opportunity. Who knows, I may even outlive you. We never know what's in our future, my friend. We can only live today. I read a quote by John Burroughs this morning." He picked up a book from the side of his bed and shuffled through the pages until he found what he was looking for.

"Here it is: *'I still find each day too short for all the thoughts I want to think, all the walks I want to take, all the books I want to read, and all the friends I want to see. The longer I live the more my mind dwells upon the beauty and the wonders of the world.'* My days have been lengthened. I will still have time to do all these things. Think of the miracle, Jeremy, think of the miracle that has been given me."

"I see Bob has told you of his miracle," said Nadine as she poked her head through the door. "Now put on a happy face and join us in our celebration." In a cardboard cup holder she had three milkshakes. As she placed a shake in front of Bob, she laughed. "Somehow I knew you would be here so I bought you one too." She placed the second milkshake in front of me, then started drinking from the third.

There was no way I could be sad in this cheerful room. We spent the next hour just talking about things that mattered. I told Nadine that my mother was anxious to meet their family and was looking forward to a visit from them. She promised that as soon as Bob was well enough to travel they would make Missouri their first stop.

I had promised Shana I would call her after 12:00 noon. It was already 12:30 PM. I hugged my friend Bob one last time before I turned to leave the room.

"Let me leave you with one more quote before you take off." He picked up his book again and turned to a page he had earmarked. "This one is from Don Quixote. Listen carefully to his words. *'Where one door shuts, another opens. We come to an end and find a beginning. Often we worry about arriving at an end with too little faith in what follows.'* Remember that quote, not only when you think of me, but also when you think of yourself. Have faith in the decisions you will be making over the next few months. They will decide the rest of your life."

"I love you, Bob Goldberg," I said as I gave him a careful hug.

"And I love you, Jeremy Carter," he said, his eyes beginning to mist.

Nadine walked me to the elevator. "You know something, Jeremy, Bob would have died of a heart attack long before the leukemia would have taken him. I'm grateful for that. Through all of this he has realized what is important in his life. He is the Bob I married and I can't ask for more than that."

"Then I can only feel joy for you, Nadine." I kissed her on her cheek and gave her a warm hug that would have to last until they were able to travel to Missouri. "And I can only feel joy for myself because of his friendship."

"Tell Shana 'hello' for us and, just in case you want my opinion, I think she's perfect for you."

"Just in case you want to know, I value your opinion."

I remembered, just in time, about the apartment. "Before I go, what do you want me do with the key to the apartment? I still have my luggage there. Shall I leave the key on the table?"

That would be just fine, and don't you do any cleaning or change the bedding or wash the towels. There's a housekeeper who will do all that after you leave." She paused and her eyes softened. "One more thing I need to say before you step into that elevator, Jeremy. There are no words to tell you how grateful I am to you. All I can say is thank you, and it hardly begins to express my feelings."

"I love you too, Nadine." The elevator doors closed as we waved goodbye. What had John said? "Love can make you feel sad sometimes, yet there is a joy that comes also. A joy that we don't connect with happiness at that precise moment." I was feeling that sadness and joy right now. I wish I could describe the feeling, but I couldn't.

As I left the hospital I punched "redial" again to get an update from the airport. The recorded voice gave the same information as before. I was relieved in a way, disappointed in another.

Next I called Shana's cell phone. She answered on the third ring. "Jeremy, I hope," she shouted through the receiver. The background noise almost drowned out her voice.

"What's going on there?" I shouted back.

"They're remodeling a room so I'll have an office. Have you found out what time you are flying out yet?"

"Still on schedule for 7:00 PM. What is your schedule like?"

"Can we meet about 3:00 PM and find a quiet place to eat before we go to the airport? I want to wave to you as you fly away to Missouri."

"I can't think of anything I would like better except that you would be in the seat next to me instead."

"The noise is too loud. I can hardly hear you." Her voice was barely audible. "Can I meet you at 3:00, at your apartment?"

"See you then," I shouted.

"See you then," she shouted back.

A taxi was sitting outside the hospital just waiting for someone like me who was in a hurry. I gave him the address of Ground Zero, then settled back in the seat and dialed home. When my mother answered I was happy to hear her voice.

"Hello."

"Hi, Mom."

"Please tell me your plane is on schedule," she begged.

"So far the plane is on schedule."

"Thank you, dear," she sighed. "Those aren't the exact words I wanted to hear but I'll have to accept them for now. Have you been to the hospital?"

I felt a flood of emotion come over me and I couldn't say anything.

"Are you there, Jeremy?"

"I'm here, Mom," I answered. I told her about the tests and how incredibly Bob was handling the whole thing. I told her about my conversation with John earlier and how his words seem to fill in the voids that existed in my feelings. I told her how Grandma's words had come to me at the right time and how they'd helped me get a grip on what was happening. "I'm so grateful for a grandmother who was so full of wisdom and so thankful she raised her daughter to be my mother," I said into the phone. "I don't think I tell you often enough, Mom, that I love you and how grateful I am for your love and your support, especially since Addie died. I've learned so much here that has helped me understand who I am and what I am about."

When I finally stopped talking, there was a pause on the other end. "Hurry home, son. We miss you." Her voice was full of emotion and I could tell she was crying. "Hurry home."

I put the phone back into my pocket and paid the taxi driver as he stopped near Ground Zero. It was almost 2:00 PM. I went to the Salvation Army Tent and found John's coat so I would have it ready for him.

I didn't have long to wait. I looked toward the west and saw his profile outlined against the sun as he walked toward me. The scene seemed so familiar to me, yet I couldn't remember why.

"Ah, my jacket," he said as he approached. He reached out and I handed it to him. "How is your friend doing?"

"He has leukemia." Every time I said that word, I shuddered with disbelief. I told John all about Bob's experience and how he thought of his injury as a miracle that had brought the real problem in his body to the surface.

"Do you see the miracle?" John asked.

"I didn't want to at first. I wanted to be angry. I couldn't understand why John would be saved from death only to die from cancer. But, the longer I sat with Bob, the more I began to see the miracle through his eyes."

"Have you ever considered that we, as humans, want to blame God when things go wrong, yet we seem to forget Him when things go right? In the scriptures it tells how God works in a mysterious way, His wonders to perform. God is His own interpreter, Jeremy. He needs no one to do it for Him, though many try. Bob did receive a miracle and understood the purpose of his miracle. He accepted the beauty of the miracle without question. At that point he and God became one.

"Have you considered there may be a purpose to what has happened here in New York City? A purpose beyond that which you can conceive?"

"I can't think of a purpose for this tragedy," I responded, shaking my head.

"Would you consider the thought that perhaps five thousand had to die so hundreds of thousands would live? Would you consider that it took a tragedy of this magnitude to wake up the world to the evil that eats at its very core? How many times have there been warnings of terrorism, yet we thought we were too powerful to be touched? How many other nations have been warned and haven't listened? All this time, those involved in this evil undertaking were growing more powerful. We fail to recognize the miracle, Jeremy. We fail to recognize the miracle.

"God can only send the warnings; the world has to acknowledge them as such. Yet there were those who blamed God and asked where He was when this happened. God was there that day. His arms reached out and enfolded all those who came to him and there was great sadness in His heart also. But there must have been great joy because the people in this great country united as one in love and reverence for Him. When we become one, one in love and unity, we are more powerful than all the evil in the world. There can be no division of color, race or religion. There can be no division in rich and poor. There can only be one people, one nation, under God, indivisible, with liberty and justice for all. Those are divine words and they mean exactly what they say. They need no interpretation."

I hung on to every word that came from John's mouth. In those few moments I sat with him, I realized I had been taught one of the greatest lessons of my life. Everything he said was truth unfolded and my life would never be the same again.

"You are a man of tremendous ability to reach out to others and to love, Jeremy. Use that ability to serve others." He stood and reached his hand out to me. My eyes lifted to meet his gaze. "I must go now, but before I do, I have something for you." He reached into his jacket pocket and withdrew a package, wrapped in plain brown paper. "Open this when you are in flight to Missouri." He turned, and for the last time, walked away. For a brief moment I felt the depth of his love, a feeling I shall never forget.

I looked at my watch. It was almost 3:00 PM. I wasn't going to get to say goodbye to Chris and Lenny, but I had their addresses and their telephone numbers so I would contact them as soon as I arrived home.

I would have to hurry to get to the apartment before Shana. As I walked down Liberty Street, there was an empty space where the bicycle had been. I smiled and said aloud,

"I'm glad someone found you and took you home." I began to whistle a tune of freedom and I was happy, truly happy for the first time in two years. I, like everyone else in this nation, had grown up. It felt good.

Shana was walking across the street when I reached the steps to the apartment. I waited for her, put my arms around her and kissed her. Nobody seemed to mind as they passed by. We walked to the apartment and I punched "redial" to the airport and found the same message. If the flight was going to be cancelled it would have been by now. If it was delayed, I could certainly wait.

We closed the door to the apartment and walked to the big front room window. There we just held each other and watched the people move along the streets of New York.

"It's a beautiful city, isn't it?" Shana whispered in my ear.

"It's more beautiful because you are here," I whispered back. "I will miss you."

"I've made arrangements to fly to Missouri in two weeks. It will be the longest two weeks of my life," she smiled through the tears that flowed freely.

It was time to leave. We did so reluctantly. We decided it would be better to eat at the airport, making sure I had everything taken care of in time for my flight.

Once at the airport, I checked in my bags. In my carry-on I had the statue, the pictures and the package John gave me. I didn't want any of them to leave my side. Shana couldn't go beyond that point so we found a restaurant with a table in a quiet corner. We sat for awhile, holding hands, without saying a word. The waiter came and left the menus, and then in a few moments returned and took our orders. Still we sat holding hands, not speaking. Finally I broke the silence. "Do you still feel the same way you did when we talked on the phone last night?"

"When I'm actually with you, it's even worse," she smiled.

"Good. I wish we had more time." I smiled in return.

"We don't need more time. We already know what we want. Let's just make it happen." Shana reached up and touched my cheek. "Is December a good time for you?"

"December is a great time for me," I answered. "My parents love December weddings. In fact December 3rd is when my Grandparents were married."

"Then, let's make it happen on December 3rd." We ate our dinner without really tasting it. Our thoughts were elsewhere. When it came time to leave, I didn't feel sadness. I felt joy. This time it was a joy that happiness brings.

"I'll wave to you as you fly away," Shana said softly.

"And I'll wave back," I promised. We kissed one more time, then I walked over to have my luggage x-rayed and my body metal detected. I was grateful for the extra time it took to get through security. That meant there was tight security.

As I stored my carry-on in the overhead, I removed the package John had given me earlier. I settled into my window seat, making sure I had strapped myself in before taking the package into my hands again. I decided I would wait until the plane left the ground before opening it. I didn't want to miss waving at Shana. As the plane lifted I looked out the window and waved, knowing she was waving back.

Once the plane was safely in the air, I relaxed and untied the cord that held the brown wrap. As the wrap fell away, a white book revealed itself. I was stunned.

If I opened it, what would it reveal? Then, in my mind, I could see John's clear calm eyes and I was not afraid to discover what the book contained. Inside, in a handwriting I didn't recognize, I began to read the events of my week in New York City. All the things I had done. All the things I had learned. Nothing was left out. I was fascinated and I read with enthusiasm all that was written. In the book I became acquainted with a man I didn't know existed until today.

It came to me, as I finished the last page, that this was a book about waking up to all the things that bring love to life. It was a story of love. It was a beautiful story of connecting one soul with another until we become one, in love. I closed the book. I didn't question how the book got into the jacket when all the time I had the jacket. That was the purpose; I had to keep the jacket in order for the book to be written. How I knew that, I don't know, but it was as plain to me as the book itself. I smiled because I now remembered who John was and I wondered why I was so blessed to have him with me for that week.

I looked at my watch and was amazed that only an hour had passed from the time the plane had begun its flight. I still had a few hours in the air so I decide to close my eyes. When I got home there would be so much excitement, no one would get to bed before midnight.

"We will be landing in ten minutes. Please make sure all seats are in an upright position and all seat belts are fastened." The flight attendant woke me with her announcement. I had been asleep for over two hours. I reached down to get the book and its wrapping but they were not there. There was no one in the seat next to me to ask if they had seen it, but I didn't need to ask. I knew. The book wasn't mine for the keeping. "Thank you, John," I whispered. "Thank you for everything."

Author's Notes

"How prudently most men sink into nameless graves, while now and then, a few forget themselves into immortality."
    — William Jennings Bryan

Although I didn't see with my own eyes, the fire fighters or the police officers go through those doors of the Trade Center, in my mind I envisioned the scene. These men forgot themselves into immortality. To forget one's own life to save another's is an act of love that defies all others. No man can give more than this.

Love is constant, never changing. It is reliable and secure. Love is the force that drives a person beyond his or her own physical abilities to protect or aid another.

To show love is to show courage, to be accepting. To love means to take responsibility. Love is the graciousness of gratitude and the element of commitment.

Love cannot be found in hate nor can it be found in evil. Evil and hate cannot endure its presence.

Some think that to show, outwardly, the tenderness of love is a sign of being submissive or weak. Water may seem submissive and weak, yet it can wear down the hardest of things. Never doubt the power of love and always be awakened in its presence.

Love is not found only in the beginning or at the end,
It is also the journey along the way.
It cannot be borrowed nor bought,
For love is a priceless gift from God.
Love cannot keep us from tragedy;
It cannot stop a hurricane or silence a storm —
It cannot keep a loved one from dying;
That is not its miracle.
The miracle is that it's there when all this happens.

If only man could hear love's plea for peace
And let it chase away the hate and bitterness
That would destroy and decay a world.
Then the world would be as one,
A world where there is no division —
There is only love.s

Epilogue

I arrived at the airport thirty minutes early. I wanted to make sure I was there the minute Shana stepped off that plane. It had been two weeks since we'd waved goodbye and it seemed forever ago.

My parents and kids had welcomed me home with my favorite dinner, balloons, cards and love. They'd made a special place on the mantel for the statue and pictures as I'd told them the stories behind each one. I told them about Bob and Nadine and how courageous they both are. I told them about Chris and Lenny. I told them the wonderful things I had learned from Sam. I told them about Flint and the hundreds of search and rescue dogs that spend hours sniffing the polluted ground without protection, for the scent of a human body. I didn't tell them about John or Shana. I needed to wait to tell them about the two people who had touched my life more deeply than I could explain right now.

My life has gone back to the normal pace of a fire chief, except I now have a deeper appreciation of my job. The men under me say I seem older. I am. My parents say they see a change in me. There is. My son and daughter say I'm even a better dad than I was before I went to New York. I hope so.

Maybe the change in those of us who were there that day is a little more dramatic than even those who have volunteered their time, money and resources. But I think we have all felt "survivor's guilt" to a certain degree and we have used that guilt to motivate our desire for more sincere patriotism, and more commitment to ensure personal freedom and the freedom of a nation. Perhaps that is our way of paying tribute to those who died. We will not allow their deaths to be in vain.

I talked to Chris and Lenny last week. They are both working twelve-hour shifts every day searching for more bodies with some success. The men, women, dogs and equipment will never be able to find all the bodies. That's a fact. But they won't quit looking until they have exhausted every resource. That is a fact also.

When I told Kyle and Kaylee about Shana, I told them separately. I needed the conversation to be one on one. I gathered up the fishing equipment the second day I was home and invited Kyle to go fishing. We sat on our favorite rock and Kyle reached into the bag for the bait.

"So, Dad," he had said, looking at me out of the corner of his eye, "what is it you want to talk about?"

"What makes you think I want to talk about anything in particular?" I replied, surprised that I was that obvious.

"How often do we go fishing without bait?" He grinned.

We laughed and threw out our lines anyway and I began to tell him about John. It seemed this was the time and the place to mention him to Kyle. He listened with great interest to my story. Then I began to tell him about Shana. I watched his body stiffen but as I continued to talk about her, the muscles in his face began to relax.

"I'm glad you told me about John first," he said. "It made the next part easier to listen to. I knew this day would come and I understand that is the way it should be, but don't ask me to be happy about it right now, please Dad, because I can't be."

"I understand." I put my arm around him and drew him close to me. We sat in silence for awhile, watching the water as it created white foam each time it bounced off a rock in its path, and listening to the soothing sounds of the river.

"Do you love her as much as you love Mom?" Kyle asked, breaking the silence.

"I will never love anyone like I love your mom," I said, "because there is no woman in this world who can compare to her."

"Does Shana know that?"

"Yes she does, and she feels that is the way it should be."

"Then I think I should meet her," he smiled as he looked at me. "Now, let's go home. I don't think these fish are going to be fooled into biting without bait. Let's stop and get some burgers and fries on the way home, sound good?"

"Sounds good."

Telling Kaylee was a different story. She doesn't like to go fishing so we went to the mall instead. You can't talk about something this serious in a mall so I had to wait until we were on the way home. I decided to stop at the park where it was quiet. We found a quiet bench, sat down and began munching on the candied almonds we'd bought in the mall. I started with the story about John and what I had learned from him, and then I told her about Shana.

"Oh Daddy," she cried, big tears running down her cheeks, "I'm so happy for you because you need to be happy again, but I'm so sad for me because I miss Mom so much every day here in my heart."

I noticed her small hand was shaking as she placed it over her heart and I wanted to cry too. I took her in my arms and let her tears fall on my shirt until there were no more tears left. Then she looked up at me and with quivering lips, whispered. "I hope she likes us even if she doesn't love us."

"I think she will love you, not in the special way your mother loved you but in her own special way which will be plenty love enough," I smiled.

My parents, of course, are very happy about Shana. She had written to them and sent them a picture of her. After I told Kyle and Kaylee, she wrote each one of them a letter and sent a picture. That helped in easing their anxiety.

I received a large packet of pictures from the sweet woman who was volunteering at the Salvation Army Tent and taking incredible pictures at the same time. That helped put things into prospective for the kids. There were fifty pictures that put together a visual story about Ground Zero.

"Look, Daddy," Kaylee cried when I dumped them out of the packet onto the coffee table, "it's a picture of you and a dog. Is that Flint? Is it?"

I couldn't believe my eyes. That woman was quick with a camera, for which I will be eternally grateful. "That's Flint," I smiled.

"He's beautiful, isn't he?" she said softly.

"Who is this?" my dad asked as he handed me a 5"x7" picture of two young people. The picture was professional.

There was a note on the back which read, "Janet and Brad, July 11, 2001."

I looked at the picture for several minutes, remembering that day. Then I told my family the miracle I had witnessed.

"What a beautiful miracle it was," my mother said, touching her cheeks with her handkerchief.

Today, they are at home waiting to meet the woman who will become a daughter-in-law and stepmother. They took a vote and decided it was best if I came to the airport alone. I thanked them in my heart.

I heard Shana's flight number being called over the sound system, announcing the plane had landed. I stood there, my heart in my throat, waiting until I saw a beautiful woman with auburn hair walking towards me. She was slim built, about five and a half feet tall, approximately thirty-five years old. She wasn't dressed too classy nor was she dressed too casual. She was perfect.

PART TWO

Eight Steps to Personal Freedom

Chapter One

Defining What Freedom Means to You

Think for a minute: how would you define *"freedom"*? In that definition you will find what freedom really means to you.

Freedom can be defined in several ways: *"The condition of being independent," "exemption from defeat," "living unrestricted," or, "not a slave."*

I suppose we've all become slaves to one degree or another. We do things we really don't want to do. We do things because we feel obligated. We do many things because of our fears.

The fact is, the only thing we truly are slaves to, is our own *self-created* fears. When living with fears, we alone take away our personal freedom.

So, what is freedom?

Freedom is being able to do what we want to do, when we want to do it without restriction. Wouldn't you agree?

Freedom is living free of our fears. In reality, true freedom is simply learning how to manage our fears. In managing our fears we are free of the stress and emotional conflict that attempts to control our life. The ability to manage our fears is the single most important component for having peace of mind, the first step to personal freedom.

Freedom begins with a choice. We must first decide to become the predominant force in our own life, and not be a victim of our fears... of our circumstances.

Yes, things are going on in the world around us that can interfere with our sense of freedom. But it's our choice as an individual whether or not we allow these things to interfere with our personal freedom. It's not what happens to us that takes its toll. It's what we do about, or how we respond to what's happening, that makes all the difference.

Freedom begins with responsibility. Freedom and responsibility are inseparable. You can't have freedom without first taking responsibility for the outcome in your life as an individual.

Responsibility is defined as *"the ability to respond,"* or *"response-ability."* If we don't take responsibility for our individual freedom, we don't have the ability to respond when our freedom becomes threatened, either as an individual or as a nation.

In order to take full responsibility and move forward into the future we want... in order to be free, we must ask ourselves an important question: which do I honor the most, my circumstances, or my freedom? Do I honor my problems, my fears, the problems going on in the world, or do I honor my vision of the life I want to live?

Here are some critical questions for you:

Why do you desire freedom?
What does having freedom mean to you?
Why is freedom important to you?

These are questions for which we should all have answers. Once you know the answers, you'll understand freedom. With that knowledge, you'll know what values run your life.

If you could design your life from the ground up without restrictions, what would it be like? *That* would be freedom. If you could create for yourself a perfect day, *that* would be freedom. If you can have perfect freedom for a day, you can have it for a lifetime. When you can know *that,* you'll know freedom.

Here are some important steps in finding freedom in your life. First, is to let go of the past. The second is to let go of the future. The past is the past. The future is the future. Neither exists. Only the present exists. It's where the *action* is taking place in our lives. It's where our lives are taking place. You can't build current freedom on a foundation of past mistakes and old beliefs, or with anxiety about the future. In the present is the only place we will find true freedom.

In order to truly live in the present, we must let go of the past. I'm not saying that we should forget what has happened to us, either as an individual or as a nation. What I'm saying is to let go of the pain, anxiety, grief and anger of the past, and the fear of the unknown future that lies ahead.

We only experience two emotions, love and fear. The question is, which one do you experience in relation to your freedom? Do you love it or fear it? Is it possible to have freedom and fear of losing it at the same time? No, of course not! You might be thinking that the fear of losing our freedom is a good thing. It keeps us motivated to do the things necessary to maintain our freedom. That's called fear motivation. If we are feeling fearful about losing our freedom, we have already lost it by "honoring" our fear.

As human beings we create on three basic levels: our thoughts, our words and our behaviors. Our thoughts create on one level, our words on another and our behaviors on still another. As we begin to think, we start the creative process. All creation begins with an idea, and an idea is simply a thought.

As we begin to add emotion to an idea or thought, we begin to create on even a deeper level. We are putting creative energy into motion. We are putting creative energy into the thought. As we verbalize our thoughts, the creative process begins to take on a new level, or a new energy, or a new motion.

Our thoughts, plus our words, will begin to influence our behavior, which takes the creative process to a whole new level... thoughts + words + actions. As we begin to act in a certain way, a result is produced. The results we produce will come from the actions we take, backed by our thoughts and words. This holds true for an individual or a nation.

If we take action from a place of fear, we will produce results that will show us more of our fear. Just observe yourself closely for a day and you will see what I mean. Observe yourself feeling fearful. Notice how it restricts your energy, lessens your creative thinking and dampens your spirit.

As we produce results, a feeling is created, which supports our original thought or idea. Fear produces a feeling of doubt and uncertainty. The feeling supports our fear, which produces more of the same. Uncertainty brings forth uncertainty.

Over time and with repetition, here's what happens. Our thoughts support our beliefs. Our beliefs support our feelings. Our feelings influence our behavior. Our behavior produces a result. Our results influence our thoughts once again. That's how we sometimes get caught in the trap of not knowing what to do next, where to turn for answers.

If we continue to stay focused on the events around us that threaten our freedom, instead of focusing on a solution, we become part of the problem. Our surroundings actually harmonize with the way we feel. If we feel fear, we attract the circumstances that will support our feeling of fear. When we talk about a problem, we will attract those into our lives who want to discuss problems. Even if we don't know the solution to a problem, just our intent to know will attract others that will lend their support in finding a solution. If we live our personal freedom, we will attract others who will support our freedom, and in turn we can support theirs.

Terrorism is not the problem. It's self-sabotage. Because, when we think something long enough we eventually begin to believe it. When we believe something, we usually verbalize it, which creates on an even deeper level. And when we believe something and verbalize it, we begin to feel it, and as we feel it, we begin act on it, and when we act on it we begin to attract it into our lives.

We are literally sabotaging our own freedom. Look at your own life. Do you have any repeating patterns or habits that do not support your freedom? Look at the nation. Are the feelings *you* hold inside, part of the problem or part of the solution?

Think of any conflict in your life as a red light flashing, indicating it's time to stop and consider a new approach before proceeding. Look at your "red lights" as an alarm clock. Time to wake up! Time to take a new look! Is this thought, feeling, belief or action supportive of my freedom or not? And, if not, let it go and move on!

Look at it this way. You wouldn't think of coming to a red light with a sign that reads "right turn on red after stopping," and not stopping before you proceed, would you? The same applies to your freedom. Stop. Observe the signs. Should you proceed, or take a new approach?

What we need to do is to "self-correct" by seeing the *truth* of our situation, let go of what dis-empowers us, and move on! Choice is the key. It's a choice to hang on to and to focus on what's not working, on what's happened, or to let go and move past it!

The very first step in experiencing freedom is getting rid of our internal conflicting dialog. We have to make a firm decision about what freedom means to us and then, as they arise, and they will arise, let go of all the imagined fears that jeopardize that freedom. This holds true both as an individual, and as an individual contributing to the freedom of a nation.

Your freedom as an individual starts with you. Our freedom as a Nation starts with you as well. No one can mess up your world or our world unless you as an individual allow them to. It is your choice. It's as simple as that!

Back to that important question: "Which do you honor most, your fears, or your vision of what you would love to have in your life? Your dreams or your circumstances? Your fear or your freedom?

Do you hope for freedom, or do you know freedom?

Benjamin Disraeli once said, "Nothing can resist the will of a human being who will stake even their existence on the extent of their purpose." Will you stake your existence on your desire for freedom?

Just remember with each action, you are building a foundation for your future. Freedom depends on three things. One, is the clarity of your conviction. Two, the amount of effort you put forth toward living free. And three, how well you manage your fears.

Living with freedom basically boils down to this: It's your individual ability to manage your own thoughts, feelings, emotions and actions. It's developing the capacity to always remain resourceful despite your circumstances… to be able to see a resourceful solution to challenges, instead of being blinded by them. It's managing your fears instead of being controlled by them.

Chapter Two

Making Courage Your Natural State

To find courage in the face of fear, we must learn to think and act differently. To have courage doesn't mean we are never afraid. It means we are willing to act in spite of being afraid.

A certain amount of fear is necessary to survive in the world in which we live. In some ways fear actually protects us. When we feel fearful, we become more cautious and grounded. Fear tempers our impulses to act and when necessary, can even make us a bit more balanced and sensible. Fear will always be present, because it dwells within. Some people never learn this; they will just keep fighting away at this imagined villain, thinking that to be afraid is to be cowardly. They spend their whole lives being motivated by fear and never really understanding what it is.

However, if we leave fear unchecked, it can become devastating and controlling. When this happens, we resist it and perceive it as undesirable, something that should be totally eliminated instead of having a place in our lives. But when we are motivated to totally eliminate our fear, we then suppress it. And when we suppress fear, we enter into a self-destructive cycle of self-rejection. It then builds in our minds until we become completely obsessed with it.

When several conflicting realities surface at the same time, there will be mixed feelings, which produce anxiety. Anxiety is a mixture of fear, anger and depression. Fear tenses your body and holds you back. Anger tenses your body and pushes you forward, and depression tenses your body and holds you inward. Anxiety is the most serious form of suppression. When we experience it we feel that there's something we must do to relieve it, so we busily put our heads down and move forward in all directions looking for the ultimate solution to our feelings.

What we don't realize is that the only way to relieve anxiety is to stop everything. That requires courage and trust, the courage to do nothing and then trust that the right solution will come to you.

Fear is simply trapped energy wanting to be released. Courage is the antidote to fear. The first step to getting rid of fear is to accept it, feel it, without resistance. Open yourself up to it in a controlled way. In other words, begin to observe yourself feeling fearful. Stay with your fear. Observe it until you feel a shift in your energy. If your fear is buried deeply, you will probably have to do this several times.

Our culture has warned us not to open "Pandora's Box," but they did not tell us if we don't clean out the box, our lives will become like its contents.

Fear manifests itself as anxiety, apprehensiveness, anger, paranoia, depression and worry, to name a few. We become fixated on what's going on around us in the outside world and forget to realize that we are the ones in control of our own fears and circumstances. As we become obsessed with fear, we then project it onto inappropriate situations. We become paranoid, imagining threatening situations and circumstances when there are none. We then begin to rearrange our personal reality to fight our fears.

The real purpose of pain and fear is a warning sign. If we refuse to listen by suppressing the warning, it will only grow in intensity, preparing for a later surfacing. Know this: pain will not be ignored, whether it is physical, mental or emotional. Sooner or later it will get your full attention and you will follow its guidance to make the necessary corrections. So, why not deal with it sooner rather than later?

Trying to get rid of your pain without dealing with it is like cutting the wires to the fire alarm. The fire alarm says, "Hey, there's a problem over here! This place is burning and needs some water sprayed on it!" The alarm is telling you there's a problem. What if you refuse to listen to the alarm and you just shut it off without investigating? Sure it gets quiet, but the fire still rages. And sooner or later it will eventually surface, making you aware that it is still burning. The longer it takes you to recognize where the fire is, the longer it will take to extinguish it and the more damage it will do. Turning off the bell has nothing to do with putting out the fire.

Taking a pill to make it go away is not the answer either. That's the same as turning off the bell, which can eventually lead to total destruction. The only reason for pain of any kind, 100% of the time, is to get us to look deeper into ourselves and to deal with whatever we have hidden there. Remember, what you cannot feel, you cannot heal.

It takes courage to look at our lives and to accept the fact that we are truly in control of our feelings and our world.

Courage is an inner feeling. It is choosing what you want instead of being a victim of circumstances. It is being the captain of your own ship. It is making the choice to own your own life instead of turning your life over to someone else or to circumstances to dictate how you live. It's deciding to be in charge. Courage is essential for joy to be present in your life. Any time you feel trapped, or your rights have been taken away, you cannot experience joy.

It takes courage to let go and allow the emotional hurts and pains to heal. It is not an event that simply happens to you one day, but rather a process that results from being responsible for your own individual world, the one inside. When you become aware of behavior patterns that no longer serve your highest good or the good of others, you are now in the position to change them. That's called empowerment, both for yourself and for others.

That kind of courage is already living inside you. All you need to do is set it free. Just like your freedom, courage is not something that is given to you and it cannot be taken away. It is you. You can choose to claim it, or you can choose to give it away, but others cannot take it from you. Living with courage, just like living with freedom, is a choice we make. We can choose to hang onto our fears or we can choose to be free.

Anger is actually fear in disguise. Initially, anger does its part in helping us to focus, to see the problem before us and take action. But the longer we hang on to this anger, the more it interferes with our freedom and peace of mind. It becomes the problem, not the solution to the problem. Only when we let go of the anger, can we discover the real solutions. That's the key to healing.

The fear we are experiencing right now in America is only a Phantom, a lie that we've bought into. I believe it is time for all Americans and the people of the world to confront the lie and to face ourselves, to face reality. It's time to confront the lies and the structures that support mental, emotional, spiritual and physical violence. I'm talking about hostility and violence in any form, within ourselves, our families, our cities, our nation… violence in any form must come to an end if the human race is to survive, let alone have peace.

Some think that peace is not possible, and for some we know it is not even desirable. They think that violence is not only natural but it is necessary! The person or mind that promotes such a barbaric and insane dogma is unwilling to be responsible for dealing with their own hurt or pain. Those who cannot, or will not, take responsibility for their own feelings, thoughts and actions, rationalize violence by saying that peace is not possible until their perceived enemy is dead.

From this day forward, let us have the courage to recover our freedom, our peace of mind, and do the unthinkable… question everything, especially our own reaction to what happens in our lives.

Facing our own issues is how we will heal and how our nation will heal. It will heal one person at a time, by each person having the courage to take full responsibility for their part and for the whole.

The world's brainwashing says you are powerless over what is happening. You're only one person. Why don't you just give up and go along with whatever "someone else" comes up with as a solution? I invite you to consider that the only part you need to play is your own. You have as much power as any human being. You are very capable of making changes in your life, both within as well as without.

The first step is to accept that you are in control of your own world, that nobody can mess up your world unless you let them. The second step is to accept how you feel and not to blame yourself or anyone else for how you feel. Just accept it. The third step is forgiveness, and this is where having courage comes in. Courage means "having strength of heart," and true forgiveness comes from the heart.

"To forgive" has a powerful meaning. The word itself translates as "to cancel," to "let go," or to "lose one's hold on." It is a tool for changing a reality in your mind and heart. Forgiveness is not even about the other person involved. It's about letting go of how you feel toward the other person. Forgiveness is all about you. It's about letting go of the resentment, anger or any feeling that is less than loving, and returning to a loving state yourself.

Right now is the time. Feel the freedom inside. We do not have to be tormented by fear. Consider the eagle and why it was chosen as our nation's symbol of freedom. Courage is the way of the eagle. If you feel lost, look to the eagle.

What is the eagle? The eagle represents an inner courage present inside each of us that knows no bondage. It represents our resolve to live free. The eagle is vision and power, courage and tenacity. It's the energy in each of us that refuses to be bound. It's the consciousness that knows only freedom and will settle for nothing less.

Listen for the eagle and you will hear the call to freedom, the courage to be free. When you know the sound of the eagle you shall lift above fear and anxiety, you shall soar above it all and your heart will be opened to love once again. Now is the time for the gathering of eagles in preparation for flight

Chapter Three

Accepting Yourself, Accepting Others

We can see what we have in common with another, or we can focus on our differences. You have heard it said, I'm sure, that we are all the same. We are all one. Although this may be true in one sense, the world is actually made up of infinite variety. It is the differences that we see, the feeling of differences that keeps us from feeling connected, and from accepting one another for who we are.

Let me ask you a question. How many musical instruments are there in a symphony orchestra? There's the horn, the percussion, the strings, etc. Now let me ask you another question. What if you were listening to an orchestra perform, and suddenly you decided you didn't like the horns? So you said, "Out with the horns!" All the horns left. The orchestra started playing again, still making music, but not quite the same. Then the next person comes along and says, "Out with those drums. They aren't music; they are just creating a lot of noise." Before long you wouldn't have music at all, would you?

My point is this. The whole world is a symphony orchestra and each person, no matter what kind of sounds they make, beliefs they hold, religion they practice, plays an integral part.

The Dali Lama was recently asked which religion was the right one. He said there should be as many religions as there are people on the earth, because everyone is unique in their own beliefs and how they apply their chosen faith to their life.

Everything in life touches the same center through its uniqueness. No two souls are the same, although every soul breathes the same air and shares the same home called Earth.

When we fall into the illusion that one creation is better than another — my religion is better than yours, my way is superior to yours, my truth is the only truth — we remove ourselves from the miracle of life and enter into the mind's worst disease. That disease is the endless deciding between right and wrong, good and bad, want and don't want — the endless internal war between "for" and "against." We enter into judgment.

The real truth is that there is no right and wrong, no good and bad. It's like hot and cold. What may seem cold to one seems warm to another. What's right for you based on your truth may not be right for me. What's bad for me may not at all be bad for another.

Accepting others for who they are and what they believe in, is one of the most difficult things to do. I'm not saying we should accept the act of another, like those who so violently attacked our country on September 11, 2001. If someone is doing harm to another, you never accept that. You take immediate action to stop it. What I'm saying is, to accept that even those who performed this act of terrorism did so based on their truth, what they thought was right. When you enter into a state of acceptance instead of judging, you enter into a state of love and resourcefulness. Then you can take action from there, with a clear head, instead of from a confused state of fear and anger. When you operate from fear and anger, there seem to be no answers. The reason is that we are completely focused on the problem instead of the solution to the problem.

No feeling takes over our lives more suddenly and more completely than fear. It seems to come from nowhere, and in a blink of an eye, can infect everything.

The wider our view, the less isolated we become. The more we stay connected to everything and judge no man for his differences, the less turbulent our lives will be. Take delight in differences. Share your journey with others. In doing so, we all become a chorus of voices, each speaking a different language, but all making up the whole. The stress of going it alone lessens, once we discover we are not alone.

Our first inclination is to try to change another. "Why doesn't bin Laden see how wrong he is? Why doesn't he believe the way I, we believe?" There is nothing you or anyone else can do to make him believe the way we do. That's his individual choice. But the one person you can affect is you. You can control how you feel, and that's the most important issue here. When you are focused on the problem, on how wrong he is, based on your belief system, you become part of the problem. When you hate another for something they've done that you believe to be wrong, your hate actually supports the hate he has for us, and it also breeds hate within.

Here's an example. How many people does it take to have an argument? Two. Right? It takes two. What if you choose not to buy into the other's issue and not to argue? Where is the argument now? It doesn't exist because you have taken yourself out of the partnership in that argument.

If we fear terrorism, if we fear bin Laden, he has already won. Yes we should take action to stop him or any other criminal, but not from a place of fear.

I was presenting a seminar for a group of Jewish women in Los Angeles a few years ago. The day before, I was using a reference book called *This Day in History*. I looked up the next day's date, the day I was to speak to the Jewish group and it said, "On this day in history in 1937 Hitler was elected Chancellor of Germany." I thought it was interesting and stored it in my mind for later use.

About halfway through the day everything was going very well. It was a very responsive audience. They were very attentive. Then all of a sudden I remembered what I'd read the day before, so I asked, "Do you know what happened on this day in 1937?" I said, "This is the day Hitler was elected Chancellor of Germany."

That was a big mistake. At least I thought it was at the time. The words were no sooner out of my mouth when a young girl, I would guess about 23 years old, stood up and began yelling at me. She said, "That son-of-a bitch killed my grandparents!" Then she began to take it out on me for bringing it up. I won't mention some of the things she called me. This went on for a few minutes. All I could do was sit there. My first thought was, "Well I guess this is the first audience I've ever lost." I figured the day was over at this point. But then the resourceful side of me took over and I decided to just sit back, listen and see what unfolded. When she finally stopped, she was picking up her belongings, preparing to leave and encouraging others to do the same. Most were following her lead.

All I could think to say was, "Wow! You feel pretty strong about that, don't you?" Well, that lit her up into a rage once again. After she again calmed down and was walking out, I asked if I could ask her a question before she left. Angrily she agreed. "My question is this," I said. "Where is Hitler right now?" Her response was, again with a lot of anger, "He's dead, and that's where he should be. And I'll hate him for the rest of my life."

My response was, "Well, it sure doesn't sound to me like he's dead. It sounds like he's very much alive in this room."

The room went totally silent. Everything seemed as though it had been put on "pause."

Suddenly the young woman began to cry. And with her tears, she was repeating, "Oh my God, Oh my God." She said, "We are the ones keeping him alive. We are still fighting the war with him and he's still winning!"

She again paused in deep thought. Then she said to me, "Thank you. Thank you so much." She said, "I am going to make a commitment to share this message with as many of my people as I can. I am going to devote my life to sharing what I discovered today."

Here's my point, if you haven't already figured it out. She had bought into hatred, a belief that had been passed down two generations, and she would have carried it with her to her death if I hadn't let go of my own fear and asked the question I asked from a place of love and resourcefulness.

The first place to start is to accept yourself. Accept your situation in life. Accept what life has given you, good or bad. Accept your feelings. Accept your anger, fear of the unknown, your grief, your confusion about what to do next. That's called accepting what is. What is, is. That can't be changed, so you might as well accept it. The sooner you can accept what is, the sooner you can let that go and move into how you want your life to be. By being trapped in what is and not accepting that that's where you are, you remain trapped in your circumstances, only creating more of the same.

Not accepting yourself, your feelings, emotions and circumstances is called self-denial. It's like wearing rubber gloves before you touch something. Then when you do touch something, you complain because it doesn't feel right. We become hardened to life and the beauty it holds. A kiss from a loved one feels like it came from a stranger. A conversation with a friend sounds like they are your enemy. A moment alone feels like an eternity. You become lost in your own emotions, feeling like you are someone else. Our greatest challenge in life is to go forth each day without the gloves, to touch everything, to feel everything, to let everything, every experience, every encounter touch our lives.

Next is to accept others. There will always be false teachers, using religion and other means to manipulate others. They do this under the guise of a promise to save or liberate people from present and future pain and suffering. They use threat and fear tactics to drive people deeper into their trauma. They use fear to keep people on the hook.

Accept that there are people like this in the world who believe this way. That doesn't mean you have to allow them to infect your world.

Life is like walking through a department store. Who informs you of what to choose from the shelf? There's no doctrine telling you that you must choose one item over another. When you walk into a restaurant and look at the menu, no one is there to tell you what you must order, to the exclusion of every other entrée. When you were in school, did you pick one subject to the exclusion of all others? You might be thinking, "This is silly." Well, indeed. In school you were a student, a young empowered human being ready to learn about the world. It never entered your mind to choose one subject at the exclusion of all others. You wanted to learn everything, until one day you made a choice about where you wanted your education to take you in life. Then you focused on the area of study that would support your belief. But just because you decided to become an engineer, you didn't condemn people who wanted to become a doctor or an accountant, did you?

That's what I'm talking about. Accept the differences. It doesn't mean you have to believe the way someone else believes. It doesn't even mean you have to condone someone's actions. All I'm saying is to accept that they are that way and don't let it mess up your world.

Again, if someone else's beliefs and actions are bringing harm to another, physically, mentally or emotionally, accept the person but not the act. Then go to work to change the situation.

You don't have to like something in order to accept it. Acceptance means opening to your feelings, whatever they are. Accept your dislikes, but don't hold another person accountable for what you dislike.

If you fight an event that has already happened, you are simply fighting yourself. If the event has already happened, who else could you be fighting? When you understand this, you put a different perspective on your struggle. On the other hand, you should not be complacent about confronting a condition that does harm to others. Accepting only means that you accept conditions now, as they are at this moment in time. Acceptance has no bearing on the past and future. Accept your condition and the painful feelings associated with it, but also take action to improve the condition, if necessary.

The World Trade Center Towers have fallen, the Pentagon had suffered severe damage, and several thousand people were murdered in the process. No matter how hard you try, no matter how much you wished this would never have happened, it happened. There's nothing you can do to change that fact. What I'm saying is: accept the fact that it happened and then go to work to improve the lives of those who were affected by the tragedy, and to insure that it never happens again.

Let me ask you a question. How many times have you re-lived the attack on the World Trade Center in your mind? The more we relive it, the stronger the fear and uncertainty becomes within us. It's like being caught in the middle of a disaster that never ends. Once we all accept it, the required changes will take place without struggle.

I want to emphasize one last point about acceptance that people misunderstand. They think that to be accepting, they have to resign themselves to unwanted circumstances, and then try to force themselves to like what is happening. This is not true. Intellectually, you are free to have preferences. We all are. What I'm saying is to accept your feelings, as they are, about the circumstances. Be non-reactive. When you react with negative emotions, it reinforces the event's power over you, and therefore strengthens the negative pattern. Non-reactiveness means that you do not react to, that you are not motivated by negative emotions. You first let them go and then take action to improve conditions.

When you let go, you are now in a state of love. Just as water fills every hole it touches, when you let go of non-love feelings, you allow love to fill every empty space it touches, allowing whatever it touches to heal.

Most things break instead of being transformed, because of their resistance to love. The quiet miracle of love is that without our interference it accepts whatever is tossed onto it, embracing it completely and fully. When you accept what is, you heal yourself with love. That's where peace and happiness begin and end — with you.

Chapter Four

Taking Responsibility, Making a Difference

Responsibility is defined as "the ability to respond," or "response-ability." If we refuse to take responsibility for the outcome of our lives, we will always be living a life that seems totally out of control. We will not have the "ability to respond" to a conflict when it presents itself.

If you pretend your life is the responsibility of others and you have nothing to do with creating the painful emotions you may be feeling, or with creating the repetitive dis-empowering patterns in your life, having peace of mind will be a virtual impossibility.

You might be thinking, "I am only one person. What can I do? I may as well just go along with whatever 'they' tell me to do."

I would invite you to go a little deeper within. Look at your own power. You have as much power as any human being alive. You are capable of making changes both within and without. You're probably thinking, "Yes, but I don't know what to do." It doesn't matter at this point. Thinking that you have no power to make a difference, or that you don't know what to do, is what's blocking you from knowing what to do in the first place. The place to begin to re-discover your own power is to take responsibility for how your life turns out.

What I'm suggesting is that every person must look at how we, as human beings, collectively and individually, have created the insanities in our world. That may seem a bit overwhelming, but being overwhelmed is a great place for healing to begin. Remember, I said before, if you can't feel it, you can't heal it.

Not taking responsibility for our own behaviors is the source of the confusion that leads people and organizations to acts of violence. It is the root cause of domestic violence, divorce, hatred, crime, terrorism and war. We must decide to become the predominant force in our own lives if we are to survive and thrive as we are meant to do.

This is not at all complicated. All it takes is first, deciding to become that predominant force in your own life, to take responsibility for the outcome of your life. Second, is deciding how you would like your life to be, how you want your life to feel. Just stop for a moment. What would living a perfect life feel like? That's rather difficult to imagine, isn't it? Just begin with a perfect day. What would living a perfect day feel like to you? When you can feel that, you can reclaim your power. And third, is to let go, to remove the realities in your own life that do not serve the vision of how you want to live your life. I'm talking about dealing with and letting go of all the false realities that lead to confusion and suffering... the thoughts, feelings, emotions, beliefs and behaviors that do not support the vision of your perfect life.

Once you've made the decision to take full responsibility for how your life turns out, the next step is to realize that every thought you think, every belief you hold, every emotion you feel and choose to deal with or to suppress, and every action you take, is either moving you closer to your desired life, or it's taking you further away. That's where peace of mind starts. That's where peace in the world starts. That's how you reclaim your personal power to make a difference. It begins and ends with each individual taking responsibility for their part.

The blockage of truth is a mind in denial. A mind in denial cannot see information and circumstances contrary to what it currently believes, which may or may not be truth. I would encourage you to challenge your existing beliefs: personal, religious, family... challenge all beliefs until you know them to be true from your own experience. Only then, take action. A responsible mind takes action only when they know that it's based in truth.

Stop right now. Take a look at your last five years. In hindsight, how predictable have they been? What about your next five years? My point is this. If you want to produce a different result in your life, in your family, in your world, in our world, you have to do something in a different way. All action should be based in truth.

A mind that is unwilling to see the truth is a mind without choices, or a mind that will remain a victim of its insane choices. On the other hand, a mind, or person who takes responsibility for any disturbance within, creates a healing space for themselves and for others.

Taking responsibility requires developing new brain cells. It doesn't happen overnight. Remember the first time you drove a car? You thought it was going to be easy. I remember, in my own case, watching my Dad drive. I thought, "This is really simple." But the first time I got behind the wheel it was a whole different story. The steering wheel seemed a lot bigger and the car went where it wanted to go, not where I wanted it to go. I couldn't get the brake, gas and clutch to be coordinated. In other words, the first time I drove, I couldn't get the car to perform the way I wanted it to. But once I drove it a few times and got some expert instructions from my Dad, I could get it to perform much better. I had to develop the brain cells to operate it correctly.

And, of course, even after I learned to drive, I discovered I still didn't know it all. I had to become aware of my surroundings and the other drivers on the road, etc. Finally one day, driving became just a part of my nature. You don't even have to think about holding it on the road or watching the other drivers; you do it instinctively.

Taking responsibility and looking for the truth before taking action may seem a little foreign at first, but after practicing and seeing the results it produces in your life, it too will become second nature.

When you challenge a belief that someone else, a parent, or someone you looked up to, told you to believe, it will be difficult at first. It may seem a little foreign to you. After all, you've been doing it this way all your life. Ask yourself, how did I come to believe this? Who told me to believe this way? How did they come to believe this way? What if they didn't know the truth? What if it's not true? That's what I mean by challenging your beliefs.

That's the only way to make changes in your life. If we want something different in our lives, we must do something in a different way. I can't tell you what truth is for you or what you need to change. Only you can do that. You have to take responsibility for how your life turns out. No one can do that for you. And if someone tells you they can, challenge it, because it's a lie, a false belief.

This all sounds pretty simple, doesn't it? It's easy to know that you have certain feelings, easy to know the burden of feeling fear, anxiety or sadness. But it is altogether another matter to truly feel your feelings, to let them penetrate the fiber of your being, to let them fully surface. However, this is absolutely necessary, because if you don't allow yourself to feel your feelings all the way through, they will never leave you. And if you don't fully feel your feelings, it becomes difficult, or next to impossible to see and to know which beliefs you hold and which ones need challenging.

There is really no end to our growth. Literally, every thought and action adds to the life you are living. But for most, because they choose to live a life of sameness, because they operate more out of habit or from the influence of others, they continue to bring up the same thoughts, the same actions, the same results, day after day, wondering why their life is so painful or is not taking them where they want to go.

I have had people approach me in my workshops who say, "I just can't believe I am the creator of my circumstances, for I certainly would have not done this awful thing to myself. My answer is this: You do not do these things to yourself deliberately, but it is absolutely your doing that brought on your condition, whatever it may be. It's called "creation by default." It's called applying the law of "cause and effect" in ignorance and getting results you don't want. And of course most want to deny responsibility when they create something they don't want; is that not true?

The bottom line is this: Until you are willing to accept the responsibility for everything you are currently creating, both the good and the bad, you will not be able to recognize or to live your true freedom. As long as you believe that something outside you is controlling you or creating your experiences or feelings, you are not free, but rather, you are bound by what others think and believe.

Freedom awaits you. Absolute freedom abounds, and you are free if you choose to be. In fact, you are so free, every thought that you think creates a different future for you. Every action affects your individual experience of life. There is no greater freedom than that.

Theodore Roosevelt once said: *"Far better it is to attempt mighty things, to win glorious triumphs, than to rank with those poor spirits who never enjoy much nor suffer much, because they live in a gray twilight that know not victory nor defeat."*

This freedom is called "deliberate creation." If you want your life to serve what is important or correct for you, then you must think and act deliberately and consciously. You are in the continuous process of creating your life. In fact, you cannot stop the creation process. But, you most certainly can, by intent, send your thoughts and actions in the direction of the things and experiences you want, rather than in the direction of the things that you don't want.

Chapter Five

Trust in a Higher Power

Consider for a moment the miracle of nature. The miracle of the sun, the seed, the soil and the process of creation. The rain cleanses the earth and nourishes every living thing. The sun heats and the clouds dissipate, the grass grows and the mountains crumble when no one is looking.

When we are present in the moment and trust the process of creation, the clouds in our minds will disappear and our passion for living will reappear. Our walls will crumble when no one is looking.

All creation is ongoing. It never stops. It begins brand new, day in and day out. Creation is a miracle that doesn't make a sound, but it changes everything if we can still our minds long enough to feel it happening. When we can be a participant in this ongoing process of creation, we can begin anew each day as well. All life continues and refreshes and renews so subtly if we just trust the process… if we let it. Each time you blink and when you open your eyes, you can begin again anew. Only *this* moment is the moment of resurrection.

Our inner work can be demanding, especially when we are afraid or confused, as many are now. We can become so easily overwhelmed by the power of our own emotions. When this happens we can lose sight of our vision, our freedom, our own inner power, and give in to the false reality that we've bought into.

If you just trust the process of life, eventually — tomorrow, next week, a year from now — somewhere along the line you will see the benefit of what we are all going through now.

Life seems to have a way of carrying us along, whether we are aware of the journey or not. Life carries both the confused and the awakened heart into a brighter tomorrow.

Trust is defined as *"assured anticipation: dependence upon something future or contingent, as if present or actual… hope."*

When you let go of resentment, anger or any non-resourceful emotion and you are afraid of that emptiness you may feel when it's gone, trust will replace that feeling. It is trust that lets you know that love will always be there to fill that empty space.

Trust is one of the most important attitudes you can hold because when you trust, doubt is no longer present. Doubt creates uncertainty and uncertainty leads to lack of vision. Doubt is the negative aspect of the mind that makes your inner work very difficult. Doubt is a form of self-rejection. Doubt has a draining effect on our energy. It shuts us down instead of opening us to growth, as trust does.

Often people ask, "Exactly what do you trust in?" The real answer, as strange as it may sound, is that it doesn't really matter. A higher power, God, Buddha, Baba, Your Higher self, The Universe, some intelligent force… whatever. It really doesn't matter. It could be anything, as long as your object of trust is basically seen as a positive force. If none of the above works for you, you can trust in scientific principles. Trust in anything you'd like to — as long as you trust.

When you trust in something beyond yourself, you open yourself to receiving guidance from a source the conscious mind cannot provide you.

You've heard me use the word resourceful several times throughout this book. It is, I believe, the most powerful word in our language. Listen to it as you say it. *Re-source-ful.* It is defined as: *"Once again full of source."* If you define the key word within resourceful, "source," it is defined as: *"where all things originate."* Not some things, but where *all* things originate. All things originate in source.

You might be asking, "So what is source?" I discovered a definition in an ancient text in Europe many years ago that defined source as "Love." Source is Love. Love is where all things originate. All answers to your or my problems, or the problems of the world, will originate in source, in love.

When you trust, you are turning yourself over to love for the answer to come in its appropriate time. When you trust, you exist in a state of love. And if all things originate in source, in love, what better place to hang out?

When you let go of a "non-resourceful" feeling or emotion, trust that the empty space will be filled with love.

I trust that what has happened to me over my life, good or bad, has a purpose. I trust that what happened on September 11, 2001 will reveal a higher purpose and direction for us all. I trust that the evolution of each individual is awakening all of us collectively to higher capacities of creativity and a deeper sense of love. I have experienced this in my own life and I know it to be true. This is why I want to keep moving forward into the unknown with no clear idea of where it might lead. I trust there is a higher power beyond my conscious abilities that will work in my favor if I let it.

Chapter Six

Gratefulness, the Magnet That Attracts

We all have so many memories, so many wounds of the heart, it's sometimes difficult to know what we are feeling and why. One of the painful memories for me was when my brother died of cancer at the age of thirty-seven. I never got to know him. He left home on his seventeenth birthday to join the navy. By the time he got out of the navy four years later I had left home. Shortly after that, we both ended up living in two different parts of the country, only seeing each other on a rare occasion.

Just a few months before he was diagnosed with terminal cancer we had re-connected and we were getting to know each other as brothers. We had three great months together before he died. I am grateful for those three months.

A few years later my father died at the age of fifty-nine. He was always in poor health for as long as I can remember. The last few years of his life I think he knew his time was short. He told me he loved me more during that time than in all the rest of my life with him. He hugged me like he'd never hugged me before, with so much love, during those final years. I am grateful for those moments of time. While I was growing up my father taught me how to work, how to fish, how to relax, and how to create something out of very little. He was a warm, kind and loving father. I am grateful for the time I spent with him. I'm glad I chose him as my father.

I am grateful that I had a mother like mine. There was no other mom like her. She was kind, loving, nurturing and giving. I loved my mom. Everybody loved my mom. My mom died without notice. The morning my youngest son Walker was born, I called my mom to let her know that we'd had a baby boy and that everyone was okay. The last thing we said to each other before we hung up the phone was an exchange of "I love you." Thirty minutes later she died. I am grateful for that last telephone call.

When my younger sister died I had the opportunity to look into her eyes and to say, "I love you, and I'm grateful for having you as my sister."

I am grateful for having an older sis, whom I love and who loves me so much. I am grateful for my six sons and all the gifts they have brought into my life. I am grateful for my beautiful, loving wife and the joy she brings into my life.

I'm grateful for my friends. I am grateful to be living on this earth at this time. I am grateful to be alive. I am grateful for each day. I am grateful for each meal I have, for a bed to sleep in, for having a roof over my head, for the books I've read, and the thousands of other things I could name.

If you find yourself feeling down; if you want to bring yourself out of a bad space; if you feel drained or depleted of energy; if you have been around someone who has upset you; you can quickly change by looking at all the things you have in your life that you are grateful for.

If we would all wake up each morning and spend just five minutes giving thanks, we would all find ourselves having a much better day indeed.

What is gratitude? It's not just something that your parents told you to do, to say "thank you" to be polite. It's not just about the holiday Thanksgiving, although that's a good place to start.

There is a more profound reason for giving thanks and being grateful. When you say thanks, it literally sends out a call to the higher power that you trust, to send you more of the same. Whatever you appreciate or give thanks for will increase in your life.

Have you ever noticed how much you like to be around people who acknowledge you, who thank you for something you've done for them? That's because it comes from a place of love. Have you ever noticed when someone does something nice for you, you want to do something for them in return? Whenever you stop to thank yourself, God, or someone else for something, the universe will provide you more of the same. It's called "The Law of Cause and Effect."

When you thank someone, you connect with that person heart-to-heart, because as you give thanks you open your heart and when they receive your thanks the other person opens their heart, allowing the two of you to connect heart-to-heart. The heart is a connection to the soul. Gratitude and thanks are paths straight to the heart. They provide nutrients for the soul.

Gratitude allows you to be open to receive more of the same. It opens your heart, connects it to your conscious mind and heals the body and the emotions with the radiance of love. It literally magnetizes you to attract the things you want in your life and repels those things you don't want.

There are many different ways of saying "thanks." It could be verbal, written and even mental. No matter how you choose to do it, if it's done idly, without feeling it in your heart, then it is not as effective as it could be. You can even "think" a "thank you," but it won't be as heartfelt for you or the receiver as when you say it verbally. When you write a thank you, it can be even more powerful, because you have thought it and taken the time to write out your feelings. It can be even more powerful than the spoken word.

Take a moment right now. Think of all the things you received during your day. It could be something as simple as a smile from a stranger, a surge of energy, someone you met, a call from a friend, a beautiful sunrise or sunset, a sale you made in your business, some money you received. You will be absolutely amazed, when you stop and consider all the things you've received to be grateful for.

Take another moment and write a note or call someone and express your appreciation for them as your friend or for something they've done for you.

Take a moment and send a message to the cells in your body by acknowledging your health. If you want to heal a problem in your body, don't focus on the problem; thank your body for all the wonderful things it is doing well. If you send it gratitude, you will find your body doing more to support your overall good health. Acknowledge the prosperity in your life, your freedom, the opportunity to live in America and the free enterprise system.

When you begin to have gratitude for all the incredible things life is giving you, circumstances will begin to re-arrange themselves like magic! You will become a human magnet for attracting good into your life.

Also when you are giving thanks, do not expect something in return. An attachment is based in fear. The more detached you are to the result, the easier it will become to attract more things to be grateful for.

The human will is an energy that flows through each of us constantly like an endless stream. When you give thanks, you increase the flow and strengthen the will. I'm not talking about "will power." I'm talking about *will* that is linked directly to the heart, a will that increases the level of love in your life and in the lives of those around you. The more you acknowledge everything in your life, appreciate yourself, the more you link your heart with your will. This allows you the opportunity to create those things your heart has been longing for you to have.

Grateful is defined as: "Good will." Gratitude is defined as: "Kindness awakened."

Chapter Seven

Commitment, a Resource That Never Fails

The questions I get from people regularly are, "Who am I?" and "What is my purpose for being here?" These are important questions, for without knowing who you are, it becomes difficult to interpret your surroundings.

In one sense we all know who we are. You have observed yourself and how you react or respond in different situations. You know how you utilize your time. You know how you are around certain people.

You may also have a vision of who you wish you were and how you would like your life to be. You know how you would like to be utilizing your time, what your ideal job would be, your ideal income, the ideal relationship, what foods you should be eating to stay healthy, what you want your body to look like. These are all visions of the person you wish you were, not who you are.

In order to truly know who you are, you must seek the quietness of your mind. Knowing yourself requires time alone, time to reflect, time to be quiet and listen to your own thoughts, time to listen to your heart, time to reflect upon yourself.

The first commitment you make is a commitment to knowing yourself. Without knowing yourself on an intimate level, there is really nothing else you can know for sure.

Some people think that commitment is using your willpower to force yourself to live that vision of who you think you should be. You may think that being committed is standing firm and inflexible; that once you've decided on that person you want to be, nothing can stand in the way of that decision.

Making a commitment to yourself means listening to your feelings and acting upon what is right for you in the present time. The projections you make about how you would like your life to be, involve projecting yourself in the present into a future that does not yet exist.

Commitment in the truest sense is being true to yourself in the present time, acknowledging to yourself that you know what to do at this moment in time. Commitment is about trusting yourself. It is knowing that you don't have to worry about what is going to happen tomorrow or next week, or next year, or ever. It is trusting that you will know how to handle things in your life as they arise, instead of worrying yourself over whether or not something is going to happen.

It is important to plan for your future, but once the plan is in place, live for today. Trust that the events of today will unfold those things that you have committed to having in your future.

Commitment is about being fully connected to something without the fear of losing it — like your freedom. Commitment is about love. The true essence of the word commitment is "love." When you are fully committed to something, you are existing in a state of "love" with it. To commit means *"to entrust."* To entrust means *"to turn over to."*

Making a commitment to yourself is to know the appropriate action to take at any given time, based upon how you would like your life to be. To do this, you must be in touch with your feelings and know that you have the power to change them when needed. You cannot be in your true power unless your first commitment is to yourself. If you do not make your life, your time, your feelings, your goals and dreams, your thoughts a priority, who else will? You will simply get lost in a sea of others' expectations of you.

Making a commitment to yourself is making your life a priority. It's acknowledging your feelings and emotions and then acting upon them in the appropriate manner, based upon how you want to live your life.

I know some people who worry that if they do what's right for them, they might be perceived as acting selfishly. The most important person on this planet is you! And you will be even more important to others when you begin to understand the effect you have on others. When you honor your commitment to your higher path, whatever that may be for you, you always honor the higher path of those around you, even if it doesn't seem so at the time.

When you have a higher vision of serving mankind and when you take a stand for that vision, you always serve the higher good for those around you. When you are happy, others around you are much more likely to be happy. Is that not true? On the other hand, when you are sad or fearful, you will have a tendency to pull others down with you.

Most of us feel as though we are actors on a stage performing a part in this giant play called life. You believe everyone is watching and judging you. In reality, the only one who is watching and judging you is, guess who?... You! In reality it is only you who have put yourself on the stage in the first place. Everyone else is too busy with their own act to pay much attention to yours anyway.

Do not feel responsible for everyone's happiness; only they are in control of that.

Only they can choose it. You cannot choose it for them.

Commitment is loving and accepting who you are, not who you think others want you to be, or who you think you should be in the eyes of others.

This is why when you find what you love to do and you start to do it, you are building a life full of passion. For what makes you alive, what you are committed to, is what will keep you alive. And a life of passion is what makes us a healthy contribution to the world.

If you love only who you would like to be at some point in the future, then you are living in a future over which you have no control. Look at who you are and look at who you want to be. Ask yourself why they don't match. Ask yourself, "Is who I want to be really who I want to be, or is it "that someone" I was told I should be? The more you can clear yourself of others' expectations of you, the more you will become committed to the person you are and the person you want to become.

The more in harmony you are with yourself, the closer you will be connected to source, to love. The closer you are to love, the more peace of mind and joy you will experience in your life. With all of this comes the capacity for loving and being loved. There you will find contentment. This should be your first and greatest commitment. But until you step into the arena and test it and live it for yourself, commitment will remain a word on a piece of paper.

Chapter Eight

How to Live "in" Love

Darkness is the absence of light, just like fear is the absence of love. When we turn on the light by letting go of our fears and non-love feelings, all we have left is love.

We do have some misconceptions about love, however, so I would like to spend some time discussing love on a deeper level.

The first misconception about love is that it comes from outside us. The second is that it is secured through relationships.

If we narrow love down to these two things, we are cheating ourselves out of the endless possibilities that exist within the power of love.

Love is always present. It has no opposite. Love is literally an energy that travels so fast, it's everywhere at once. Even in the darkest moments love is always present.

The non-love feelings that we all experience come from not being present with ourselves, right here, right now. They come from looking outside oneself, or into the future somewhere, or looking to someone else for our happiness.

Love is a word that many of us find difficult to comprehend. I've heard it used to explain pleasure: "I love chocolate chip cookies." or to express an intention: "I'd love to have this or that." It's used as a measure to show how much we care for someone: "If you really loved me, you wouldn't treat me this way." Even in the songs we hear, we use it to express an addiction: "I'm hooked on your love," or to express pain: "Love hurts."

Being "in" love doesn't ever hurt us. Being "in" anger, fear and anxiety is what hurts us. What we really get from being "in" love is joy. In fact, to be "in" love means to be full of joy, to be deeply connected to source. And the depth of that connection becomes stronger as we let go of the fear, doubt, anxiety, anger and blame that we allow to run our lives.

The love that we all search for is always present inside us. It is the spirit that lives within. It has only been covered up by all our fears.

It's been said that love is the most powerful force in the universe and that it can overcome all obstacles and heal every pain. If this is true, and it is, then love should relieve us of all our problems. If love can truly solve all our problems, then perhaps we should begin to look at it in a whole new way.

Let's start with the true definition of love. Webster defines love as *"God's benevolence toward mankind."* I'm sure if you asked 100 people for their definition of love you'd get a hundred different answers. Some might say, "Love is happiness." "Love is caring for another." "Love is sharing." "Love is caring for yourself." "Love is having empathy and compassion." Love for some might be friendship, kindness or believing in God. These could all be definitions of love and I'm sure we could come up with many more like them.

Yet isn't it amazing that if we asked the same hundred people to share with us their experience of love in their lives, what do you think we would hear? From as far back as they can remember until now, do you suppose we would hear a story of happiness, sharing, caring, kindness and self-love? I would think not. In fact, from a great deal of them we would hear a story of heartache, pain, sadness and broken hearts.

The real truth is, either we don't know the correct definition of love or we simply don't know how to experience it. Maybe we could gain a better understanding if we looked at love from a different point of view.

Just for a moment I'd like to ask you to put all your beliefs aside and consider another approach to understanding love. I'm not asking you to believe me, but just to have an open mind and see if this rings true for you.

Maybe a good place to begin is by asking, "What or who is God?" I'll bet if you asked the same hundred people the same question, a good portion of them would say that "God is love." Wouldn't you agree? Certainly if you asked most of the religious and spiritual teachers from around the world, I'm sure you would find that at least one thing they all agreed upon is that "God is love."

Now, consider this: If God is love and God was there in the beginning, then love was there in the beginning as well. It is still here now, and it shall be for all time. And if love is *now*, has *always been and will always be* for all eternity, then it must surely be everywhere.

Love is not reserved for a chosen few, is it? And we shouldn't have to go to some chosen place to experience it, should we? It's okay if you do; that's everyone's choice, but we shouldn't have to... not if love is everywhere and available to everyone.

If God's love is everywhere, then God's love must be present in Europe, in Africa, in the Middle East, in Pakistan, behind prison walls and inside every home. If God's love is everywhere it must be inside the church as well as outside the church. It must even be inside the body we live in. It must also be inside every atom as well as outside. And if God's love is inside of every atom and we are made of atoms, then we must also be made of love. And if God's love is in every human being, then that love must be equal for every person on earth, wouldn't you agree?

When you look at love that way, then it must be equal for the prisoner and the guard, the priest and the congregation, the parent and the child, for the enlightened and the ignorant, even for the Christian and the Atheist. It must even be the same for those you love and those you hate. It is the same on Sunday as it is on Wednesday or Friday... and December or July wouldn't matter either, would it?

Love would also have to be present when you are happy or not, sad or not, rich or poor.

If love is always equal and is always present in all things all the time, then maybe the truth is that everything exists "in" love. Love is not in us, but rather we are "in" love. And, if God is love and God is everything, then just perhaps, God's love is the only love there is which, of course, is everyone's love... your love and my love equally.

If this is so, and I know it to be true, at least it is my truth. It doesn't have to be yours. If this is so, then we must ask the question, how do we become more aware of or experience more love?

Perhaps the answer is in the message that introduced the world's greatest representations and teachers of love, "joy to the world." You see, joy and love are the same. One cannot exist without the other. When you en-joy anything, you might say that you are "in" love with it as well.

This is the exact reason we have so many definitions of love. We call it compassion, caring, giving, sharing, sex, making love, just to name a few. This is perhaps the reason we love so many things.

I love my boat. I love my cat. I love fishing. I love my BMW. I love my house.

Because joy and love are inseparable, we have an experience of love anytime we enjoy something. I enjoy fishing. Therefore I am in a state of joy, or love, when I am fishing. The problem arises when we begin to believe that the things we enjoy... our BMW, for example, is the source of love itself. Our love then turns into an attached form of love: "I love chocolate"; "I love cars"; rather than a source of our joy.

When we become romantically involved in a relationship, it is because we en-joy certain things about that person. Since they are the source of the joy, we believe they are also the source of the love, so we say I am "in love" with you.

Perhaps it would be better to say, "I am in God's love with you."

Enjoying one another in a relationship is the key to experiencing more of God's love. It is also not necessary to do things that the other enjoys in order to experience joy in the relationship. If you want to experience more love in your relationship, then learn to experience more joy. If you want the other person in the relationship to be more loving, then help them to experience more joy. You don't even have to be involved in what they are enjoying.

Maybe you can relate to this: When I take the time to work out at the end of the day, it helps me to relax. I en-joy exercising. My wife knows that I enjoy working out, so she encourages me to do so. As a result I am almost always more loving, which makes our relationship more en-joyable.

When either person in the relationship does something that they truly enjoy, they naturally become more loving... and lovable, and the other person will experience more love as a result. This is simply because their enjoyable experience, whatever it might be, will make the person more aware of the experience we call love, and they will naturally share that experience with everyone in their presence without even trying.

The wife doesn't need to go fishing with the husband in order to experience the joy he experiences while fishing. When either experiences something they en-joy, they become more of a loving person and a more lovable person.

So if you want to experience more love in your life, do more things that you enjoy, and on the other hand, let go of the things you do not enjoy... beliefs, incorrect thinking, old habit patterns, feelings, emotions, etc. When you do, everyone around you will experience more love as well.

I'm sure you've heard it said that "when you give love, you receive love in return." I personally think it should be the other way around. "When you receive love, you can give love." You have to first be open to receiving love before you have any love to give. And when you are doing the things you enjoy, you are receiving love and giving love; it happens automatically.

Fortunately, God has provided so many ways for us to be "in-joy"... laughter, flowers, a smile, sunshine, clouds, rainbows, snow, children... if we would only take the time to be "in-joy" more often.

Many traditions and religious disciplines teach that getting in touch with the spirit aspect of our true nature is a long, drawn-out process that requires a great deal of discipline and "special" techniques. The fact is that it is simple and easy. Nothing is so intimately a part of us as our own spirit, or our own true nature... love.

The love that we are all searching for is right there all the time. It can't be lost. It can't be separated from us. It *is* us!

Many believe we are imperfect and need to develop ourselves into perfection, when the opposite is really true. *We are already perfect.* All we really have to do is to let go of our beliefs about our imperfections, which then allows our own true nature to shine through. Love and happiness are our natural state, and for that reason we continually search for them. The fact is, love and happiness are one and the same.

We intuitively feel a pull toward our true nature. We recognize love and happiness because they vibrate within us. That longing we feel is simply homesickness.

Living with this knowing will bring complete fulfillment. However, this can only happen when we release the layers of fear, anxiety and emotional conflicts that create our resistance to love in the first place. When we resist the natural flow, by giving our attention to our fears, we are resisting our own self-love, our own true nature. We are resisting the love that is always with us.

Trying to "earn" love by "acting" or "being" a certain way will always end in failure, because once we stop behaving in these "conditioned" ways, we are still left with self-doubt; which is exactly where we started in the first place.

In order to end the search for real love, we have to go beyond behavior and start looking inside. When we do, we'll discover our real self, the self who knows on a soul level that love is all there is and that "I *am* love."

When we uncover the layers and reveal our old beliefs for what they really are, we discover the most basic truth of all — that compassion, happiness, peace of mind and love are our natural state. And before we can fully realize this fact, before we can experience being filled with love, we must first be emptied of all that is non-love. In order to be reborn into a new way… in any area of our lives, we must first die to the old ways.

Of course, one of the most basic fears we have about letting go is the fear of the emptiness we believe will be there when we do. But in reality, when we die to the old, a vacuum is created for the new. That empty space is instantly filled with love.

Trying to chase love is like trying to vacuum the carpet with a full dust bag. When we surrender a false belief, the vacuum is then filled with love, and it happens without any effort whatsoever.

We seem to be constantly looking back into our past, hoping to find some kind of guidance that will provide us with more love in our future. Only when we stop viewing the future through the filters of the past, do we have freedom from our past and no fear or anxiety for the future. Only then do we truly exist where everything happens — including love — and that's in the present moment.

When we begin to see that every seemingly painful event is truly a gift designed to show us the power of love, our true nature will then unfold.

Remember: *"What you pursue will always elude you. What you become is what you'll attract.* If you *pursue* love, it will always be "out there" somewhere, in the next relationship, job, or outside event. When you *become* love through the process of letting go of non-love, you then step into the universal broadcast of love.

When you exist "in" love, you begin to discover it in everything. You'll begin to transmit it in all you do… through your touch, your thoughts, your words, your eyes, your feelings, your handshake, your smile and your very presence.

With one act of real love you can cancel out thousands of acts of non-love. When you give love in this way, you attract more love into your life.

Remember, in order to truly give love to another, you must first be open to receiving it — because how can you give something you have not yet received? Receiving comes first, then giving. As you receive and give to others, you also give to yourself in return. And of course the reverse is also true: what you withhold from yourself, you withhold from others — and again from yourself as well.

Think of someone you would enjoy giving love to today. By simply considering giving love to someone, you will automatically open yourself up to receive love, so you can then give it.

Here's the most important point of all. *Love only operates in the present.* By living more fully in the present, you send love into your future and you also heal your past. When you exist "in" love, your whole life will become an endless stream of miracles.

In the bible there's a saying, *"and time shall be no more,"* which simply means "one day we will all live in the present." Only our ego speculates about what will happen tomorrow, or relives what happened yesterday.

Another of my favorite quotes from the bible is, *"Many are called and few are chosen."* This simply means, "Few listen." We seem to spend a great deal of our time pondering two questions. The first is, "Will I get something out of this?" and the second is, "Will this cause me pain?" We may appear to be calm, but under the surface, these two questions are always lingering. In order to avoid the pain and find our happiness, we take the same old habit patterns we've used all our lives and attempt to create a new framework from which to live. It's like putting on dry clothes over wet ones and expecting to get dry.

The key is to enjoy each moment. Each and every moment is complete and full just the way it is. Right now, what does your moment hold... happiness, anxiety, pleasure, discouragement? Each moment is just as each moment is. It can never be anything more than what it is. Our real mission in life is to truly exist in this moment, whatever it may bring. Another way to say it is, *"Wherever you are, be there!"*

We only think of the emotional upsets we experience as problems because of the pain they create, and we want to avoid the pain. But in reality, the pain we feel is the result of our expectations, which are created by remaining focused on the past and projecting it into the future. When you are willing to just *be* there, exactly as you are, life is always okay. If things go right, that's okay. If things go wrong, that's okay too.

I'm not suggesting for a second that we shouldn't take action to improve our circumstances. What I'm saying is that if we don't get the results we want, we should accept it in the moment, then take action to change it.

If we take our story and the story of the world around us personally, we'll get stuck in all the little things in life. Life will become a race with no finish line!

In order to help the world, we must first help ourselves. We cannot show others unless we know the way.

Hopefully, one day all of humankind will be constantly aware of being "in" love together. And with that will come the joy of loving every person in every relationship we have.

Remember that love is not separate from anything. It has no boundaries or limitations. Perhaps, just perhaps, love is not separate from anything, not from you nor from me. It has no boundaries or limitations. It heals all, and *is* all there is.

THE GIFT*

Dear friend,

I just want to let you know how much I love and care about you.

I saw you yesterday while you were walking with your companions. I waited all day wishing that you would walk with me also.

As the evening drew near, I gave you a beautiful sunset to end your day, and a pleasant breeze to rest you while you slept. Again I waited, but you never came. I want so much to be your friend.

I watched you as you fell asleep last evening and I longed to touch your brow, so I spilled moonlight upon your pillow and face. Again I waited patiently, wanting to get close so we could talk. I have so many gifts to share with you.

You awakened late and quickly rushed off to start your day. My tears were in the morning mist. Today you seemed sad. So alone. It made my heart ache, because I understood.

I await you. My love for you is everywhere.

I whisper it in the peacefulness of a quiet green meadow, the beauty of a rainbow and in the color of every flower,

I light the stars for you and hang them in the nighttime sky.

I am the smile that brightens the face of every child.

---

*This poem grew from the inspiration of a few lines that a friend sent to me many years ago.

My breath is in the whisper of the leaves in the trees and in the silence of a floating cloud.

I am the shadow that walks with you on a summer afternoon.

I fill the air with the fragrance of honeysuckle and clothe you in warm sunshine.

I give the birds love songs to sing for you.

My love for you is all around and it is more powerful than you can possibly imagine.

You and I will spend eternity together. I am here for you when you choose.

I know how hard it is here on earth, and I will always be there for you.

It is your decision. I have chosen you, and because of this I will wait for you to join me.

I am your life's most precious gift.

I am all there is and all there ever was.

I am love.

Let go and walk with me.

Let go, your gifts await.

ABOUT THE AUTHOR

JIM BRITT

Jim Britt is also the author of *Rings of Truth* and *Unleashing Your Authentic Power*. He is an internationally recognized leader in the field of personal development training and highly sought after as a seminar leader, keynote speaker and success counselor.

His background includes all levels of experience, research and application. Jim served as President of Dr. Denis Waitley's Psychology of Winning, Vice President of Jim Rohn's Adventures in Achievement and President of Dr. Maxwell Maltz's Psycho Cybernetics, International. In addition, he founded Immuno Systems, Inc., a company involved in nutrition, immune enhancement research and observing the effects of emotions on our overall health, with clinics across the United States.

Since 1970, he has shared his life-enhancing realizations and "breakthrough technologies" with thousands of audiences, totaling over 1,000,000 people from all walks of life. Jim is more than aware of the personal and professional challenges we face in making adaptive changes for a sustainable future.

Jim has served as a human behavior specialist, trainer and counselor to more than 300 companies throughout the United States, Canada and Europe, helping their employees to access their true potential professionally, find personal happiness and a feeling of true fulfillment.

Contact information for Jim Britt:
Jim Britt, International, Inc.
P.O. Box 1743
Grass Valley, CA 95945
Tel: - 888-546-2748
Web Site: www.jimbritt.com
Email: info@jimbritt.com

Other Works By Jim Britt

Also available through www.GoOff.com
Rings of Truth

Rings of Truth is a novel (based on a true story) about one man's journey to find truth, happiness and himself. It is literally packed with true-to-life lessons, principles and examples that are truly nourishing and enlightening to the reader.

Matt, the main character in the book, after having achieved great success begins to face many challenges, causing him to ask deeply felt questions about truth, self-love, forgiveness and his life purpose. His quest takes him from the red hills of Sedona to the majestic waterfalls of Kauai, and ultimately, to a powerful discovery that will change his life forever…

The story is guaranteed *to invigorate your mind, open your heart and touch your soul.*

Unleashing Your Authentic Power

In this powerful book, you'll discover how to create a new approach to happiness. You will learn how to let go of emotional baggage, unravel disempowering beliefs and perform at a level of "high action" and "low attachment." You will find simple, yet powerful methods that will allow you to live and exist in an ongoing state of resourcefulness, happiness and self-love. You will be able to move away from a painful past, release anxiety in the present and live a life of love toward a future that is ripe with possibilities.

The Power of Letting Go Home Study Course I & II

In this program Jim Britt will lead you on a powerful journey of self-discovery and personal change that will touch every area of your life. You'll learn how simple it can be to erase non-productive programming, to let go of the blocks that restrict your success and happiness, to feel calm and in control in any situation, and to break free of self-limiting beliefs and self-sabotage. You will receive answers for making your career more successful, your relationships more fulfilling, your family life more harmonious, your financial status more abundant, and much more! In this amazing program you'll learn how to break free of the pendulum of negativity and hold true to your hopes and dreams.

Standing Ovation Success! When Jim Britt is the Featured Speaker for Your Next Convention, Training or Special Event

Rings of Truth Workshop
The Power of Letting Go Workshop, Seminar or Keynote
MONEY, How to Earn it, How to Make it Grow, Seminar or Keynote
Other Keynote Seminar and Keynote Subjects Available
Custom Presentations and Training Available

ೞೲೞೲೞೲ

Jim Britt, International, Inc.
P.O. Box 1743
Grass Valley, CA. 95945
Tel: 888-546-2748
Web Site: www.jimbritt.com
Email: info@jimbritt.com

IF YOU LIKED THIS BOOK, YOU WON'T WANT TO MISS OTHER TITLES BY DANDELION BOOKS

Available Now And Always Through www.GoOff.com And Affiliated Websites!!

Non-Fiction:

America, Awake! We Must Take Back Our Country, by Norman Livergood... This book is intended as a wake-up call for Americans, as Paul Revere awakened the Lexington patriots to the British attack on April 18, 1775, and as Thomas Paine's *Common Sense* roused apathetic American colonists to recognize and struggle against British oppression. Our current situation is similar to that which American patriots faced in the 1770s: a country ruled by 'foreign' and 'domestic' plutocratic powers and a divided citizenry uncertain of their vital interests. (ISBN 189330227X)

Seeds Of Fire: China And The Story Behind The Attack On America, by Gordon Thomas... The inside story about China that no one can afford to ignore. Using his unsurpassed contacts in Israel, Washington, London and Europe, Gordon Thomas, internationally acclaimed best-selling author and investigative reporter for over a quarter-century, reveals information about China's intentions to use the current crisis to launch itself as a super-power and become America's new major enemy..."*This has been kept out of the news agenda because it does not suit certain business interests to have that truth emerge...Every patriotic American should buy and read this book... it is simply revelatory*" (Ray Flynn, Former U.S. Ambassador to the Vatican.) (ISBN 1893302547)

Shaking the Foundations: Coming of Age in the Postmodern Era, by John H. Brand, D.Min., J.D.... Scientific discoveries in the Twentieth Century require the restructuring of our understanding the nature of Nature and of human beings. In simple language the author explains how significant implications of quantum mechanics, astronomy, biology and brain physiology form the foundation for new perspectives to comprehend the meaning of our lives. (ISBN 1893302253)

The Last Atlantis Book You'll Ever Have To Read! by Gene D. Matlock... More than 25,000 books, plus countless other articles have been written about a fabled confederation of city-states known as Atlantis. If it really did exist, where was it located? Does anyone have valid evidence of its existence – artifacts and other remnants? According to historian, archaeologist, educator and linguist Gene D. Matlock, both questions can easily be answered. (ISBN 1893302202)

The Last Days Of Israel, by Barry Chamish... With the Middle East crisis ongoing, The Last Days of Israel takes on even greater significance as an important book of our age. Barry Chamish, investigative reporter who has the true story about Yitzak Rabin's assassination, tells it like it is. (ISBN 1893302164)

The Courage To Be Who I Am, by Mary-Margareht Rose... This book is rich with teachings and anecdotes delivered with humor and humanness, by a woman who followed her heart and learned to listen to her inner voice; in the process, transforming every obstacle into an opportunity to test her courage to manifest her true identity. (1SBN 189330213X)

Fiction:

A Mother's Journey: To Release Sorrow And Reap Joy, by Sharon Kay... A poignant account of Norah Ann Mason's life journey as a wife, mother and single parent. This book will have a powerful impact on anyone, female or male, who has experienced parental abuse, family separations, financial struggles and a desperate need to find the magic in life that others talk about that just doesn't seem to be there for them. (ISBN 1893302520)

The Prince Must Die, by Gower Leconfield... breaks all taboos for mystery thrillers. After the "powers that be" suppressed the manuscripts of three major British writers, Dandelion Books breaks through with a thriller involving a plot to assassinate Prince Charles. The Prince Must Die brings to life a Britain of today that is on the edge with race riots, neo-Nazis, hard right backlash and neo-punk nihilists. Riveting entertainment... you won't be able to put it down. (ISBN 1893302725)

Unfinished Business, by Elizabeth Lucas-Taylor... Lindsay Mayer knows something is amiss when her husband, Griffin, a college professor, starts spending too much time at his office and out-of-town. Shortly after the ugly truth surfaces, Griffin disappears altogether. Lindsay is shattered. Life without Griffin is life without life... One of the sexiest books you'll ever read! (ISBN 1893302687)

The Woman With Qualities, by Sarah Daniels... South Florida isn't exactly the Promised Land that forty-nine-year-old newly widowed Keri Anders had in mind when she transplanted herself here from the northeast... A tough action-packed novel that is far more than a love story. (ISBN 1893302113)

Weapon In Heaven, by David Bulley... Eddy Licklighter is in a fight with God for his very own soul. You can't mess around half-assed when fighting with God. You've got to go at it whole-hearted. Eddy loses his wife and baby girl in a fire. Bulley's protagonist is a contemporary version of the Old Testament character of Job. Licklighter wants nothing from God except His presence so he can kill him off. The humor, warmth, pathos and ultimate redemption of Licklighter will make you hold your sides with laughter at the same time you shed common tears for his "God-awful" dilemma. (ISBN1893302288)

Adventure Capital, by John Rushing...South Florida adventure, crime and violence in a fiction story based on a true life experience. A book you will not want to put down until you reach the last page. (ISBN 1893302083)

Diving Through Clouds, by Nicola Lindsay... Kate is dying... dying...dead; but not quite. Total demise would have deprived her guardian angel, Thomas, from taking her on a nose-dive through the clouds of self-denial to see herself in the eyes of the friends and family she left behind. A spiritual journey from a gifted fiction writer. (ISBN 1893302199)

Return To Masada, by Robert G. Makin... In a gripping account of the famous Battle of Masada, Robert G. Makin skillfully recaptures the blood and gore as well as the spiritual essence of this historic struggle for freedom and independence. (ISBN 1893302105)

ALL DANDELION BOOKS ARE AVAILABLE THROUGH WWW.GOOFF.COM AND AFFILIATED WEBSITES... ALWAYS.

Disclaimer and Reader Agreement

Part I of this book is a fiction work. Any resemblance of fictional characters in this book to living or deceased individuals is purely coincidental. Neither the author nor the publisher, Dandelion Books, LLC, shall be liable for any damages or costs related to any coincidental resemblances of the fictional characters in this book to living or deceased individuals.

Under no circumstances will the publisher, Dandelion Books, LLC, or author be liable to any person or business entity for any direct, indirect, special, incidental, consequential, or other damages based on any use of this book or any other source to which it refers, including, without limitation, any lost profits, business interruption, or loss of programs or information.

Reader Agreement for Accessing This Book

By reading this book, you, the reader, consent to bear sole responsibility for your own decisions to use or read any of this book's material. Dandelion Books, LLC and the author shall not be liable for any damages or costs of any type arising out of any action taken by you or others based upon reliance on any materials in this book